HERE'S TO
TOMORROW

TEAGAN HUNTER

Editing by Editing by C. Marie

Formatting by AB Formatting

For my B.
You were the first person to ever read my words, so guess who gets the first dedication.
Trusting you with Rae and Hudson was easy from the start. This one is for you.

CHAPTER 1

RAE

"SHOULDN'T you at least buy me dinner before you screw me?"

"Um...what?"

Yep. I, Rae Kamden, just said that. Out loud. Not on purpose, of course—it was just my luck and lack of filter. Foot, I'm sure you're well acquainted with mouth by now, but just in case, say hello.

"Nothing," I spit out as I avert my gaze down to my light pink Converse shoes to avoid the most amazing pair of amused green eyes staring down at me.

Mr. Hot Bod Mechanic standing in front of me is not an unpleasant sight—at least from what I can tell through the curtain of hair I'm currently hiding behind.

I peek up and see that his lips are smashed together tightly like he's trying to keep something—probably his laughter—in. I can't say I blame him. I've spent the last five minutes pacing and rambling.

Unfortunately, he's currently letting me know how much this latest round of repairs is going to cost since my car decided to break down just a mile up the road—again. This is killing his hotness factor.

I used the last of my cell phone battery to look up the nearest mechanic and then hiked here to beg someone to tow my car for as cheap as possible. I ended up in a little locally owned shop that has an awesome setup, which I only know because I scoped the place out while I was waiting in the office earlier—just to make sure I wasn't in some sort of car-stripping shop, because you never know these days.

Now I'm kind of just standing here, pretending to stare at my feet while I steal glances to check him out. I can justify this, though, because he's staring right back, taking me in from my feet to my slightly tilted head.

He gives a crooked grin when he takes in my Transit shirt. The band is local, so he must be a fan—I'm hoping so because that means he has good taste in music, which kind of drives my life. Add another item to the *Reasons This Guy is a Total Stud* list.

He cocks his head to the side, that crooked grin still in place, and waits.

Get your shit together, Rae, and stop making fake lists.

"So, it's the transmission?" I manage to ask once the red in my face subsides. I look back up, trying to keep my eyes darting around the shop because I'm still embarrassed about my little outburst, and he's still hot.

He clears his throat. "Yeah. It looks like whoever fixed your car last just threw that shit together. You're looking at a new tranny and a tune-up all the way around. Like I said, my best guess is eighteen hundred after all the repairs. That's if you want to keep it on the road."

Despite his gravelly voice being the most beautiful thing I have ever heard, I'm pissed. This is the third time in three months that I've brought my car in for repairs. On top of that, eighteen hundred dollars is lot of damn money for a fresh college graduate. Hell, in this economy, it's a lot of money period, and I'm not about to ask my dad for more. Sure, he can afford it, but I've just spent the last two weeks convincing him I can make it on my own and to let me do my own thing for once. If I were to ask for more money now, that entire conversation would be rendered pointless, and I would fail in my quest for independence. *So not happening.*

"Dammit! I knew I shouldn't have trusted that guy. I just spent two grand three months ago on a new one. Ugh! I don't have the time or money to deal with this. I could just use the rest of my savings, but then I won't have any padding. I'd have to pick up extra shifts at work to replenish it and then I'm just going to be overworked and stressed out even more than I already am and that just leads to—" I stop, realizing I'm pacing and rambling like a lunatic in front of this poor guy... again. *He probably thinks I'm a complete freak now. Just wonderful.*

To my surprise, he starts laughing.

"Whoa. Take a deep breath, relax. It's all good. We'll get something worked out with payments if you need to pay that way. No big deal. We're a small business wanting to help people and all that."

"Bullshit."

"Excuse me?"

"I call bullshit. No one is *that* awesome and lets clients do payments on car repairs."

The grin returns and he bends at the waist until his mouth is close to my ear. "I'll make an exception for you."

He pulls back, his eyes lit with humor.

Wait, I know that look—he's *flirting* with me! *Me!* Is that even ethical?

You know what? I don't even care. He's offering me a sweet deal, not asking me to suck his dick for a discount. I'm in.

"I don't think I'll need to do that, but just knowing the

option is there would help me sleep a lot better tonight. Thank you."

"Don't sweat it. We'll get you fixed up."

He spins on his heel, but not before dropping another sexy-as-sin grin. He heads toward the front of the shop and I follow like a lost puppy. Stopping at the door, he turns my way. "So, Miss..." He trails off, wanting me to provide my name, which is odd because it should be on the clipboard he's holding.

"You can just call me Rae." I hate when people call me *Miss*.

"All right, Rae. You got lucky because we just had to push another job back by a week, so we can get the work done and give you a call in about four days. Is that okay? Do you have anyone you can call to give you a ride or do you need me to take you somewhere?"

"Four days is perfect. Thank you so much. If I could use your phone—since mine conveniently died just like my car—I can call someone to come get me."

"Sounds good, Rae. I'm Hudson, by the way. Just ask Tucker at the front desk. He'll grab you a phone to use and push more paperwork your way." Hudson points toward a door and looks down at his clipboard, starting to fill info in.

"Thanks, Hudson," I say, unable to stop myself from using his name out loud. His head jerks up and our eyes collide for more than half a second for the first time, and holy hell was this worth the wait.

They're beautiful swirls of dark and light green with a smidge of blue. The colors blend together perfectly, like the ocean on a stormy day—which sucks, because I'm terrified of the ocean. Though, if I'm being completely honest, there's something about his eyes that doesn't scare me but calls out to me with familiarity and protection—which is beyond strange because we *just* met.

Just like that, his eyes become my favorite part of him. They *speak*, and I'm liking what they're saying.

He's interested.

I am too.

We stand there staring at one another, locked in one of those moments you read about in romance novels where only seconds have passed but it feels like a lifetime.

He's the first to shake it off, giving me a somewhat strained smile. I attempt to smile back, but it comes out as more of a grimace and I likely look like a psycho as I move around him toward the office.

I walk through the door and spot the man I assume is Tucker. Sitting at the front desk playing on his phone, I can't argue that he's almost as attractive as Hudson—almost. He has beautiful, dark blond hair that's been carefully arranged to look messy. I can't tell what they are, but he has two full sleeves of all-black tattoos. You can tell, just from the sheer beauty of them, they clearly mean something important to him.

"Hey, um, Hudson told me I could use the phone. Apparently you can help me out with that." I wait as he looks up and stares at me for a second. I raise my eyebrows at him.

"Sorry." He shakes his head slightly. "I didn't catch that. I'm on this super hard level of Mad Maxwell and I wasn't paying any attention. What can I help you with?" He looks a little embarrassed that he's making me repeat myself. I want to roll my eyes, but it's kind of cute that he is so distracted by his game.

"I need to use the phone so I can get someone to come pick me up. Mine died. Do you have one I can use?"

"Oh, sure." He hands me a cordless phone from below the counter. "Just press 9 to dial out, wait for the tone, and enter the number."

"Thanks," I mumble as he focuses back in on his game. I

dial my sister-slash-roommate—hers is the only number I can remember—and pray she picks up.

"Hello?" Haley asks, her voice trembling with caution.

"Hales, it's Rae. My car broke down. Again. Think you can come give me a lift?"

"Dude, again? You have crap luck, Rae. Of course I can come get you. Where are you? The caller ID just said 'Jacked Up'. Is that the name of the shop? Because, girl, that doesn't sound too promising to me."

I laugh. "Yes, that's the name of the shop. Before you get your panties in a wad, they are pretty cool so far. Some guy just told me he would even work with me on payments if I needed it. I've never heard of a place doing that before, so I guess I was lucky to break down where I did."

A throat clears, grabbing my attention. Tucker quickly ducks his head, but I know he was just looking at me. Strange.

"Hmm...seems kind of odd," Haley says in my ear. "I've never heard of it before and I've been around a lot longer than you."

"Two years, dude. Two freakin' years. Hurry up. I have to be at work by six." I hang up.

Being the younger sister in our relationship, I'm used to her weird thinking. Haley is an outspoken, protective, and demanding person. She drives me crazy with her incessant questioning and assumptions, but she's the best sister ever. She lets me live with her for next to nothing and never complains about being my personal taxi or my lack of ever doing the dishes. Just with that last one alone, I got lucky in the sister department.

I return the phone to Tucker, thanking him again, and plop down in a chair in the waiting room to start filling out the paperwork for the repairs.

I can feel eyes on me.

Lifting my head, I see Tucker staring at me like he's unsure what to make of me. *Odd.* I look away then glance back, watching as he gets up and walks out of the room.

Suddenly, I see Hudson in the window of the door leading to the shop, talking with Tucker. They look a little uncomfortable, and with that look that Tucker just gave me, I can't help but think it has something to do with me. I hope they aren't arguing over my repairs or the cost, because that's the last thing I need right now. I don't think I would be able to cover much more than I already am. I'm still trying to catch up from missing work two weeks ago when I had the flu, and I don't want to risk having this mess up everything else I have planned.

Besides, my father would probably strangle me if I came to him for money right now. We've been having this ongoing "conversation" about me moving to Boston with Maura, my best friend. I want to live in the city, not thirty minutes out where I currently am, all part of my *growing up and doing things on my own* plan.

I'm not saying where I live is bad, because it's truthfully a great town to live in. It's not too big and not too small, but I'm in need of a change of scenery, something more fast-paced...I think. I feel like I'm *supposed* to move on, but I don't know if I *need* to.

Either way, he agreed last week on one condition: I have to get a "real" job.

Sure, I'm an adult and don't need his permission, but I want to have it. He's the only parent I have ever had, and I don't want to mess up the fantastic relationship we've built by moving away—even if it's only thirty minutes—without his blessing. Doesn't feel right to me.

So, at his insistence, I've been putting in applications at a few different marketing firms over the last two days, since I graduated with a degree in marketing. I'm not sure if I'm completely cut out for an office setting, but I'll have to make myself be to get a start in the industry.

Glancing up from my paperwork, I see Tucker opening the door with a slight smile on his face. *Guess it didn't end up so bad.*

"Rae, was it?" I nod. "Right, so we're good to go on starting your repairs. Should only take about four days since we have an opening. We'll give you a call when it's done or if anything comes up. Were you able to find a ride today?"

It's kind of sweet that he acts like he wasn't eavesdropping on my conversation with Haley.

"Yep, all set. They should be here shortly to get me. Here's this." I hand him the clipboard with my completed paperwork. "I'll just go wait outside. Thank you again for doing this so quickly. If you guys ever have a free night, come up to the bar where I work and I'll get you some beers on the house."

"Yeah? What bar is that?" he asks.

"Clyde's over on 25th Street. You ever been?"

He shakes his head. "Can't say that I have. Might have to stop in some time."

"You should. We have some kickass wings. Plus, free beer on me."

Tucker chuckles. "You drive a hard bargain. I'm in."

"Sounds good. Guess I'll see you in a couple days to pick up my POS in there."

"Hey, cars have feelings too," he jokes.

"All that one has is anger. So pissy all the time, breaking down on me constantly."

"You got me there. I'll give you a call when she's done."

"She?" I ask.

He shrugs. "Most people say cars are girls because they can be a big pain in the..." He trails off, noticing my now glaring eyes daring him to finish that sentence. "Right. Bad idea to go there."

"I'll see you around, Tucker," I say on a small laugh.

Shaking my head, I walk out the door and over to the edge of the parking lot. Knowing Haley, she'll probably pick me up on a drive-by, so it's pointless to wait around inside.

I kick around the rocks lining the edge of the lot, trying to convince myself Tucker understood my invite. I don't just want him. I want Hudson too.

Because I am already dying to get a glimpse of those gorgeous green eyes again.

————

Hudson

HUDSON TAMELL, you're a straight-up creeper.

I'm standing inside the open garage, staring at this girl as she waits outside for her ride. Luckily, if she were to look over, she wouldn't be able to see me. It shouldn't matter, because I shouldn't be watching her anyway, but I can't seem to look away. I've already tried.

She's beautiful. Not the in-your-face, runway beautiful, but a subtle kind of beautiful—the best kind of beautiful.

That's not even the real reason I can't pull my eyes off her. No. It's her mouth. She sucked me in with that whole dinner before screwing her thing—not because I'm a perv and was thinking of screwing her, but because who says shit like that? People don't usually spout off random stuff like that. It makes her different.

I like different.

And honestly, even if her weirdness didn't draw me in, the rest of her would have. A girl in a Transit tee and Chucks with a mouth that damn kissable? Add in her voice—which is a strange, smooth sort of husky—and that stare of hers—which had me captivated for far too long—and you can count me in.

That stare. I can't get over it. Her forest green eyes were speaking, if eyes can do so, and they were saying, *I'm wandering.* She seemed lost...and undeniably familiar to me too.

This odd urge to protect her washes over me. I have no idea where it comes from or what it means, but I want to do something about it right away.

But I can't. I have too much already on my plate—too many responsibilities, namely my daughter, Joey—that I'm not about to flake on for a spitfire girl with a wicked mouth and beautiful eyes.

"Are you shitting me, man? You're just standing there staring at this chick? Fucking creeper."

"Would you keep it down, asshole? The doors are open," I whisper through gritted teeth.

"If you would quit being weird I wouldn't have to keep my voice down."

He comes to stand next to me, looking over at Rae. He was in here earlier asking me questions about her. I guess she said something to whomever is picking her up about the payments I offered, and he was worried about it because that's not something we have offered at Jacked Up before.

I couldn't help it, though. She looked like she was going to blow a fuse. Plus, all her pacing and rambling was making me dizzy.

Oddly enough, it was also cute. Why? I have no clue.

Who in the fuck finds that shit attractive? Me. That's fucking who.

"I'm not creepin', you dick." He gives me a look, telling me he knows I'm full of shit. "Fine, I was, but only a little. I was worried she wouldn't find a ride." He knows I'm still lying. "I can see she did, though. Good."

Just then, a car pulls up and she hops in, so I walk away and start working on getting her car prepped before Tucker starts questioning me any further.

Now I'm wondering who was in the car. Her boyfriend? Is it serious? Was it her fiancé? How long have they been engaged? Shit. Was it her *husband*? She looked a little too young to be married, but you never know these days.

Dammit. I have no idea what's going on with me. I don't care either way. I shouldn't care. I don't have time for girls, for dating. I have Joey to worry about, and that's enough. There's no reason for me to get my brain all jumbled up over a gorgeous girl.

Don't care, don't care, don't care, don't care. I repeat this in my head until I almost start believing it.

But...I do care, and that's evident since I've spent the last five minutes repeating my new mantra and it hasn't done anything to help get rid of the image of Rae's beautiful stare that seems to be burning holes in my head right now.

Don't care, don't care, don't care, don't care.

I'm a liar.

CHAPTER 2

FOUR DAYS HAVE PASSED, but I feel like I was just here, standing in the middle of Jacked Up, waiting for my car. I don't know if it's the lack of sleep I've been getting or my rumbling stomach, but I'm starting to get irritated standing around.

"Miss Kamden?" All the irritation I'm feeling drains from my body with those two words. I turn toward the same gravelly voice I've been secretly craving to hear again since I walked out of this shop the last time.

Standing before me is Hudson, the insanely hot mechanic that witnessed my lack of filter and crazy rambling. I realize then that I find uniforms to be very sexy, and it has everything to do with Hudson. Even in his navy jumpsuit, he's hot, and the smudge of oil on his cheek does nothing to take that away from that fact. Hell, it adds to his overall appeal.

"Just Rae," I say, finding my voice.

His lips tilt up at the corners. "Just Rae. Right." Hudson rakes his eyes over me quickly. Something along the lines of interest flicks in his gaze, but he pushes it away. Clearing his throat, he shifts on his feet, taking on a more authoritative pose. "We have her all done for you. I can have one of my guys bring her around front while we go over any last-minute paperwork in the front office."

"Sounds good. Lead the way," I tell him, my voice steady and calm, feeding off the professional vibe he's now giving off.

We walk through the same doors as before, though I notice this time that Tucker is nowhere in sight. Hudson walks around behind the counter and I follow his movements from the other side.

"So, just looks like you need to sign off on a few things," he says, handing me a clipboard. "Here." He points to the bottom of the page, and I quickly scan it then sign it. We do this three more times before I swipe my debit card and he declares us done.

As I'm handing the pen back to him, his rough, calloused finger grazes over mine, and I'll be damned if those stupid romance books weren't right—I feel it. A small zing shoots up my arm, the feeling so sharp, I almost wince.

I peek up to find Hudson staring back at me intently. I feel it again—that weird pull I felt last time we gazed at each other like this—only this time it's stronger than before.

In this moment, something changes. Looking into Hudson's eyes, I feel *something*, and it's big. It's something that could change...well, everything.

I clear my throat and look away hastily. "Right. So, anything else?"

He shakes his head once. "No, you're all set. Let me go tell the guys to bring the car around for you."

I fold my arms over my chest and wait for him to come back. I don't have to wait long at all.

"All ready. It's out front," Hudson says, walking back in the through the doors. He hands me my keys. "She runs great, by the way."

"Yeah? I'll believe it when I see it," I say, failing in trying to keep the bite out of my voice. I just can't help it. I've been burned by one too many mechanics that have said the exact same thing.

"You want to go for a test drive then?" Hudson asks, a small smile playing on his lips.

"Know what? I do. Let's go," I tell him, already moving toward the front door. I don't hear him following me so I look back. He's bent down behind the counter, reaching for something. "You coming?"

Hudson stands, holding a piece of paper with footprints on it. "Wanted to grab a mat so I don't get your car dirty. We did just clean it, you know."

I look him up and down, making it obvious I'm eyeing his dirty jumpsuit. "What a gentleman," I deadpan.

He laughs at my blatant sarcasm and unzips the getup right there in front of me, stripping out of it in seconds. I won't lie, there's a huge part of me that was hoping he was naked under there, so I'm a little disappointed to discover he's in a pair of black running shorts and an orange t-shirt.

Hmm...guy doesn't look too bad in my favorite color.

I click the unlock button on the key fob as we approach my car. Hudson jogs ahead of me to the driver side door at the sound.

I stop a few feet from him. "Um, shouldn't *I* be the one driving?"

He gives me a smirk—something I feel is his secret weapon —and opens my door for me. "Just living up to my gentlemanly duties."

My lips betray me and a smile breaks out across my face. "Right. Gentleman. I forgot," I say, walking past him and climbing into my car.

I unabashedly admire the way he moves as he jogs around to the other side. He's a big guy, tall and muscular, but he moves with ease. Hudson folds himself into the small car and immediately pushes the seat back, stretching his legs out. Hell, even his legs are sexy, and I've never paid any attention to someone's legs before because there's nothing sexy about hairy man-legs—except Hudson's, apparently.

He clears his throat, and I realize then I'm still staring at his legs. I force my eyes to meet his and find him still smirking. *Stupid smirk.*

"You do know how test drives work, right?"

It takes me a second to understand what he's getting at—I haven't started the car yet. I lower my eyes to slits and stare him down. "Yes, I do."

"Just checking," he says, laughing lightly.

Meeting someone you like right away, someone you click with instantly is an unusual event. To have that person just happen to be the hottest guy you've ever seen? Unheard of.

But it's happening. Right now, with Hudson, it's happening. Our grins come easy and the teasing rolls off our tongues. You don't get that often with a stranger, especially since I know I come off as snarky and sometimes rude to a lot of people. Hudson seems to understand what sarcasm is, a language I'm fluent in, and I *so* appreciate that. *I'll add that my list of winning attributes for the dude.*

"You sure?" he prods.

Shit. I'm still just sitting here. Luckily, this time I was staring out the front window instead of at him. Granted, I *was* thinking of him, but that's not the point...not entirely.

I slide the key into the ignition and she fires up beautifully.

"Good so far," I mutter.

Hudson chuckles from beside me. I ignore him and make my way out of the parking lot, turning right. I make it to the first stop sign, about a quarter mile down the road, before Hudson speaks again.

"Where you taking her?"

I shrug. "Probably just a drive around the block."

"That's it? After insulting my ability to repair a car, you're just going to '*drive around the block*'? That's...a letdown. I figured we were going for a nice long drive—you know, to make sure I know how to trade out a transmission adequately."

I love the way he teases me with ease, love the way it feels... familiar. I make a split-second decision to continue straight instead of making the turn I had planned. "Well, I thought about going to visit my MawMaw in Boston, but I figured you had some work to do—unless you want to meet her, of course. It is the middle of the afternoon, so traffic may be heavy. We could be looking at an hour-long road trip, at least, and I'm telling you, if you plan on meeting her in *that* outfit... Ugh." I roll my lips up in mock disgust. "It's hideous and you could probably use a bath. MawMaw would never appreciate your grease-stained fingers the way I do."

"You appreciate my fingers, huh?"

I nod, loving how he doesn't miss a beat. "Very much so. They got this POS up and running again. I'll be forever grateful for them. Magic fingers, I tell ya. Magic."

My seat starts vibrating from his silent laughter. I glance over to find his face red from trying to contain it. *Damn. He's even hot when he looks like a cooked lobster.*

"That's..." he starts, still laughing too hard.

It hits me then what I said and how that can be easily misconstrued.

"I swear to God if you say 'that's what she said' I will pull this car over and drop you off on the side of the road and never look back," I tell him, only half kidding. "What are you anyway, fucking twelve?"

He's *still* laughing. My stupid, stupid lips betray me again, a small smile forming. I don't know if it's his immature reaction or his laugh that makes me smile, but either way, I like it.

God, I don't remember the last time I clicked with someone like this. Maybe with Maura? It's been twelve years since we became best friends. That's a long time ago, which is why it's so surprising that everything has seemed so easy with Hudson.

It sounds stupid and sudden, but hey, it's true, and I like it. I *really* like it.

"I am most certainly *not* twelve." *Don't I know it.* "I just don't get a chance to goof around often so I make sure to take full advantage of it when the opportunity arises."

"Sounds fair, I guess."

"And don't you know it's rude to ask someone their age?"

"Correction. It's rude to ask a *woman* her age, not a man."

"Women are excused from this question because?" he challenges.

"Because...well, because I said so. So there."

I can see him staring at me from my peripheral. I glance over to see that he has his dark eyebrows raised, trying to hold his smile back. I mimic his expression and flick on my blinker, inching close to the side of the road as if I plan to pull over and give him a piece of my mind.

"Are you going to argue with that, Hudson?"

The smile breaks through. "No ma'am."

I laugh and ease back into the middle of the lane. "Smart guy."

Hudson

RAE IS SNARKY AS HELL, and I fucking love it. It's like she doesn't care about—or just doesn't catch—the words that come out of her mouth. It's adorable. I'm sure it would be a turn-off for most, but not for me. I find it...refreshing. She's like a little stick of dynamite or some shit—small, but feisty.

I think my favorite thing about her by far is the confidence she exudes. I could tell right away she wasn't someone who needed to be constantly reassured or coddled. She seems independent and to have a good hold on who she is, which isn't typical for someone her age. It makes her seem older, more put-together, and if I'm being honest, with where I am in life—single father and all that—her confidence is like a beacon to me.

Rae is driving me wild in the best way possible.

We drive another mile away from Jacked Up and I'm starting to wonder if she's truly going to keep driving to Boston or turn around at some point.

Since I didn't tell anyone about this impromptu test drive, I pull out my phone and shoot Tucker a quick text.

> **Me: Went for a test drive. If I'm not back in 30, call the cops.**
> **Tucker: Dibs on your office furniture!**
> **Me: Thanks for having my back, Tuck. I knew I could count on you.**
> **Tucker: Always.**

I shake my head and slide my phone back into my pocket. I look over at Rae, who seems to be concentrating on the road.

"Are you really taking me to your MawMaw's? Or do you plan on finding some woods to dump my body in?"

She jumps at my question, like she was lost in thought or

something, but recovers quickly. "Honestly? The woods would probably be better. My MawMaw is kind of nuts."

"Yeah? How so?"

"We're talking collecting those creepy-ass porcelain dolls, and by collecting, I mean having two entire rooms dedicated to them. It's weird."

"Yikes. Woods it is."

She looks down at the dash and winces then flicks her blinker on again. She pulls off into a gas station and parks at a pump.

"Do you mind?" Rae asks turning toward me. "I didn't realize how low on gas I was and the little light just popped up. I don't want to risk driving you back and then running out of gas. I've done enough hiking this week."

"No, no at all. Do you mind if I run inside? I'm thirsty." I'm not, I just want to drag this out as long as possible because I'm enjoying being around her.

"Nope, but you have three minutes or I'm out of here," she teases.

"You need anything?" I call out as I walk toward the building.

"I'm fine!" *Yes you are.*

And there I go being the perv I said I wasn't. Even if it doesn't feel like it, this is supposed to be a professional test drive we're taking, not a *check-out-the-hot-chick* kind of thing. To be fair, I haven't been ogling her too bad. The only thing I've looked at for a pervy amount of time is her ass, which is *real* nice, if I do say so.

Perv.

In my defense, she was walking ahead of me, so my eyes just sort of drifted on their own accord.

There's really no denying that Rae is attractive—no, wait, that's too bland of a word. Rae is...gorgeous, sexy, beautiful, *perfect.* She's everything I'd be looking for in a woman if I dated —but I don't, and I'm not looking to.

I grab a soda since that's what I came in for and make it back out to the car in under two minutes. Rae's just screwing the gas cap back on when I approach the car.

"How's that for timing?" I ask over the roof.

She gives me a beautiful smile. "Perfect." *Yes you are.*

See? That wasn't bad. You're doing good, dude.

We're quiet as she drives us back to Jacked Up. It's not an awkward silence, but a pleasant one. It feels normal for us to be this quiet, to drive without even the radio filling the stillness between us.

I frown, knowing our time is coming to an end. The entire ride with Rae has been so...easy, something I'm missing in my life right now. Nothing's been easy for the past seven years. So this? This short laugh-filled car ride with Rae? It feels damn good.

"So, Rae..." I begin as she pulls into the parking lot.

"So, Hudson," she retorts.

"What do you think?"

"Of you or the car?"

"Well, I was talking about the car, but, please, answer freely."

She thinks for a second.

"I like."

Curious. "You like? Which is that directed to? Me or the car?"

Rae looks over at me, a playful smile on her lips. "Both."

"Blunt. I can dig that."

"Most don't."

"I'm not most."

She grins. "No, I guess not."

Now, I've been smiling and laughing since the moment Rae

walked into the shop today, but this smile? The one plastered across my face right now? It's different, because that answer— that one four-word answer—it just made my heart do some weird-ass flippy thing it hasn't done in years.

"Good," I say, still smiling like a damn idiot. "I guess this is it then. Thanks for the...uh...test drive."

"Thank *you* for fixing my car, Hudson. I think it may last this time."

I cock my brow. "May?"

She rolls her eyes. "I'm not one to count my eggs."

"Your eggs? You mean your chickens, right?"

"Eggs, chickens, whatever. It's all the same."

"Right," I mumble through a chuckle. I climb out of the car as she rolls down the window. I bend down and lean on the door. "I guess I'll see you around then?" It comes out a question, but I don't know why.

"I guess?" Another question.

"Bye, Rae."

"Bye, Hudson."

Neither of us moves, not wanting to go just yet. We stay frozen, gazing at one another and soaking up our last moment together before we each disappear back into life.

I do my best to memorize her face in case I never get the chance to see her again. A tiny, miniscule part of me hopes something else will break on her car just so she has to come back. I don't want to not see her again because I know—*I know* —she's something special. I don't want to let that go.

Even though I'm not looking to date right now, something is screaming at me, telling me to make an exception for Rae, that she could handle the single father part of my life.

As inappropriate and unprofessional as it is to mix business and dating, I *have* to get her phone number.

"Yo, there's a call from Mr. Anderson." Tucker's footsteps

slam against the pavement, against any chance of getting Rae's number. "He says it's urgent."

I let out a sigh and silently curse him for his timing. Turning back to Rae, I can see the disappointment on her face. I nod once and tap the side of her car. She gives me a small wave in return.

Watching as she pulls away, I can't help but feel the odd weight that was lifted when she was around fall back onto my shoulders slowly.

"Great timing, dude. I was just about to ask for her number," I tell Tucker, walking past him into the front office.

"Like her phone number? For what? A date?" I nod. His eyes widen. "You shitting me?"

"Nope."

"Well, hell. Sorry, man, but Anderson is on the line. I figured you'd want to deal with him directly. Besides, can't you get it from her file or something?"

"I may be weird sometimes, but I'm not *that* weird."

"I'd do it," he mutters as he walks back to his chair behind the counter.

"So would I!" calls Liam, another coworker, from the door connecting the office and main shop.

I'm surrounded by a bunch of fucking weirdos.

CHAPTER 3

RAE
Two Weeks Later

WORKING AT A BAR SUCKS ASS. It may seem glamorous to some, getting lots of tips and checking out hot guys all night long, but it's not. Not even close. It's mostly catty women, and to be honest, there's too much ass-grabbing and not enough hot guys.

In the four and some change years I've been working here, I've only ever had a problem with Clarissa, another waitress working tonight, and it's not that *I* have the problem. She has a major one with me. What is it? I have no freakin' clue. She just doesn't seem to like me and thinks everything I do is wrong, but I'm not one for confrontation so I let it all roll off my back.

I'm currently on the receiving end of a glare and a fierce finger-point from my beloved Clarissa.

"What the fuck, Rae?" She has me cornered in the back hallway, shoving her too-long bright pink fingernail in my face. "You stole my table! I was just about to walk up to them. You saw me! I could have earned some serious tips from them! They've been eye-fucking me all week and you took the table!"

I smother a laugh because I know what Clarissa means by "serious tips" and it's *not* money. She's talking about hooking up. However, the table I apparently stole belongs to my cousin Perry and his friends, none of whom would give her the time of day.

I'm not trying to judge Clarissa, because what she does on her own time is her business, but when she does it in the parking lot at work, it kind of becomes my business—especially when I've had to witness it a few times when I'm on break or leaving for the night. She seems to think no one can see inside cars when it's dark outside.

She's wrong.

Anyway, I don't like it. It gives off the wrong kind of vibe for Clyde's Bar & Grill. This place doesn't deserve that kind of reputation. It's not too rowdy or too quiet, but perfectly mellow. The orange-and-blue theme of the bar keeps it bright and friendly—definitely not a sexy atmosphere. Simply put, she needs to stop boning in the parking lot because this is not the place for it.

"I'm sorry, Clarissa. I didn't see you walking up to them." Not a lie—mostly because I try to ignore her, but whatever. "You can have the next two that come into my area. I promise."

It doesn't work that way, but whatever. At Clyde's, the first one to the table gets it. We all try to stay within our own little area, but in all honesty, every table is fair game. It's different than the last place I worked, where we had our own sections. The owner here likes the spontaneity of it all, likes that we all work the whole floor. It seems to do the job so far, and it's fun. Makes the night go by faster.

"Damn right I get the next one." She gives me one last glare and flounces past me. I swear I can hear her mumble "bitch" as she goes by.

I press out my apron and mentally roll my eyes before walking out of the hallway into the main bar. I'm tired and so not in the mood for her shit. My mind hasn't been focused for a couple days now and my infamous nightmare is back so I haven't been sleeping well as of late. On top of all that, after two plus weeks of not getting calls back on applications, I'm starting to feel like I'm never going to get out of here, and I *really* want to get a move on with my life.

Last year I started to feel...lost. Even though I know exactly where I am, I feel like I don't, which doesn't make much sense —not even to me. I want out. I want to start my life because it feels like I haven't been living, like something is missing.

I just can't figure out what.

Shrugging off my doom-and-gloom thoughts, I look around the bar, taking in the customers and how my tables are doing.

"Yo, Rae!" Benny, the bartender and our unofficial bouncer, calls out.

Benny's huge, so huge that I'm positive his muscles have muscles. He's kind of scary-looking at first, but once you get a glimpse of that blinding white smile on his face, you can see he's nothing but a big teddy bear. I would know, since I've been working at Clyde's for over four years now and we've grown close. He's a big softy and so sweet; he's easily one of the most caring and giving people I've ever met. He'd be the perfect boyfriend, too, if he weren't almost as old as my dad and gay.

I give him a quick high-five and place the drink order for my cousin's table. It's an easy order of just one Coke so far since the guys are still fighting over what pitcher of beer to get.

"How's my girl doing? You look down, honey." An unnatural frown appears on his face. "You been sleeping okay?"

Of course he would ask that. "Not really. *It's* back," I huff, referring to my nightmare.

"Same as always?"

I nod. "She's always in it."

"She did a number on you, huh?"

"She's my mom, Benny. Yeah, she did a number on me."

"You need to get out of that head of yours. It can't keep coming and going like that. I wonder what triggered this round."

He knows me all too well, because he's right. Something triggered it. It usually stays away for months at a time, then something happens, causing it to start up again. I'm never sure what it is. It's been almost eight months since I've had one, which is a record really, because it has never stayed away so long.

"I know. I can't keep trucking along on two to three hours of sleep." I shrug in an *I give up* kind of way, causing Benny to throw me a sympathetic smile as he hands me my drink.

I turn to bring the Coke to my cousin, taking a few steps forward and glancing around, checking each of my tables to make sure I have everything I need.

Holy shit!

I apparently have some untapped superhero powers because I just had some serious Spidey-like reflexes going on to catch this Coke midair, without looking.

Those devastatingly perfect green eyes? The ones that belonged to that insanely hot mechanic? Yeah, I just caught them staring at me.

Hudson is here.

My chest feels so heavy and my breaths come in rapid succession. I'm frozen to the spot.

And then I'm not, because I'm stumbling sideways.

"Shit, Rae! Sorry!" Maura, my best friend, rushes out and runs right into me, in front of Hudson. She grabs my arm to help steady me. "What the hell, woman? You were just stopped right in the middle of the floor."

She's now looking at me with a mixture of concern and slight aggravation. I guess concern wins because then she looks over in the direction of where I was staring.

"Who is that? Why's he staring at you? Do you know him?" She starts firing off questions, looking back and forth between Hudson and me. I pull her to the side, out of Hudson's view.

"Remember when my car broke down and I told you about that hot mechanic guy?"

She nods her head. "Henry?"

"*Hudson*," I correct her. "Well, he's here." She steps over to look again. I pull her back. "Stop it! He's going to know we're talking about him. I can't believe he's here. *Holy shit.* I can't believe he is here. I invited them in two weeks ago! That's *forever* ago! What in the world is he doing here, Maura?"

This is what most would call "freaking the fuck out", but in all honesty, it's normal for me, so Maura doesn't even bat an eye.

"Looks like he's waiting to make his drink order, possibly order some food, with hot friends. Why didn't you tell me he had hot friends?"

She *would* focus on that. I can say with one hundred percent certainty that Hudson's friends, no matter how attractive they are, won't measure up to him because he's beautiful. It's not just because of his looks, though he's not lacking in that department with his ink-black hair and towering, well-built frame. It's his eyes that put him in the front of the pack. The eyes that talk and flirt with me. They'll draw me in every time when it comes to him. I can tell already.

"I didn't know. Well...I kind of did. His friend Tucker wasn't bad to look at. But back to the important thing here—HUDSON IS HERE!"

Cue mini panic attack. My lungs are on fire and the air I'm sucking in rapidly does nothing but fan the flames.

I'm not even sure why I'm so worked up. I met this man two weeks ago. Two entire weeks. We didn't even spend that much time together, didn't exchange numbers. It was just a short car ride. Sure, we laughed and smiled a lot, but that shouldn't lead to this freak out.

I mean, sure, it could be because I've spent the last two weeks thinking of nothing but him. I don't know what happened in that shop or during our test drive, but *something* passed between us—something nice, something I know I'm going to like if I ever get the courage to ask for his number, like I almost did before his buddy interrupted us.

Now he's here, at my place of employment, sitting in my "section" and looking like he belongs in *my* world.

And fuck me if I don't want him to.

"Snap out of it, Rae!" Maura shakes my shoulder, jolting me out of my own head. "You need to put on those old-ass big-girl granny panties you wear, go out there, and ask him what he wants to drink. Keep it light. Wait for him to say something about seeing you again first. God, I feel like I'm back in high school all over again."

With that, she walks off, leaving me standing in the hallway still holding this damn Coke.

———

Hudson

THE WOMAN I've been thinking about nonstop for the last two weeks just froze in the middle of the bar when she caught my eyes burning holes into her.

The internal battle of whether that's good or bad has been warring inside me since.

No matter the answer, I don't think I care. She's still beautiful, still has that weird magnetism about her. I still feel like I know her, even though I don't, and she still makes me wish I did.

I have a feeling that if the other waitress hadn't crashed into her, she would still be standing there staring at me. I'm positive they were talking about me in that hallway because I saw the other little blonde waitress peek around the corner to look at me, which I have to admit makes me feel a little...giddy.

I'm not a giddy kind of guy, not about this sort of shit.

"Dude, Hudson, what the fuck are we doing here?" Tanner spouts off in his obnoxiously loud voice.

I've never been fond of the guy. He rubs me the wrong way and gives off this asshole vibe—not the fun asshole everyone secretly wishes they could be, like Tucker, but the asshole that's...sleazy? Yeah, that fits him. A part of me thinks it's a front, like he's trying to hide the real him for some weird macho reasons, but I'll be damned if he doesn't come off that way all the time. I think it's more alienating than anything else.

What's the part that keeps him around? For starters, he's Tucker's older brother so we kind of have to. Also, he's a soldier, and no matter how much of a dick he is, you don't fucking ditch soldiers because they keep your ass free.

"Wing night, man!" Tucker shouts, saving me from having to explain to Tanner that we're here for a girl. Then he shoots me a look, telling me not to let his brother know of my interest in Rae.

How does Tucker know? Easy. He's my best friend and can read me better than even *I* can sometimes. He knows something's up and that I've been off my game for the last two weeks because all I can seem to think about is Rae when I'm not supposed to be thinking of anyone other than Joey right now.

It's almost scary how well Tuck knows me. We've been there for each other since we were fifteen. He moved into the oldest, most beat-up house in the neighborhood and some kids started giving him crap for it. That didn't last too long after I took him under my wing and he ended up whooping those kids' asses. It was hilarious watching those little hoodlums run away from a kid half their size, because they totally deserved it.

Since then, he's been glued to my side, sticking with me through all the shit that's been thrown at me—and it's been some deep shit considering I became a father when I was still in high school.

I look back over to where I last saw Rae just in time to watch her walk out of the darkened hallway. My eyes follow her as she carefully avoids our table to drop the soda off about five tables away.

She must know the people sitting there, because she seems to be cozy with one of the guys. Touching his shoulder, she bursts into fits of laughter and I swear my heart stops.

I'm not sure if it's because she's touching some other guy with obvious familiarity or if it's her laugh. It's breathtaking. I've never known a laugh to be breathtaking before, but Rae's is.

The fact that I don't even know this girl and I'm so damn drawn to her scares the crap out of me. I've never—and I mean never—been so tuned in to another person before. It's fascinating—and terrifying, because I'm in a difficult place in life. I have a daughter to think about, so I have to play my cards carefully. No matter how drawn I am to Rae, no matter how badly I want to march over there, drop to my knees, and beg her to date me, I can't. I have to make sure she's worthy of Joey first, worthy of being in our lives.

And, of course, if she's game to date a single father.

Before I can even clear my head and start breathing again, she's standing in front of me. Tucker throws an elbow into my side and I snap out of my haze then exhale.

"Hey, what can I get you boys tonight?"

We all start talking at once.

"Dr. Pepper."

"Coke."

HERE'S TO TOMORROW 31

"Sam Adams."

"Water."

She blinks rapidly and then repeats it back to us. We all nod like idiots. "Great! I'll be right back with those drinks."

"Isn't that the same chick you were checking out when we first got here, Hudson?" Tanner asks once Rae's out of earshot. He noticed. *Awesome.*

"I wasn't checking her out. She just looks familiar. I think we did a job for her a few weeks ago."

I look to Tucker, hoping he'll go along with me. He dips his head, letting me know he understands. Then I eyeball Gaige, my other best friend, letting him know too. He shrugs and goes back to picking apart the napkin he's been playing with.

Gaige is very...quiet. He comes off as shy, but he's not; he just chooses his words carefully, and I completely respect that. Words are important, and he's not into wasting them. He's been this way for as long as I can remember. He's the prettiest asshole among us, but doesn't use his charm, like Tucker does, or attempt to, like Tanner does. It's not his style. When I met him at seventeen, I thought he was moody and antisocial. After getting to know him better, I realized he's just thoughtful, and a damn good friend.

"We did. Transmission, right?" *Thank you, Tucker.*

"Yep!" Gaige pipes in.

These dudes are lifesavers.

Once Tanner catches wind of anything of this sort, he doesn't just let it go. He's like a middle schooler all over again.

"Oh, cool."

He buys my reasoning, but then I realize I'm now going to have to say something to her because if I don't, he will, and that will end in nothing but disaster.

CHAPTER 4

RAE

NOT SURE IF I'm unlucky or lucky Clarissa didn't snag their table first. Lucky sounds good, because at least the likelihood of finding her out in the parking lot with one of them later is smaller, which makes me breathe easier.

I load the tray up with their drinks while Benny eyeballs me from behind the bar. He can tell something's up, probably because my hands are shaking so badly. I can't help it. My heart is pounding hard from just being *near* him. I have no idea how I'm going to serve them all night.

Breathe, Rae. Just breathe. I repeat this over and over and over again until it starts working.

By the time I make it back to their table, my hands are almost steady as I pass out the drinks.

"Were you ready to order or did you need a few minutes? We have a great wing special tonight. Ten cents each for traditional and twenty cents for boneless, all you can eat." I do my best to put some pep into my speech and clear my voice of the shakiness I'm still feeling.

This time Hudson speaks up. "Uh, I'll take twenty boneless hot wings, please."

Eight words. After two whole weeks of thinking about this

insanely attractive man almost nonstop, eight words are all I get (because I'm *so* not counting his request for Dr. Pepper).

Fantasy over.

"Also, I know this might sound weird, but you look familiar. Did you happen to get your car fixed at my shop a couple weeks ago?"

Fantasy back on...kind of.

I'm not sure if he's just playing dumb or if I'm that forgettable. If he truly doesn't remember me, I may have to cry later because I don't think I imagined our connection. Perhaps that's why he was staring earlier, because he doesn't remember me and was trying to place me.

Crap. Just play it cool.

"I did. Jacked Up, right? You're Hudson." I point to the guy next to him. "And you're Tucker. Ever get past that level of Mad Maxwell?"

Tucker grins. "I did. How's your car doing? 'o1 red Toyota, was it? Miss Kamden?"

It seems I've been focusing on the wrong Jacked Up employee. Tucker just became a whole lot hotter with all his remembering—not that he was bad to look at in the first place with his blond hair, tattoos, and golden eyes. That's a dangerous combination for some, but not for me. Even though he clearly remembers me, I'm all about Hudson—or at least my head is because Hudson is all I've been replaying these past few weeks, not Tucker.

"You're right, and it's just Rae."

"Right. I knew all that," Hudson puffs out, looking at Tucker with a murderous glare.

Huh, apparently he does remember me. Guess I wasn't the only one trying to keep my cool.

"If you're done reminiscing with these two douchebags and want to get to know a real man, I'd be more than happy to help." The mystery man sticks his hand out. "I'm Tanner, Tucker's older and sexier brother." He waggles his eyebrows at me and I have to fight hard not to laugh.

I'm guessing by the huge grin on his face, a smile slipped through. *Great.* Dude probably thinks I'm interested and I'm *so* not. He's more Maura's type than mine with his buzz-cut hair and big build. I check him over quickly because I know she's going to be asking about him. I spy a chain around his neck. Dog tags, maybe? Probably. He looks military.

"Hi," I reply with a tight-lipped semi-smile. "Did you want to take advantage of our Monday wing special tonight?" As soon as the words are out of my mouth, I regret them. The wolfish grin he's wearing is a dead giveaway that I *should* regret them.

"Oh, sweetheart, there's a lot I'd like to take advantage of tonight. Cheap wings, cheap beer, and some sexy-as-sin willing waitresses. Know any?"

Called that shit.

"I'm sure there are few floating around here somewhere."

"I'm sure there are." He eyes me like I'm one of them. Yeah, no. *Big* no.

Ignoring anything else that comes out of his mouth because I'm starting to find this dude annoying, I turn to the other guy I don't know, the quiet one. "Were you ready to order?"

"Um, yeah, can I get twenty bold traditional wings, please?"

"Sure thing. Tucker, were you ready?"

"Yeah, I'll take the same as Hudson, please."

"I'll do thirty *super* hot traditional wings," Tanner chimes in, doing a good onceover, apparently liking what he sees because he gives me another creepy smile.

I nod. "All right, boys, I'll be back in a bit with your food. Flag me down if you need anything in the meantime."

I'm not entirely sure, but I think I hear Tanner say something about needing me all the time as I walk away. Asshat.

As soon as I walk through the doors to the back, I'm verbally attacked by Maura.

"Holy shit! That guy on the outside is so hot! Who is he? Is he single? Can I have him? Oh, how'd it go with Henry?"

Now I know she's just being a brat about his name. "It was okay, I guess. *Hudson* acted like he didn't know me, but then Tucker, the one next to the guy you're drooling over, spouted off all kinds of info about me and Hudson didn't seem to like the fact that he knew all that."

"Well it seems like he was trying to play it cool, something you should have done. I watched you the entire time and I could see you sweating and shaking from here. I guess it wasn't too bad of a start. Now, what about the hot guy?" She's bouncing up and down by the end of her question.

"His name is Tanner, he's Tucker's older brother, and I'm almost positive he's a soldier."

She claps her hands together and bounces even more. "Ohhh, I like soldiers! Right?"

She's getting all worked up and it's cute as hell. Maura just started coming out of her shell last year and now she's boy crazy as hell, which I find amusing.

"Settle your ovaries, woman. He seems like a player, so maybe this one isn't a good guy to get invested in? Plus, like I said, he's probably a soldier and soldiers leave a lot, so there's a good chance he won't be around long."

"Perfect. I'm not looking for anything serious anyway. That dillhole Aaron screwed me over and I'm still trying to recover from that. We can just have some fun in the meantime, okay?"

I'm reluctant to agree, but I find myself doing so anyway. "Okay," I say as she brushes past me with a wink.

As much as I love my best friend, she can be exhausting.

Maura's always been one of those quiet-in-public, loud-around-her friends-and-family people, but last year, something lit a spark under her ass and she's been on the go nonstop since. She's been dating—something she didn't do until last year either—so if she wants a little fling, good for her.

Now if I could find me a man, I'd be set. I've been single for...forever. Okay, it's only been six months, but I think I'm ready. I'm not wanting anything like meet-the-family-let's-move-in-together serious, but something steady would be nice. It's not that I *need* someone in my life, but I *want* one. Someone to talk to, to connect with, to just...be with.

And right now there's a hot as hell guy out in the dining room that could be that someone for me.

But, I don't want to get ahead of myself, so I won't be counting my chickens or ducks or whatever the hell it is people count.

Maura, on the other hand, seems to be just fine doing so. I breeze back through the doors to find her chatting it up with Tanner, not paying any attention to the other guys at the table. I laugh, because Tucker keeps glancing over at his brother and rolling his eyes. Not sure what's going on there, but it doesn't seem like he's a big fan of Maura's choice in men.

I'm gliding around the bar, refilling drinks and delivering food, when I feel *his* eyes on me again. I don't have to look to confirm that it's him. I *know* it is. His gaze makes me feel...alive.

The hairs on my neck stand up and chills run down my spine as I casually scan my area from behind the bar, stopping on his intense green eyes for only a few seconds. Intense is the right word for them too because I have never been able to *feel* someone's stare before, but his—I feel it everywhere. Every fiber of my being feels Hudson's gaze. Every fiber loves it, wants it, *craves* it.

Chill, Rae. You don't really know the guy; you just think you do.

I close my eyes briefly to try to collect myself. When I open them again, he's standing directly in front of me, causing me to jump.

"Hi," he says with a small frown. He shifts on his feet. Two seconds go by. "Um..." Four seconds go by. "Well, uh..." Two more seconds. He's nervous. "Um...bathroom?"

I raise my eyebrows, silently hook my thumb in the direction of the bathroom, and watch as he practically runs away.

I barely contain my laughter.

And I thought I was weird.

―――――

Hudson

BATHROOM? BATHROOM? That's what best I could come up with? What the hell?

I stand in the bathroom, staring into the mirror, trying to get myself under some semblance of control. I glare hard at my reflection, striving to burn her image, her laugh, and her presence out of my head. She shouldn't be in there. She can't be. If I keep telling myself she can't be in my head and that my obligations to Joey come first, then maybe I'll believe it. I cannot ask her out. I will not ask her out.

I really want to fucking ask her out.

I shake my head, take a deep breath, and head back out there.

"You good?" I hear.

I turn toward the voice. Rae's standing at the end of the bar closest to the bathroom. *Was she waiting for me?*

"I'll survive."

"You sure? You seemed a little...tongue-tied." She gives a small shrug. Her lips twitch slightly, totally giving away whatever bullshit she's about to spout. "But then again I've been known to leave men tongue-tied from time to time. It's a gift."

"Wow. Someone is totally full of themselves."

"Or just honest."

I laugh. "Fair enough."

We stand there in silence for a few seconds.

"Can I apologize for earlier?"

"What do you need to apologize for?"

"Well, I kind of only pretended to not know who you were to avoid my friend giving me shit for kind of checking you out."

"You were checking me out?"

"What happened to all that confidence?"

"It's still there. Don't avoid the question."

"Yes, Rae. You're a beautiful woman and I was appreciating that fact. I was also surprised to see you here. Tuck mentioned this place weeks ago and we only now had the chance to all get together to come out. He never said you worked here."

"And knowing that would have made a difference?" she asks.

"Yes."

My answer surprises me, and it surprises Rae too judging from the way her eyes widen.

"Oh."

"Yeah. *Oh.*"

I take a step closer to her as someone passes by on the way to the bathroom. I'm sure I'm closer than I need to be, but she doesn't back up, so I don't either.

"You having a good night so far, Rae?"

"You know, it didn't start out too hot. I have this coworker that kind of hates me and was mad I took her table, but it seems my luck has turned around. While she was off pouting or hitting on some poor unsuspecting customer, I snagged the best table in the joint." Her eyes sparkle as she says this.

"Did you now?" I ask. "What table would that be?"

She steps closer and motions for me to bend down next to her. She leans in close, her breasts brushing against my arm. She smells incredible, clean and fresh, like rain when the sun is out.

I can feel her hot breath over my ear as she whispers, "You see that table?"

"There are a lot of tables, Rae. You need be a little more specific," I tease.

I line my sight up with the finger she's now pointing, following as she scans the crowd slowly...so slowly it's as if she's trying to make this last as long as possible. I can't blame her. Being next to her like this, up close and personal, feels *so* damn good. I shift an inch or so closer and catch the hitch in her breathing. I smile smugly.

"There. That's the best damn table a girl can ask for."

"*That's* your favorite table tonight, huh?"

I feel her nod. "Yep. I'm a lucky gal."

She's pointing at a table full of some dudes that are probably in their sixties, all of them sitting around with bored expressions.

"And *why* is that your favorite?" I push.

"Because..." she starts, searching for some sort of answer because she knows I know she randomly picked that table. I bet it's not even hers. "Tips! Because tips."

She sounds so proud of herself right now. It's adorable.

"You want to know my favorite table?" I ask, taking a chance and shifting behind her more. "It's real special."

She bobs her head up and down.

"You see that table?"

I feel her laugh lightly. "You need to be a little more specific."

Very cute, Rae.

Reaching down, I place my hand over hers. I gently lift our arms and slide my hand down hers until I can extend her pointer finger. Then I match my arm over hers, lining our fingers up until we're pointing directly at my table.

"There," I whisper, my lips brushing her ear. Her heart is racing so fast and I can't help but smile. *I feel it too, Rae.* Being this close to her is doing things to me I can't begin to explain. Little beads of sweat are starting to form on my hairline and my mouth has gone almost completely dry. "That's the best damn table a guy can ask for."

"Yeah? Why is that?" she asks, her voice unsteady and thick. I lick my lips and swallow the lump that has formed in my throat. *Fuck. Maybe it wasn't such a good idea to get so close to her.*

"Because..." I tease. "It's lucky enough to have the best-looking dude in the whole place sitting there tonight. Whoever gets the opportunity to serve him is very blessed."

She laughs and steps away from me, turning back to the bar and grabbing her tray of drinks. "You're right. She's a lucky gal. Tucker is pretty hot."

"The sass that comes out of your mouth..."

"I know." She winks before rushing away to drop off her drinks.

I watch as she walks away, a smile stretched across my face the entire time.

I hear a throat being cleared next to me and turn to find a huge-ass bouncer-looking dude shooting daggers at me from behind the bar. He's scary-looking as shit. He glances over at Rae and then back at me, the look on his face lethal in a silent I-will-kill-you-if-you-hurt-her sort of way. Honestly, I respect that.

I give him a nod, acknowledging the promise.

"Yo, did you fall in or what?" Tanner asks when I get back to the table.

I ignore him. "You guys wanna come over for a card game, pizza, and beer this weekend?"

"Joey not gonna be around?" Tucker asks.

"Nah, sleepover at Charlie's."

"Damn. Joey's fun, man." I just laugh and shake my head because he's right. Joey is fun, probably the best kid ever. She's always running around doing and saying crazy stuff. I get a good laugh out of it all. "Well I guess I'm still in then."

"Yeah, I'll be there. I don't have anything going on this weekend for a change so it'll be nice to relax a bit," Gaige says.

"Wait, what day? I kind of agreed to a double date when you were in the bathroom." I look at Tucker like he's on crack. "What? Tanner got that other hot waitress to go out with him on one condition: double date."

"With who?" I ask, wondering if it's Rae. I look around the bar, not seeing her.

"No idea. He just looked at me and said I'm going. She skipped away, saying she'll find someone 'real sweet' just for me." Tucker shudders.

"You scared?"

"Maybe a little."

Gaige chuckles while I try to be a good friend and hold in my own laughter.

"What's the other waitress' name?"

"Maura, and she's fucking edible, man!" Tanner practically yells. I cringe, hating when he gets crude like this. It's one thing to talk to a woman like that on an intimate level, but another to bellow it out to your buddies.

"Anyway," I press on. "I was thinking Saturday, or is that 'date night' for you dorks?"

"Saturday is good. We're going out Friday night," Tucker says.

I can almost see the wheels turning in his head as he tries to find a way out of it. Tucker isn't one for blind dates, or dates at all. He enjoys the single life, not in a slutty guy way, and not in the Tanner way; he just prefers to be alone. I mean, dude has itches, and he gets them scratched, but he doesn't talk about it or advertise any of it. I respect him for it.

"I see you, man," I say to him.

"I see you, too," he bounces back.

We narrow our eyes at each other and then break out into grins. It's something we've been saying and doing for years. No idea when or how it started, but it's our way of saying we know what each other is thinking.

"Aw! Did you girls just have a moment?"

"Don't be dick because you're jealous of our bromance, Tanner," Tucker tells his brother.

"Whatever," Tanner mumbles. I think deep down he *is* jealous. He and Tucker have a decent relationship, but Tucker and I just seem to click in a way they don't.

They continue to bicker but I tune them out as I catch sight of Rae again.

Right now, I want to kiss whoever came up with the uniforms for this place. They're simple but sexy—or at least Rae's is. It's nothing but a pair of black shorts that somehow make her short legs look a mile long and a tight burnt-orange V-neck that is clinging to her curves in just the right way. Most places make you wear those ugly-ass no-slip shoes, but that doesn't seem to be required here because Rae is rocking a pair of blue Chucks. Her entire look is so simple and understated that she stands out in the best way possible. She looks nothing like the other girls running around who are caked in makeup and have freakishly long bright fingernails. Rae's plain, but it's a good kind of plain.

She stops at the table full of guys again and I watch as she laughs with them. I hate that I am, but I admit I'm a little jealous I'm not sitting over there just so I can hear her more clearly.

I've thought about her laugh a lot over the last two weeks. In some weird sort of way, I've missed it. It felt so good to be able to laugh and have fun with her during our little ride. I'm usually surrounded by people who have been in my life since Joey was born, and it's become a little...bland. It's not that I don't have fun with Tucker and Gaige, or that Joey doesn't make me happy all the time, but it was nice to have had that small connection with someone new—no matter how short-lived it was.

I can't even count the number of times I had to talk myself out of looking at her file to get her number. Tucker caught me with it on my desk once and proceeded to make fun of me for two days straight. I eventually had to lock him out of my office because he kept walking in at random times just to see if he could catch me again.

Rae glances up and catches me watching her again. She gives me a small smile that causes my heart rate to increase. *Damn.* Just her smile does stupid things to me. She spends another thirty seconds (yes, I count) at the table before she makes her way to ours.

"How you boys doing?" she asks in that sultry voice of hers. She peels her gaze from mine and looks around the table. "You want another Sam Adams?" she directs to Tanner.

"Bring it on, baby," her tells her before returning his attention to Tucker and Gaige.

My body tenses for all of two seconds over the "baby" part

before the look on Rae's face registers with me. She's *so* not impressed with Tanner. *Good job, Rae. The guy is a total douchebag.*

She nods politely and then turns to me. "How about you, Hudson? Need a refill? I hear you have an excellent waitress that can get one for you."

My body tenses again, but this time it's from her saying my name. I didn't realize before how much I love it.

"I'm good." The grin she gives me is adorable and I can't help but wonder what just went through her head. "What?"

She brings her hand up and pretends to zip her lips. I raise an eyebrow at her. She huffs.

"Geeze, Hudson. You can't expect a girl to just give up all her secrets."

One word—*secrets*. That's all it takes and suddenly I now want to know *all* her secrets. Every last one. I want to know *her*, want to get close to her—no, I *need* to get close to her.

But should I? Should I drag her into what's going on in my life? Can I do that to Joey? Can I let a stranger into our lives like that?

For her, I think I could.

You should probably start by getting her number, jackass.

"Listen, Rae..." I start.

"Yo, Rae! You have food, honey!" the guy behind the counter hollers, interrupting me.

She turns around and holds up her finger, telling him she'll be a minute. Spinning back to me, she squints, waiting for me to continue. I guess I've lost all courage because I don't say anything. The corners of her mouth tip down briefly. "Well, duty calls, boys. Flag me down if you need anything."

Then she disappears.

"Fuckin' pussy," Tucker mumbles next to me.

I groan because he's right. I *am* a pussy. I could have had her number ten times over now if I would just man up, but it's hard. I've been out of the flirting-and-dating game for quite some time, so I kind of forgot how to play it.

What if I'm not ready yet? I *think* I am, but what if this is a sign? Should I just put aside the way she makes me laugh, makes my heart skip? Or how her smile makes me want to tell shitty jokes all day long just to get the corners of her mouth to turn up even a fraction?

If even *thinking* about dating is this stressful, there's no way I'd survive an actual date. *Fuck. I am so screwed.*

CHAPTER 5

RAE

I COULD STRANGLE my best friend. She roped me into a double date that I do *not* want to go on.

First, I hate double dates. Second, why me? Third, did I mention my hatred for double dates?

Okay, fine. I'm in a bit of a sour mood, have been most of the week. I'm kicking myself in the ass for not being mature enough to talk to Hudson more the other night and for not growing a pair and asking for his number. This is the 21st century—girls *can* ask for a dude's number. I was just too much of a chickenshit to do it.

So, yeah, I've been a sourpuss all week, bitching and moaning about everything, especially this bullshit double date and my lack of balls.

"Knock knock! You ready yet?" Maura lets herself into my small room, making herself comfortable on my bed. I glower at her. "Hey, don't be mean. You're going and that's final."

"You won't even tell me who my date is!"

"That's because I don't even know who it is, you loser. That's the whole point of a *blind* date."

I grumble and spot her sporting a satisfied smirk in the mirror as I swipe on the last of my mascara. Maura looks adorable in a cute white and black strapless romper with a cropped black cardigan, a bright red belt, and black flats. She's the only person I know in real life that can pull off a romper. She looks so sexy and edgy all at the same time with her blonde bob, bright red lipstick, and sultry body. She's one of those naturally gorgeous girls, and I'd envy her if she wasn't the world's sweetest person.

Well, except for right now, because she won't let me out of this horrible date.

"Let me get my flats on and I'll be ready. Do I look okay? Am I dressed appropriately? I'm not sure since you still won't tell me where we're going." I'm wearing simple skinny jeans, a fancy, silky army green tank top, and my usual minimal makeup. My curly auburn hair is spritzed with hairspray and hanging naturally. The whole look makes my green eyes pop out more than normal.

"You always look good, girl, and yes, you're fine. The outfit is perfect."

I trust Maura with every fiber of my being, so I don't argue or double-check like most girls would. I nod and slip my feet into my slightly sparkly black flats. "Ready!"

"Good. We're meeting the boys there. Want to take my car or yours?"

"I'll let you drive since you know where you're going and I have no idea at all—because you still won't tell."

"Works for me. By the way, you should know me well enough by now to know your passive aggressive remarks aren't going to get you anywhere." She smirks at me.

"Bitch."

She winks at me over her shoulder as she opens my bedroom door, walking out into the living room. "I learned from the best."

I laugh and follow her out, spying my sister relaxing on the red loveseat of our small two-bedroom apartment. She has a bag of cheese popcorn in one hand, a bag of Skittles in the other, and her e-reader sitting in her lap. She's wearing lime green sweatpants, a Disney t-shirt, and has her hair up in a messy bun. I'm guessing she's not going out tonight.

"You look fabulous, ladies! Those boys are gonna have to pick their tongues up off the ground by the end of the night," Haley tells us as we make our way to the front door. "Please be careful, and never leave your drinks unattended. Are you wearing underwear? You should always wear underwear on the first date. You never know what the guy may try, especially on a blind date. I can't believe *you* agreed to a blind date, Rae. That's absurd and completely out of your norm. Just please tell me you're wearing underwear."

Maura and I exchange mildly surprised looks and burst out laughing.

"How much sugar have you had tonight? Better yet, can I have some of whatever the hell it is you're smoking? You're nutty as hell, woman—and yes, we're both wearing underwear." I'm not sure if I just lied for Maura or not, but I know *I'm* wearing underwear.

"Good girls. Now run along. I apparently have some more sugar to eat and joints to smoke!" She waves as we walk out the door.

As I close the door, Maura turns to me. "Dude, your sister is so weird, and I love her so much for it."

"I HEARD THAT! I LOVE YOU MORE, MAURIE!" Haley shouts through the door. That one sends us into another round of belly laughs.

Once we sober up, we begin making our way out of the building. I can feel Maura's stare on me so I peek over at her and raise my eyebrow.

She sighs. "I know this isn't your thing—it's not even really *my* thing—but you can back out. I can't. Last chance...you in or out?"

This time I really look at her. She's biting her lip; it's her tell. She wants me there, and I truly want to be there for her. She's going to need some support. Am I excited about this blind date? Not really. I kind of figure the dude I'm being set up with is Tucker, and I'm not terribly excited about that. Truth be told, I want to wish for a miracle and pray Hudson is the one I'm being set up with. But, I highly doubt that's the case. Tanner and Hudson didn't seem buddy-buddy, and it's logical to assume Tanner will bring his brother, even if neither of us are into each other.

But this isn't about us. This is about Maura and Tanner, and I'm going to be there for her—even if I go kicking and screaming the entire way.

"Of course I'm in, goofball." I pull her out the front door of the apartment building.

I push all my nerves aside as we climb into the car.

The ride is quick, leaving me no time to regret my decision. We pull into a relatively new open mic joint appropriately named Mic's. It surprises me that Tanner would pick something like this—not that I really know the guy. This just doesn't seem like a place he'd hang out.

"Tanner picked this? This doesn't seem like a Tanner place," I ask as we approach the front doors.

"I know, but honestly, he only acts like a player around his friends and brother. He's been really sweet in all the texts and phone calls we've had this week." Maura beams as we walk into the club.

I want to question her, ask why he feels like he needs to hide his sweet side around everyone else. Is it a macho man thing? A manipulative thing? I don't know, but I'm not crazy about it—but, this isn't about me and Maura seems happy, so I brush it off and walk in behind her.

"They're here!" Maura squeals and hurriedly makes her way to our table, launching herself into Tanner's arms, leaving me struggling to catch up.

As I approach, I'm surprised to find the table empty. Apparently Tucker isn't here yet.

Tanner catches me looking at the empty chair, so he supplies the answer to my unasked question. "He's in the bathroom. He'll be right back."

I nod and grab a stray napkin to give myself something to do while I wait for my date to come back.

"This is a cool place. I've been wanting to come here since it opened but never had a reason to before," I say, trying to drum up some sort of conversation.

"The drinks are good and that's about it. Not a place *I* would have picked, but I did agree to it. This was your date's idea," Tanner confesses.

I knew he wouldn't have picked a place like this!

"I like it. Gives off a good moody, sexy vibe," Maura says as she eyes Tanner. He waggles his eyebrows at her, causing her to break out in giggles.

Giggles—like a schoolgirl, not a twenty-two-year-old. I realize now that Maura may like Tanner a little more than she's been letting on. Truthfully, I can kind of see why. He's smooth, charming even, and I'd fall for it too if he didn't give off a *don't-trust-me-as-far-as-you-can-throw-me-and-I'm-big-so-that's-not-really-far* kind of vibe. This concerns me for Maura.

As they cozy up next to one another, I sit back and enjoy the soft music coming from the stage. It's good, very fitting for a place like this. I'm lost in the music, so I barely hear Tanner when he speaks up.

"Ah, he's back." Tanner nods his head at me to indicate I should look behind me. Maura gasps.

I don't look, because I can tell it wasn't a good gasp that just came out of her. Is it not Tucker? I assumed it would be him. *Shit.* What if it's one of his soldier buddies? I'm not big into the whole soldier thing. I mean, it's amazing that these people do what they do for their country, but that's one of the things that scare me off: the uncertainty of everything involved.

I don't want to turn around. I don't want to know who it is, because it's clearly not who we were expecting, which leaves me to believe it's a stranger, someone I don't know. I'm going to have to make idle chitchat with some random person, and I'm not one for idle anything.

The urge to be immature and bang my hands on the table washes over me. I just want to go home because I hate dates. I hate *blind* dates.

"Sorry about that." The voice slides over me, and I freeze as my date sits down next to me. "I went to the bathroom and got a phone call I couldn't miss."

I know that voice. It's a voice that's been haunting me for the last three weeks. A voice I can't seem to get enough of. A voice I've been dying to hear again. A voice that makes me want to *love* blind dates.

I suddenly don't want to go anywhere. In fact, I kind of want to stay here forever.

I turn and say, "Hudson, good to see you again."

Hudson

I LOOK LIKE A FUCKING FISH. My mouth is hanging open, and I can't seem to get it to shut.

This is not what I was expecting. Rae is not *who* I was expecting, and judging by the look in her eyes, I'm not who she was expecting either.

I didn't even know she and Maura were the double date type of friends. Hell, I didn't know they were friends in general. I assumed they were coworkers when I saw them talking at Clyde's.

So, Rae? Yeah, kind of the last person I was expecting.

As I had guessed, Tucker managed to get his ass out of the date and get me to go in his place. To be fair, he couldn't really help it. I heard him puking his guts up at work earlier today, and he says he's been at home vomiting since I sent him home earlier. So, I took his place because he didn't want to let his brother down. I can respect that, but it's not going to excuse him for leading me to believe this date was with someone other than Rae.

Fucking asshole! He *knew* that would be a big deal to me, knew I would have prepared more, wouldn't have dragged my feet in agreeing to go in his place. He also knew I would have tried to wiggle myself out of this mess at the last minute because I'm so worried about screwing everything in my life up, I'd have let this opportunity pass me by.

So, I kind of want to kiss that asshole because I have a feeling he completely set me up.

I finally give myself a little headshake and find some manners. "Rae, it's good to see you again, too. I had no idea you were my mystery date for the night."

"Trust me, I'm equally surprised." She looks over at Maura, who seems to be trying to discreetly shake her head back and forth.

"It was supposed to be Tucker!" she confirms, looking at Tanner with accusing eyes.

"He got sick at the last minute and asked Hudson to step in," Tanner says defensively.

I chuckle. "Well, I'm very pleased with the outcome. I apologize for not being here to greet you. Like I said, I had an important phone call to attend to."

"That's okay. Is everything all right?"

"Yep." My mother had called about Joey, who was complaining of a tummy ache and wanting to talk with me. Honestly, I think Joey just missed me.

"Good. This is a nice place you chose. I really like it."

"I'm glad you do. It's one of my favorite places to come for drinks and good entertainment."

"It's a fucking *performance* club! That's weird as shit. Why anyone would want to embarrass themselves in front of a bunch of strangers is beyond me," Tanner interrupts.

"It's not that bad, Tanner," Maura says in a reserved tone.

"I think there's something brave about it—strangers performing for strangers, opening their hearts on the stage, leaving it all up there, airing their dirty laundry. It seems freeing and brave," Rae says, peeking over at me. I dip my head, agreeing with her wholeheartedly because that's the exact reason I like the place.

"Whatever. You're all on crack," Tanner huffs.

I look at Rae and roll my eyes. "I completely agree with you."

She smiles and picks up the menu. "I'm starving. What are you getting, Maura?"

I watch her, not even bothering to look at my menu. She's not like most girls, that much I know. I haven't been a on real date in years, but I do know that the last woman I went out with hardly touched her food and kept holding her hand over her mouth as chewed. From what my buddies say, they've had similar experiences. It's nice to know Rae's confidence carries over into something like this.

I feel like the more time I spend with her, the more I like her. I love that I'm constantly on my toes, never knowing what she's going to say next. She unpredictable and I love it. Her eyes—the darkest green I've ever seen—are so honest, they draw me right in. When you combine them with her long auburn locks, pale peachy complexion, and the dusting of freckles across her nose, she's just as gorgeous as her personality.

I'm in awe of her. Knowing this woman isn't afraid to be herself—or at least the version of herself I have seen so far—and the fact that she's impossibly gorgeous is such a huge turn-on.

To think that I barely know her, that there's more to her, excites me and worries me all at the same time. It excites me for the obvious reasons—hello, I *am* a guy—and worries me because I think I like her too much already.

I carefully pull my phone out and send a text to Tucker because I'm positive at this point that he set this up on purpose. Rae is just too much like the type of girl he'd pick for me.

Me: I see you, asshole.

He responds immediately.

Tucker: I see you, too, dick.

And then something occurs to me.

Me: Are you even fucking sick?

If not, he's a good damn actor because I *did* hear him puking earlier and he looked pretty damn sick to me.

**Tucker: Ha! Nope! Thanks for
letting me out of work early
by the way.**

I barely manage to hold in a laugh.
Yep, I'm kicking his ass.

CHAPTER 6

RAE

"MAURA, BATHROOM?" I ask sweetly.

"No, I'm good." She's not even looking at me.

"Maura!" I put a little more bite behind her name this time, causing her to finally turn her head.

"Fine," she huffs. "Would you boys please excuse us?"

I grab her arm and drag her to the restroom, turning on her as soon the door swings closed.

"What in the hell, Maura? Hudson! It was supposed to be Tucker, who I don't even like so I'm not sure why you were going to set me up with him, but still! I had prepared for him, wasn't sweating the date too bad because, again, I'm not into him. I wasn't *date* date ready. Then you go and surprise me with Hudson and you didn't give me a single heads-up. I mean, hey, thanks for this because I *do* like him, but why no heads-up?"

"Chill, woman! It *was* supposed to be Tucker, but only because he's Tanner's brother. Tanner wanted him here, not me. Besides, I figured we could grill Tucker on Hudson, get some info or something. If I'd had any choice at all in the matter, I would have picked Hudson from the start and I would have at least warned you about that. You know that. You're just freaking out because Hudson's here and you're *so* into him."

I huff and turn toward the sinks, leaning against them as I eye myself in the mirror. Maura starts primping next to me.

"Just relax, Rae. It's okay. Hudson was obviously as surprised to see you as you were to see him. It's all going to be okay. You two are cute together, by the way. Like ridiculously cute. You can tell he likes you too. He keeps leaning in toward you."

I know she's saying all this just to make me feel better, but a part of me desperately wants to believe she's right. I like Hudson, and while I don't know him all that well, I can tell I'm going to keep liking him—or at least I hope so. I'm usually a good judge of character, if I do say so myself. I can peer into someone's eyes and read them like a book almost every time, and I hope this is one of those times, because when I look into Hudson's eyes, I see determination, love, longing, familiarity, hope, and even sadness. I want to find out what causes every one of those feelings I see.

I feel like I *have* to know.

"I can see you doubting me. You think I'm just saying all this to make you feel better. I'm not. Look at me, Rae." She spins me her way, staring directly into my eyes. "I promise I'm not lying to you. I can see something there. I'm not sure what it is, but it's something, and I think you should explore it."

She knows we well enough to know about my eye contact thing. I know she's telling the truth based on that alone. I exhale loudly. "Thank you."

She nods and we exit the bathroom because that's all there is, all that's needed between us: honesty and trust.

As we walk back to the table, Hudson and Tanner are in a heated discussion of some sort. Tanner flicks his eyes over

Hudson's shoulder and sees us, causing them both to stiffen a bit and stop talking.

I mentally shrug and brush it off. Whatever it is, it's none of my business.

The table is quiet when we sit down. I'm not sure what they were talking about, but whatever it was, it's lingering. I attempt to distract them both because it looks like they may jump over the table at one another.

"So, do you come here often?" I ask Hudson. Hudson laughs, almost choking on the Dr. Pepper he's drinking. Tanner gapes at me and Maura rolls her eyes in an *oh-my-god-did-I-really-take-her-out-in-public* way. She loves me.

"Actually, I kind of do. Tucker plays here a lot, one a week or so. That's how I discovered the place—watching him play."

I'm shocked because Tucker didn't seem like the musical type to me. I mean, I don't know him well, but I pride myself on reading people and I didn't see that one coming.

"No shit?"

"Shit," Hudson deadpans. I feel the corners of my mouth tip up a bit.

"What the fuck, Tanner? Why didn't you tell me your hot brother plays the guitar?" Maura scolds, getting all death-glare-like with Tanner.

"Chill, babe. I didn't mention it because he's always trying to steal my thunder. He's not even that great at it," Tanner pouts.

"That's bullshit, Tanner, and you know it. He's damn good. Why he hasn't pursued a career in music, I have no idea. He loves this place though. Coming and watching all the different types of performances: the poetry, the skits, the comedy routines, the other musicians, all of it. I love it too. It's eye-opening, really."

"How so?" Maura asks. I may have forgotten she and Tanner were even here—Hudson's voice is so mesmerizing.

"It's kind of along the lines of what Rae said earlier. Think about it. All these people who get up there on that stage"—he points to the stage in the very center of the building—"pour their hearts out to strangers. That's amazing. Not only that, but it's eye-opening to know that those people—those brave people who can bring the room to complete silence, make others cry or laugh with their words—they're people we know. People we live next to, work next to. *Family*. Anyone, really. It's just eye-opening to know that such talented people are living among us day to day. I love it."

I'm speechless. I can't believe he just said all that. It was so beautiful, poetic, and true. I think I may have just fallen in love with his brain.

"Holy shit!" Maura exclaims. "Marry him now, Rae. If you don't, I will."

"Hey now! Watch yourself, Hudson." Tanner angles himself in front of his date. "I'm growing quite fond of this one. I don't want to have to fight you for her."

Hudson doesn't seem notice. Our eyes haven't strayed from one another since I broke in with my awesome pickup line.

"Don't sweat it, Tanner. I think I'm growing quite fond of someone myself." He gives me a cute little smirk and I turn away because I feel my face heating up with embarrassment.

I take the moment of silence to readjust my mind and observe this club Hudson's so fond of.

Mic's isn't really anything special at first glance, even from the outside. It looks like your typical low-lit bar, only there's a stage directly in the center of everything. Dozens of tables surround it with fresh flowers or candles on each one, indicating they serve a little more than your usual bar food.

When you take a deeper look, you can see how amazing

this place is. The decor doesn't match in the slightest and the walls are covered in photographs, signed set lists, and custom paintings and drawings. Each one is beautiful in its own right. You can see the love the performers have for this place plastered all over the walls, including a few action shots of Tucker playing. You can see how many patrons love this place and keep returning night after night in the worn-out furniture and chipped dishes. It's all things that are easily dismissed with a glance and sorely overlooked all too often, which is sad, because those are the things that make this place so unique.

"It's beautiful," I say, turning back to Hudson. "Just beautiful. Thank you for choosing this place."

He smiles.

I melt.

"So, Hudson," Maura says, causing him to break our eye contact. "You work at a car shop?"

"I *own* the car shop. Jacked Up is my baby." His answer is spoken with such pride.

Tanner mutters something under his breath and Hudson shoots daggers at him. He quickly shuts up.

"You own it? I had no idea!" Hudson grins at my little outburst. Now I'm sufficiently embarrassed because standing in Jacked Up with Hudson wasn't one of my finest moments, since my mouth decided to run before my brain caught up. I'm assuming from the little glint in his eyes that he remembers.

"Yep. Have since I was twenty, but I've worked there since I was seventeen. That place kind of saved my life. Old Mr. Horton knew how much I loved it, so when he was diagnosed with stage four lung cancer, he offered the place to me at a crazy affordable price. I couldn't turn it down."

"Did he make it?" Maura asks. Hudson's lips tip down, transforming his whole face. Even his eyes dim a bit. "Shit. Sorry. That was rude of me. Forget I said anything."

"It's okay, really. Unfortunately, no, he didn't make it. He was like a second father to me is all. I'm very much indebted to him."

Before I realize what I'm doing, I reach out and place my hand on his arm. He whips his head in my direction, his gaze landing on my hand.

"I'm sorry for your loss." He meets my eyes and I stop breathing; his gaze is so sad and thankful all at the same time. I don't think he's healed from the former owner's death, and I can tell how much my words mean to him. He nods, offering me a small smile.

The waiter picks that moment to deliver our food. I remove my hand and begin pushing around my chicken pasta, suddenly not quite as starved as before and thinking a little too hard about the intense stares Hudson and I have shared since I met him.

Truthfully, there have been a lot, more than I feel entirely comfortable with because they do something to me. They make my heart race, my body tingle, and my head fuzzy. It's something new and intriguing, and as concerning as it is, I like it.

His eyes are so intense, so open. I would bet they've gotten him in and out of a lot of trouble. I smile a little to myself over that, which earns me a not-so-gentle kick in the shin from Maura. I look up and glare at her. She gives me her "innocent" face, which I've grown very accustomed to over the years, and turns back to Tanner, who seems to be talking her ear off. I hadn't even noticed.

"So, Rae, what do you do? I mean, I know you work at Clyde's and all, but are you in college or anything?" Hudson asks.

I take a sip of my drink to buy me a little time before I answer, because I hate this question, *especially* since I still haven't heard back from *any* of the companies I applied to.

"I graduated in the spring. Clyde's is it for me for now, but I've put in several applications in the city. I have a degree in marketing, and there's not much to market around here." I shrug, trying to play it off as if my lack of professional career doesn't bother me.

"Marketing? That's some fast-paced stuff. I know it's not big time or anything, but Jacked Up has been looking at some advertising firms lately. We want to push our name more, generate some loyal customers so we can update our machinery a little," Hudson says.

I perk up. "Have you found anyone yet?"

"No." Hudson sighs. "Everyone wants to take it in a whole different direction. I want to keep it small, you know? Build our clientele with more advertising and a little marketing makeover."

"Well, I don't want you to feel obligated or anything, but I can look over your ideas if you want. Give you some pointers."

"That would be fantastic!" he says without hesitation. "I don't want *you* to feel obligated, though. Only if you have time."

With my lack of employment outside of the bar, I have plenty of time. "I do. It's no problem at all."

He smiles again. I melt again.

Hudson

AFTER HAVING to warn Tanner away from saying anything about Joey because I'm not ready to spring the single father card on Rae just yet, dinner went well. The conversations flowed and there were no awkward lulls. Even Tanner was on his best behavior with Maura, only telling a few inappropriate stories about his buddies in the army.

Tanner and I split the bill while the girls step away to use the restroom one last time before we leave—"girl time", apparently. Tanner approaches me with a gleam in his eye as I'm standing by the entrance.

"I'm so fucking that tonight, man! God, did you see her ass? Wait, don't answer that, because I don't want to have to punch you. You should ride home with Rae, get a little action yourself. I'm gonna offer to take Maura home, and by home, I mean back to my place, because I'm so hitting that!" Tanner's all amped up at this point.

"You're disgusting."

"She wants my dick and you know it."

"God, I hate you sometimes, Tanner. Have some fucking manners. Treat her with respect, you ass."

He scoffs and I'm about to lay into him more when Rae's laughter hits my ears.

"Maura, baby, can I give you a ride home?" Tanner asks all sweet-like when the girls approach.

I gag a little, surprised Maura is buying his shit. Tanner isn't a completely bad dude, he just has no manners.

Maura looks to Rae, asking for permission. "That cool?"

"Yes, just be safe."

"You—" Tanner begins to interrupt but Rae silences him with a stern look.

She turns back to Maura. "Now give me your keys since you drove. I do need to get home somehow."

Maura tosses Rae her keys and squeals as she leaps into Tanner's waiting arms, waving at Rae as they practically run from Mic's.

"Guess it's just me and you then, huh?" Rae asks, coming to stand next to me, watching them exit.

I smile down at her. "Guess so. Hope you don't mind driving me home, though. I rode in with Tanner. Probably should have mentioned that before."

After a brief pause, she says, "Nah, I don't mind. Where do you live?"

"Over on 152nd Street for now. In those older apartments."

"For now?"

Now it's my turn to pause, because I want to phrase this carefully. I'm not trying to hide my daughter from Rae, but I'm not ready to reveal her yet either. "Uh, yeah. I'm looking to get a bigger place. I have something secured in Pembrooke Village, but I'm waiting on some electrical stuff to go through."

"Oh, that's a nice place, very family friendly."

I smile and open the door for her, hoping she'll drop the subject. She does.

We climb into a silver mini-SUV and head toward my apartment. She must be familiar with the area because she doesn't ask for directions once.

"Are you from around here?" I ask, unable to contain my curiosity anymore.

"I am. I grew up here. I went away to college in Boston but still came home every weekend the entire four years," she says, smiling widely. I can't help but smile too. She really seems to like this little town.

"You seem fond of Wakefield. Why do you want to move to Boston? For work?"

"Honestly?" I nod. "Well, I'm not even sure I do. I think I just want a scenery change, really, something new, different. I don't necessarily want to move to Boston, but I want to move *somewhere*...I think. I just want to do some things on my own for once...maybe."

She might maybe think she wants to leave, but I almost feel

as if she feels obligated to do something on her own, and she should understand that it doesn't really have to be that way.

"That makes sense."

"Does it?"

"Sure. I can relate. When I was younger, I went through some serious shit I wasn't ready for. I felt like I *needed* to be out on my own, doing my own thing. I tried and failed miserably. That resulted in me moving back home for a couple years. I've only been out on my own again for a month. As soon as the place in Pembrooke is done, that's when shit is going to get real serious, because I'll definitely be on my own again."

She's quiet, almost too quiet.

"So you think I'm going to fail?" Rae asks in a flat voice that leads me to believe she's not as calm as she's pretending to be.

"What? No, no, no, no. That's not at all what I'm saying, Rae. I'm just saying don't rush it. You'll know when you're ready. I don't really know you that well—"

"You're right, you don't know me," she interrupts, never taking her eyes off the road.

"But I can tell you're struggling with the decision to leave this town. You don't *have* to. You don't have to leave to find happiness. You can have it here. You can have your dream career here. You just have to find out what works for you, not what works for *them*."

"Or you. I don't find it fair you're telling me what to do—or not do—handing out this advice when you don't know my situation."

"I get that, Rae. I truly do," I try to reason. "But that's not what I'm trying to do at all. I'm just saying you should do what makes *you* happy. Don't give in to everyone else, to their dreams or what you feel like is expected of you. Don't let them tell you what you want."

"Like you're trying to do? *You* have no clue at all what I want."

"Neither do you."

Then she's quiet again and I'm man enough to admit I'm a little terrified of her silence.

Finally, she huffs out a breath. "You're right. I get what you're saying now. It's just...it's a tough subject for me. I *don't* know what I want. I wish I did, and I wish I didn't feel like I *have* to move on to bigger and better things, but I do. But again, you're right, so, thank you. I'm sorry I was sort of...snippy."

"Sort of?" I ask, grinning at her.

"Ass."

Goddamn, I love her mouth.

CHAPTER 7

RAE

I'M A BITCH.

I heard the word "fail" and all other coherent thoughts left my brain so I decided to attack the dude I like because I. Am. Insane. I'm going to scare him off before we get the chance to take this anywhere.

Now that I can think rationally, I can see that he's right. I shouldn't feel obligated to move to have a career, but I do feel that way. I feel like I *need* to move away to make something of myself in a field I'm not even one hundred percent certain I can excel in. I feel like I *need* to leave to prove I can do things on my own. Who am I trying to prove this to? I don't really know. Myself? My father? My sister? My dead mother? I don't know, but I do know I shouldn't feel that way. There's really no need for me to but...shit, I do.

We settle into an easy, comfortable silence. The last hour and a half zooms through my mind.

Hudson was sweet and friendly, and sexy. He dressed in a simple, tight long-sleeved black shirt and dark jeans that fit him just right, his hair perfectly messy, and his five o'clock shadow clear on his face. He looks damn good, like kissable kind of good.

No, Rae! No kissing.

I reach over to turn on the radio to distract myself from the images of Hudson kissing me running through my mind. Maura has my Transit CD in and "Asleep at the Wheel" starts playing. I peek at Hudson, remembering him smiling at my Transit shirt in the shop a few weeks back.

"Shut the front door! You *do* know Transit!" He jumps at my outburst. "Sorry," I mumble. "You're humming along, so you know who Transit is? You know this song?"

He smiles sheepishly. "I do. They're my favorite band."

"Oh. My. God. Marry me now!"

To my surprise, Hudson starts laughing at my word vomit. I glance over at him and he's holding his stomach and slapping his knees.

"Are you gonna be okay?"

He wipes at his eyes. "Holy shit. You and Maura are two peas in a pod. Do you always do that?"

"Um, do what?"

"Just say whatever pops into that cute little head of yours? Because it's highly entertaining."

I feel my face heat up. "Um, kind of. It's a quirk of mine." I shrug and focus on my driving and not freaking out over the fact that he just called me cute...kind of.

"It's very cute," he mutters as I pull into his apartment building lot. *Okay, it's settled—he called me cute.*

I park in front of the building he directed me to and face him. "Is this the part where I walk you to your door? Because that might be a little weird, and totally bass-ackward."

He stares at me with his mouth hanging open. I reach over with two fingers and push his mouth closed. "Flies, Hudson."

He mumbles something about my mouth between belly laughs. I shrug and turn back toward his building. It's cute. Small, maybe a little outdated, but still very cute.

I hear him starting to rustle around so I glance back over at him. He motions for me to hold on a minute and gets out of the car. I watch as he jogs around the front and opens my door.

He holds his hand out. "My lady."

I stare up at him for a few seconds before my brain registers what is happening. When it finally catches up, I unhook my seatbelt and place my hand into his. He helps me out of the car, closing the door and pulling me up close to him. He has my hands in his between our bodies. We're standing in a near-empty parking lot, staring at one another. I bet someone could walk right past us and we still wouldn't lose the connection our eyes have in this moment. It's intense, but not an excessive way. It feels...natural.

"I figured we'd just say goodbye here so it's not too weird for you," Hudson says with a small smirk. "I had a wonderful time with you tonight, Rae, and I haven't had that in a while. Would you like to go out with me again sometime? One on one, perhaps?"

"Uh, um, I-I..." I stammer. "Y-Yes. Definitely yes. I didn't scare you off with my random word vomit?" I ask seriously.

He smiles. "No. Definitely no."

It's my turn to smile.

"I've been meaning to asking you this—can I have your number?" Hudson asks.

I nod and find myself a bit sad when he breaks us apart so we can get out our phones. Mine vibrates as I'm slipping it back into my pocket, and I raise my eyebrow at Hudson.

"I sent you a text. Don't read it until you get home though. Might make this a little less awkward."

Suddenly he steps back into me, closer than before, leaving no room between our bodies. He slowly reaches up and places both hands on my cheeks, gently sliding them up until he's cradling my head. We're locked in another stare.

He closes his eyes and takes a deep breath, then leans forward and places his lips against my forehead. I close my eyes and feel myself melting into him. He holds his lips there for several seconds while I attempt to draw air into my lungs. He's warm, and surprisingly soft. I don't want to let go.

"Goodnight, Rae," he whispers against my skin. He slowly lets me go and walks off toward his building.

I stand there frozen with my eyes still closed for what seems like hours, though I know it's only been seconds since he walked away.

Only seconds since I started missing him.

––––––––

I PULL my favorite teal blanket around me tighter, trying to get my racing mind to calm down.

I wish Haley were still awake because I *really* need someone to talk to about tonight. I found her passed out on the couch when I arrived home. She may have had cheese puffs smashed on her sweatshirt and melted Skittles still in her hand, and I may have taken photographic evidence.

Tonight was...well, it was amazing. I wasn't expecting Hudson. I wasn't expecting him to be so open, so sweet, and I damn sure wasn't expecting his favorite band to be my favorite band. He scored major points with that one. Everything with him was so easy—the conversation, the laughing, even the silence. I've never had that before.

I roll over, looking at the clock on my nightstand: eleven thirty. I've been lying here for twenty minutes trying to calm my brain. I notice the light flashing on my cell, indicating a notification.

The text. I completely forgot about the text!

I practically throw myself across the bed and halfway onto the floor when I grab for my phone. I unlock it and stare perplexedly at the name popped up on the screen.

FMK?

> **FMK: You better be home while you're reading this, little lady. I had a great time tonight. Thank you. Hope this is a little less awkward than walking me to my door. ;-)**
>
> **Me: FMK?**
>
> **FMK: Future Mr. Kamden. Ya know, since you so beautifully proposed to me tonight.**

I laugh, because he's got me there.

> **FMK: Lame?**
>
> **Me: Very cute.**
>
> **FMK: You think I'm cute, huh?**

I do, but he doesn't need to know that.

> **Me: I think the name you put in my phone is cute. I'm still trying to decide if you are.**
>
> **FMK: You're a terrible liar.**
>
> **Me: Fair enough. Thank you for**

**tonight. Goodnight,
Hudson. x
FMK: Goodnight, Rae.**

I fall back onto my pillow with a smile on my face. For the first time in weeks, I find peaceful slumber.

CHAPTER 8

HUDSON

I WAKE up to my phone ringing. I blindly reach over, knocking the framed picture of Joey and me off my bedside table, and grab my phone. Squinting at the bright light, I see I have four missed calls from my mom. I spring out of bed in a panic, thinking something's wrong with Joey.

"Hello?" Joey answers.

"Joey? You okay, bug?" I ask cautiously.

"I missed you. Why didn't you come home last night? You're missing pancakes."

I wince. "Sorry, Joe. I had a late night. I'm getting up now and I'll be on my way over soon, I promise."

I hear my mom shout, "Joey! I told you not to wake him up!"

"But he's missing pancakes!" Joey answers. "She's so grouchy sometimes. Hurry please. Love you. Bye." The line disconnects.

I sigh and pull myself out of bed. I go about my morning shower routine and dress for a day at my mom's with Joey. Lastly, I grab Rocky—my black Lab—and hit the road.

It's only a ten-minute drive so I'm pulling into my mom's

driveway in no time. Joey runs out of the house to greet me wearing a mismatched set of pajamas.

"You're here! Finally!" So dramatic.

"Hey, kiddo! You save me any pancakes?" I ask, lifting her into my arms for a big bear hug. Rocky tries to squeeze his way in.

"No. I was starving."

Setting Joe down, I laugh and make my way into my mom's house, calling Rocky in behind me.

"Yo, Eleanor! You better have saved me a big plate!"

"Hudson Michael Tamell! I am your mother. Call me Mom, Mommy, Mama—anything but Eleanor," she scolds.

"Yeah, Hudson," Joey pipes up.

I raise my brows at my mom. She shrugs. "Gets it from you."

"Fair enough." I take a seat the breakfast bar and fix my gaze on Joey and Rocky, who are still in the hallway rolling around. "So, bug, what do you want to do today?"

"Swimming!" I shake my head no. "Ice skating!" Again, I shake my head no—it's freaking September. "Hiking!" I shrug. "I know! The dog park!" This time I nod, and Rocky perks up. "Yes! Rocky, we're going to the dog park! Come with me while I get dressed." They go racing up the stairs.

"Don't run, Joe!" I yell after them. "Damn kids."

My mom snorts and mumbles an agreement. "Be careful with those two today. They're a handful. Joey's been hyper as hell all morning," she warns.

"Oh boy."

"*Oh boy* is right. You're in for a long day. Now, how many pancakes do you want?"

I give her my trademark grin that's gotten me out of a lot of trouble over the years. "Six."

"Dammit, Hudson." She groans, knowing she'll have to make more batter. "You're lucky I love you."

I get up and walk over to the stove where she is, planting a big wet kiss on her cheek. "I love you too, *Eleanor*."

She whacks me with a spatula. "You better go check on Joey and Rocky. I told you they've been trouble all morning. I came downstairs this morning to find them playing in Rocky's water bowl. There were puddles all over the kitchen."

I make my way up the stairs and creep down the hallway. As I approach Joey's room, I can hear her talking.

"We're going to the dog park, Rocky. It's gonna be so fun!" The door is ajar so I peek inside. Joey has Rocky's head firmly in her grasp, talking right into his face. Rocky's full attention is on Joey, and I think it has nothing to do with him being trapped between her little hands. He loves that girl. "So much fun! We went all the time with Pop and Hazard before they went to heaven. Now I get to go with you!"

Joey's buzzing with excitement as she tells Rocky—who is now curled up watching her run around the room and pull clothes from drawers—stories about how my parents used to take Joey and *their* black Lab, Hazard, to the dog park all the time.

It makes my heart swell and eyes water because I really miss my dad, but damn does it hurt more that Joey isn't getting the time with him like I had. It's not fair. She's missing out on a lot of good memories with Pop.

Just like I did.

Up until I was just two months shy of being seventeen, I had a *flawless* relationship with my father. Our relationship was more best friends than it was father/son. Then I fucked up—big time. I got my high school girlfriend pregnant.

We were never the same after that.

I ended up moving out for a little over three years because

of a big blowout we had once we told everyone the news. My parents could have easily made me move back in since I was still a minor, but I think they saw that I needed to leave for things to get better between my father and me. I want to thank them and hate them for it all at the same time.

When I left home, I met Mr. Horton and started working at Jacked Up. In a way, he saved me. I had no idea what I was doing, and him giving me that job was the best thing I could have asked for. It kept me sane and grounded when I needed it the most. He also stepped in as a father figure of sorts since I wasn't in the best place with mine. I can never repay him for all he did for me, or my parents for letting me go free, for giving me the chance to meet Horton in the first place.

I had it great with Horton and Jacked up, but life eventually came crashing back down around me and I did move back in with my parents. To my surprise, I was welcomed with open arms by them both. While things weren't perfect for us, we worked hard on building our relationship again.

As life would have it, just when everything was turning around for us, when things were getting back to where they were before I screwed up, we got "the call".

Pop had a heart attack while driving and wrecked the car.

He didn't make it.

I've felt guilty for years over our fallout even though I know Pop wouldn't want me to. He was a great guy. He was kind, patient, and all-around loving. Never so much as raised his voice at mom for anything. All he did was fix random cars out in his garage, cater to the plants, and work for thirty years as an onsite construction manager in the city. He was amazing, so humble, so free-spirited, always making people smile and laugh with the all the random stuff that came pouring out of his mouth.

Now that I think of it, Rae and him would have gotten along well just for that alone.

Wait, no. I can't do that. I can't bring Rae into these facets of my life. It's too soon.

Before the panic can set in, I clear my throat and push open the door. "You ready, kiddo?"

"Need shoes. Come on, Rocky!" Joey races past me and they go bounding downstairs like the best of friends.

I glance around Joey's room, noting all the stick figure drawings of us together with mom and Rocky. It makes my heart swell for a whole other reason. *Damn, my daughter makes me proud.*

After taking one last peek around the room, making sure everything is in order, I trudge downstairs after them. I scarf down my pancakes while Joey and Rocky run around the backyard.

"How much sugar did you give her?"

"Only two spoonfuls...after she drowned her pancakes in syrup, of course," my mom says with an evil smirk.

"That's it. You're fired."

"From being her grandmother?"

"Yes."

She laughs and pats my arm. "Oh, Hudson. Don't you know it's my job to load her up with sweets and send her off with her dad for the day? Gives me time to take a nap. She'll be going for hours."

"Yep, definitely fired."

"My nap is going to be worth it," she calls as she makes her way upstairs. I grumble under my breath about how evil she is. "I heard that!"

I roll my eyes, because of course she did, and then I gather up my kid.

"Last one to the car is a big fat loser!" I holler out the back door.

"You're always the loser!" Joey yells back, barreling through the door with Rocky hot on her heels.

And that's how my Saturday begins.

———

AFTER AN EXHAUSTING DAY at three different parks, I'm relaxed on my mom's couch. Joey's curled up next to me drifting in and out of sleep with *Finding Nemo* fired up on the screen.

Times like these are my favorite.

I had to reschedule the card game with the guys for next weekend after the sleepover was cancelled due to a sick kid.

If I'm being honest, I would have rescheduled, canceled sleepover or not. I've been trying to avoid them after my evening with Rae last night because I know those two assholes are going to question me until I'm blue in the face. I don't want to rehash it all and have them analyze every little detail. I want to keep it—keep Rae—to myself for a while longer.

I've been fighting the urge to text her all day. Even though I was out with the most amazing kid ever today, she's been right in the front of my mind. I want to talk with her, but I have no idea how to start up a conversation. I could be lame and ask for that marketing help, or I can try to think up something smooth.

Yeah right. Better stick with lame just to be safe.

> **Me: So, hey, did you still want
> to help with that marketing
> thing?**

I toss my phone onto the coffee table so I don't stare at it until she texts back. Instead, I end up staring at the clock over the TV.

It takes her five full minutes to respond.

> **Rae: Actually, no. I completely changed my mind. I'm SO swamped with work right now, I'm afraid I don't have the time. I was just being nice. Wait, who is this?**

Her sarcasm knows no bounds.

> **Me: Hudson**
> **Rae: Which one? I know a few.**
> **Me: The sexy one, of course.**
> **Rae: Shit. That could be at least two different guys. :-p**

I laugh out loud at that one.

"Why are you laughing? That wasn't even funny," Joey says, pointing to the television.

"Nothing, kiddo. I just thought of something funny."

She pats my arm and lies back down. "Okay then."

> **Me: It's the extra sexy one. The one you can't stop thinking about...**
> **Rae: Oh. Hudson Carter? How the hell are you, dude?!**

Little smartass. My phone vibrates again before I'm able to respond.

> **Rae: Fine. I give. You caught**
> **me. Yes, I'm still willing to**
> **help you. What do you have**
> **in mind?**

My fingers fly over my keyboard and I've hit send before I can take it back.

> **Me: Have coffee with me**
> **tomorrow? We can talk**
> **then.**
> **Rae: Sure. Where and when?**

Holy shit. I just asked Rae out!

"Oooh! You said a bad word! Pay up!" Joe exclaims next to me.

Oh hell. Apparently I said that out loud.

"Dang, kid. I can't catch a break with you." I dig a quarter out of my pocket and hand it over. She closes her tiny hand around it and holds it to her chest like it's the most precious treasure she's ever received.

> **Me: 10 AM? We can meet at**
> **Perk.**
> **Rae: Done. See you then.**

Score! I do a fist pump, bouncing around a few times.

"You're weird," Joey says, giving me side-eye.

"Whatever. Where do you think you get it from?" I stick my tongue out.

She taps her finger to her chin, just like she's seen me do a thousand times when I pretend to think on something. "True."

I laugh and tell her it's time for bed. She complains, but I finally get her in there.

I'm on cloud nine as I close her bedroom door and head down the hall to my soon to be old room. I still can't believe that any day now I'll be living in my own house, a house that I *own*.

Don't get me wrong, my mom has been a godsend these last few years, allowing me to live at home and save up enough money for a sizeable down payment. Hell, even when a last minute electrical issue popped up, she didn't complain that Joey and I weren't out by our planned move-out date. Instead, she hooked me up with a good friend of hers who needed someone to watch his sublet while he found a new permanent tenant. She said it was my space to use for quiet time before I don't have it anymore.

So, I stay in the apartment about two or three nights a week to make sure everything is good with it, though my time is still mostly spent at my mom's.

When it comes down to it, I'm a twenty-four-year-old single father and business owner. I should be out on my own, taking care of my own priorities, and not relying on my mom so much. I don't overload her or anything, but it's about time she moved on with her life and lived for herself for once—not looking after me *and* Joey all the time.

It's time we all moved on and started living our lives again, me included.

After a quick shower, I settle into bed. I'm close to being asleep when light spills over my face. I crack open one eye to find Joey standing in my doorway.

"What's up, bug? Bad dream?"

"No. I just missed you." My heart skips a beat.

"Well, come on then. Hop in," I say, lifting up the blanket and scooting over what little I can. Joey's only seven, so space isn't really an issue. Good thing, too, because this bed is only a twin.

"Thanks, dude." Joey yawns as she climbs into bed, curls up into a ball, and snuggles up close to me.

"I love you, kiddo."

"I love you more, Daddy."

"You little liar."

"You big liar."

I fall asleep with a smile plastered on my face.

CHAPTER 9

RAE

BANG! BANG! BANG!

"Hurry the fuck up, Hales! I have shit to do!" I yell through the bathroom door.

"Go poop somewhere else!"

"I said shit *to do*. Not shit *to take!*"

"You can still go somewhere else."

Haley's been in the bathroom for the last thirty minutes doing God knows what. It's pissing me off because I'm supposed to be meeting Hudson in twenty minutes at a coffee shop that's almost ten minutes away. As soon as I was done with my shower, she skidded in there and locked the door behind her.

"Calm your lady bits, little girl! I'm finishing up now!" she yells back. I roll my eyes because "finishing up now" probably means about ten more minutes for her.

Of course I'm right—eight minutes later, she finally comes out. I glare at her as I rush inside to brush my teeth and run a comb through my still wet hair, pulling it back into a tight ponytail. I swab on some mascara and decide I look decent enough in my plain white t-shirt and dark skinny jeans. It's obviously not going to get any better since I have to leave in about two minutes if I want to make it on time.

Even after speeding a little, I'm still about four minutes late. I rush inside and frantically start looking around for Hudson. When I don't see him, my hopes are dashed. *Did he forget?*

I take a seat at an open table and lay out some of the notes I managed to make last night after work. I check my phone as I'm looking over everything. He's ten minutes late and only has another five before I leave.

My phone buzzes. I snatch it up quickly, hoping it's Hudson with a good excuse. It's not. It's Maura, who I made the mistake of telling I was meeting Hudson this morning.

Bestie (NOT PERRY): Wellllllll?

I laugh, because the fact that it says "Not Perry" next to Maura's number means she got ahold of my phone and changed her name...again. She and Perry have this war going when it comes to who gets to be my best friend. I'll never tell Maura this, but Perry wins, though only slightly.

Me: Can't talk right now. We're about to have coffee. Call you soon. x

I switch my phone to silent as the door to Perk flies open.

"I am so damn sorry, Rae! I had to take care of something at home. I swear I'm usually on time. I promise," Hudson rushes out, throwing himself down into the chair across from me.

He's looking at me with those beautiful ocean-colored eyes. They're still perfect. He's still perfect.

Chill, Rae. He's just a guy, a possible client at that. You've been on one accidental date, that's it.

He frowns. "You're mad."

I realize I haven't said a word to him since he sat down at the table. I've been too busy staring.

"I'm not, really. It's fine. I was four minutes late myself, and *I'm* usually not late, so there's no reason I should hold it against you."

Hudson sinks back into the chair, relieved. "Thank God. I thought you were gonna be so pissed and refuse to work with me, which would suck because I really do need your help."

"Oh, so this is a work date? Not a *date* date?" I put on my best innocent face and bat my lashes at him.

He freezes, and all the color in his face drains.

If he's going to be late, I'm going to have some fun with it. I let my eyes water and bite my lip, making it seem like I'm holding in some serious tears. "I just...I thought... Never mind," I say, turning my attention to the window to gain some sort of composure because I'm about to lose it. Once I have myself under control, I turn back to a still very pale Hudson.

"Uh, I...umm...shit. Rae, listen...I didn't mean this as a *date*, just a..." He trails off in a state of confusion, doing that fish thing with his mouth again. He clears his throat and attempts to form an actual sentence.

Laughter bubbles up and spills—ungracefully, I might add —from my mouth at his attempts. I think there's a snort in there somewhere too.

Hudson begins clearing his throat and shifting uncomfortably in his chair, glancing around the café, politely smiling at other customers who are openly staring since I'm not being all that quiet.

I swipe away the tears and take a deep breath, trying to sober up some.

"I'm fucking with you, Hudson. This is just a business meeting. Come on, you're buying me a coffee for being so late—and so gullible." I grab my purse and head to the front counter, leaving Hudson sitting at the table gaping at me.

I'm looking over the menu when I feel him approach. He steps into me, his warmth falling over me like a blanket. He's nearly plastered against me, causing my breath to catch. There's no way he doesn't hear it.

"You're something, Rae. I like it," he says softly in my ear, his lips ghosting the shell of my ear.

Luckily the barista turns toward us, his words drowning out my shallow breaths.

My words are nonexistent, and I guess I stand there longer than I should because Hudson orders for me. "We'll take two large black house coffees, please."

We. The word rings in my ears, causing my heart to flutter and fill with warmth. That word sounds good...too good.

"Thank you. How'd you know what I wanted?"

"Shot in the dark. Can't go wrong with plain coffee. You can change it if you want," he says.

I shake my head and make my way to the pickup counter while Hudson pays. I take the opportunity to study him from afar. He's dressed in simple jeans and a semi-tight short-sleeved baby blue shirt, making his eyes and messy dark hair stand out against his lightly tanned skin. He must have spent the day outside yesterday because he's a bit darker than he was on Friday night.

"Here you go, gorgeous," the barista says as he slides my coffee toward me and winks.

I thank him and look over in time to catch Hudson scowling at the poor high school kid. Laughing, I pour a generous amount of cream and sugar in my coffee, topping it off with a few shakes of cinnamon.

"Cinnamon?" Hudson crinkles his nose in disgust.

"Don't hate. It's delicious." He still has a look of disbelief plastered on his face. I sigh. "Let me guess, black? No sugar or anything?"

He smiles, takes a sip of coffee, and lets out an exaggerated, "Mmmmm."

As we settle down back at the table, I flip open my small folder of ideas. "So, I'm not entirely familiar with your situation at Jacked Up, but I did a little research after work last night." I flip to my page of notes and begin reading off some facts I found. "It opened in 1985, so you're coming up on your thirty-second anniversary. It's locally owned, obviously. You have six employees total and don't seem to have much of an online presence, or at least not one that I could easily find."

"It's one of the things I want to work on. Our website is shitty and in desperate need of an update. You couldn't find us on social media because we don't have any accounts, which I know we need to remedy. Currently we have one small billboard and a tiny spot in the phone book—not that anyone really uses that anymore—but, yeah, that's about it."

I cringe. "That's it? Dang. That's not a lot. Well, you're already aware of your lack of social media presence, so that's good. I know a few up-and-coming web designers that would be more than happy to help you out for a reasonable price. It'll help build their portfolio and give you something fresh, so it's a win-win for both of you. How do you feel about a whole new look?" I ask hopefully.

He thinks on it for a minute. *I like it.* I like that he takes the time to think about what's best for his business instead of just jumping into anything.

"I can be persuaded. I'm not entirely fond of what we currently have, but I also don't want it to turn into a huge expense."

"We can talk with the graphic designer about that when we do the website. You're going to want everything to blend together anyway, so updating it all at once would probably be best, and cheapest. Speaking of that, how about business cards? I know you have them, but have you thought about passing them around town? I mean, you're a small business, and in little towns like this, the small guys like to stick together. I think if you talk with a few places about getting some counter space for business cards, it could be good."

Hudson nods. "Yeah, I think a few places might be open to doing that. Could work out well for both of us, too. I'm liking this, Rae. Anything else?"

"Hmmm...well, other than what we've already hit on, which I think would help a lot, I would strongly suggest considering getting rid of your wasted space in the phone book and put that money into advertising in the local paper and possibly even those little free thrifty magazines. Maybe even take out a few spots in Boston? For all we know they could have some real shitty auto shops over there, so it wouldn't hurt too much to stretch your advertising area."

He takes another moment to think, and then nods again. "I like this. I like it all. You have some great, small ideas I didn't think of that could help get the word out about the shop a little more. I have to be honest, Rae, I was nervous to hear your thoughts. I wasn't sure how we could help boost the business in a way that wouldn't cost me a fortune, but I think you've managed to throw out some great ideas I can work with."

His compliments make me blush a little. "You're welcome. It was no problem at all. I even did a little research on ad space prices," I say, handing him the folder.

He eagerly takes it and begins looking over the info I've gathered. I can see the approval on his face, and damn if it doesn't make me feel like I'm floating among clouds.

After several minutes, he smiles to himself. Then he turns the charm my way. "How about we go on a real date now? Not a business meeting, not a coffee date, but an actual *date* date?"

———

Hudson

"PLEASE." It leaves my mouth before I can stop it.

I just asked Rae on a date, even though I didn't plan on ending this business meeting doing so, and she's sitting here staring at me with a confused look on her face.

In reality, dating is the last thing I need to be adding to my hectic life, so maybe I shouldn't have asked her, but...I wanted to. I *had* to. There's no doubt in my mind now that I have to see where this...connection or whatever it is we have goes.

But she's not saying anything. Maybe I jumped the gun? Maybe she doesn't want to date me now...

Fuck. I'm her client now. That has to be it.

"Shit. Sorry. Just forget I said—"

"Yes."

"—anything. It was a—wait, what?"

"I said yes, Hudson. I'd love to go out on a date with you. One that isn't about a business project and that I can be prepared for. One that's not with Maura or Tanner. Yes," she says again.

"You said yes."

She chuckles. "I did. Why are you so surprised? You asked me this on Friday night. I wasn't going to let you off the hook with a business meeting/coffee date, you know."

Her teasing eases the nerves racing through me. "You're right. I don't know. I just thought maybe you wouldn't want to with us potentially working together."

"Potentially? As if. I have you hook, line, and sinker and you know it."

Though she means it in terms of business, she has me in other ways too. I don't even know this girl but feel the strangest connection to her, like her car was meant to break down up the road from my shop, like she's supposed to fit somewhere in my world, no matter how crazy it sounds.

I peer over at her to find her staring at me, her green eyes lit up with joy. "You do, Rae. You do."

CHAPTER 10

RAE

I SHOULDN'T like Hudson as much as I do, especially since I just met the guy, but I can't help feeling a connection to him. I have no idea why, but he feels...safe.

I like safe.

"How about dinner at my place on Wednesday?" he asks hopefully.

"That sounds perfect."

He shoots me a wide smile. "Good. Good." He's still smiling like an idiot. "I hate to do this, but I have to get going."

"Oh that's no problem. I have some stuff planned this afternoon anyway."

We gather our things and head toward the door together. I never really understood the appeal when those hunky heroes did it in all those romance novels I read, but the moment Hudson's hand finds my lower back, I get it. That one small touch feels so intimate.

"Can I walk you to your car?"

I dip my head and he steers me toward my little sedan, beating me to the door and opening it for me.

"Thank you so much for your help with Jacked Up, Rae. I feel like we've been stuck lately, and I think this is going to pump things up for us. I saw a card in the folder, so I'll give that website guy a call tomorrow," Hudson says, stuffing his hands in his pockets and rocking back on his heels.

God, he looks so cute when he's being shy.

He stands several inches taller than me, and I have to tilt my head back to smile up at him. "It's no problem. I'm glad I could help."

"Seven thirty okay? For Wednesday?" he asks.

"Perfect." He rocks back on his heels again, like he's not sure what to say next.

"Hudson?"

"Yeah?"

"I'll see you Wednesday."

He smiles again as I climb into my car.

When I glance in my mirror before I turn out of the parking lot, he's still standing there with his hands in his pockets and that perfect smile plastered on his face.

———

I PARK in front of my apartment and switch my phone back on. I'm not surprised to see that Maura's texted eight times while I was with Hudson, and I give her a call.

"Finally! You can't just leave a girl hanging like that! Spill. Now," she yells into the phone.

"First, calm down; you're hurting my ear," I say in my best motherly voice. "Second, I have a date Wednesday." She squeals so loud I have to pull the phone away while she gets it all out. "Ears, woman!"

"Sorry!" she whispers. "I'm just *so* excited for you! I can tell you like him a lot. Tanner told me a little about him and he seems like a stand-up guy, Rae."

I'm not sure I find anything Tanner says to be reassuring,

but I'm glad Maura approves. "Good. So, how was your *second* date with Tanner last night?"

"Glorious!" she rings out. "He's *so* sweet and funny, Rae. I know he seems like a dick sometimes but it's all a show, like he has to prove he's macho or some crap like that. I swear, he's so considerate and awesome when it's just the two of us. I *really* like him, Rae."

Though her choice in men is questionable, I'm genuinely happy for my best friend. "As long as he treats you right, I'm happy for you."

I hear someone in the background. "Damn. I gotta go, Rae. Order's up! Talk to you later, love."

"Kisses! Bye!"

I put my phone away and shake my head. *That girl. She's something.*

I sling my bag over my shoulder and make my way to my apartment.

"Yo, Hales! I'm back!" I yell as I bust through the front door.

"We're in the kitchen, Rae!"

"Do you have a mouse in your pocket? Who are you— Dad!" I yell, running to the stool he's sitting on, wrapping my arms around him and squeezing him extra tight.

"Hey, kiddo, I've been missing you," he says, squeezing me back.

Even though we live in the same town, I rarely get to see my dad. He's a bigwig accountant at a firm in Boston and he's always working. With my schedule of nights and weekends at Clyde's, we don't get much time to see each other.

This time it's only been about a month since I've seen him last, but it seems like longer.

"You're looking a little gray," I tease, ruffling his hair.

"You're the second meanest kid I have. Haley told me I had more wrinkles."

"You do," my sister chimes in.

We're both lying. My dad doesn't look a day over thirty-five. He still has the same dark hair he's always had and the same pale skin I do, and there are no wrinkles, not even lining his brown eyes.

"What brings you by?" I ask.

"He came to see me, his favorite daughter. Duh," Haley says, as if it's the only plausible answer.

We both ignore her. "Just wanted to see how my *two* favorite girls are doing. I feel like I haven't seen you in forever. How's everything going? How's the job hunt?" He turns to Haley. "How's the daycare doing?"

As close and Haley and I are, there's one huge difference between us: I hate kids. Haley, on the other hand, wants an army of them. She even manages a daycare with her best friend, that's how much she loves them.

Me? I'll pass. I'm horrible with kids. I either clam up and don't know what to say or I talk circles around them, usually saying something wildly inappropriate.

I don't have a motherly bone in my body, and I can thank my own mother for that.

"It's going very well. I may have some leads," I lie. I haven't heard back from a single firm, but I don't want to admit defeat just yet.

"And The Learning Hut is doing well. We enrolled two new kids the other day so we're maxed out until one of them ages out. We're may be looking at expanding soon."

He beams with pride. "You girls make an old man happy as a clam. Now, do you want to go out and grab some dinner?" He points a finger at my sister. "I still don't trust your cooking, Haley."

"Rude! I burn one pizza and turn noodles to paste twice and suddenly I 'can't cook'. Maybe I'd be a better cook if you didn't have such high expectations of me, Dad."

"I'm the worst dad ever," my dad deadpans.

I ignore their show and roll my eyes. "You mind if I freshen up real quick? I didn't get the chance to properly dry my hair because *someone* was hogging the bathroom," I say, giving Haley my best death glare.

She shrugs. "Shouldn't have overslept."

"I had trouble sleeping last night."

As soon as I say it, I know it was a mistake. My dad zeros in on me instantly.

"You're still having the nightmare? I thought you said it was getting better." He's frowning, the concern clear.

Since I was seven, I've had the exact same nightmare over and over again. It's cloudy and I'm floating out in the middle of the ocean. The wind whips around me, causing huge waves to crash against me and knock me sideways like I'm nothing but a piece of driftwood. The salty water is so cold that I can't feel my fingers or toes. My teeth chatter together as I try to call out for help, but it's of no use. No one can hear me over the wind and waves. I'm not that far out, but since I'm so small, it seems like I'll never see land again. I keep swimming and swimming, trying so hard to reach the shore of this vast body of water.

I'm scared and screaming for help. I can see my savior; she just can't hear me.

My mother's standing on the edge of the water, not paying any attention as the waves slam into me again. I call out as my head bobs underwater and I push back through the swell.

It's then I see a shadow of what looks like a kid running up next to her. He's frantic and yelling, even I can hear it over the noise of the water, but I can't make out what he's saying.

My mother is still just standing there, starting off into the horizon, looking right over me as I struggle.

Then, I sink.

I have no idea what, if anything, happens next, because that's always when I wake up drenched in sweat. The dream seems so unbelievably real. I feel the fear and heavy weight of the dream for days afterward, every time. It hangs heavy, like it's something that's actually happened, but I know that's not possible, because surely I'd remember something like that...right?

I train my eyes on my dad. "It did. I hadn't had one in eight months, but it started up again about three weeks ago. I have no idea what caused it to come back this time. Stress, maybe?"

I did some research online and found that stress can be a trigger. The dream itself is stressful, so maybe that's all it is—my mind projecting real life into the dream. It just seems so weird that it's coming back now because I don't feel *that* stressed.

Also, something feels different about this round. It feels *more* real than normal, so real that I woke up three times last night before the kid even arrived. After the third time, I was done. I threw on a pair of shoes and drove out to Lake Quannapowitt, my thinking spot. I sat for an hour to watch the sunrise and came back home to sleep some more, which didn't turn out so well since I woke up late.

My dad exhales loudly because he knows how much this affects me. "Yeah, that could be it. With your car breaking down, you getting sick, and now all these job applications, I'm sure you're stressed out. Maybe take it easy for a while? You're already pushing this whole moving-to-the-city thing pretty hard, and that can't be helping out at all. Just take it easy. Besides, you're not in that big of a hurry to move away from your old man, are you?"

I shake my head and answer honestly. "Well, no. Honestly, I'm not sure what exactly it is I want to do anymore. The more I keep tossing around the whole moving thing, the less appealing it sounds. I don't even know how appealing marketing sounds. Maybe I just need a break from thinking."

That was hard, admitting that out loud to my dad. I was so sure of this a few months back—hell, even a few weeks ago—but now I'm not.

Hudson helped me see that.

"Kiddo, if you're worried about upsetting me, stop. Everything will figure itself out. I'm not rushing you to find something, so don't rush yourself. Getting a job like this is a big deal. I want you someplace that makes you happy. I don't want you to settle. You're keeping your head afloat, that's the important thing right now."

"Yeah, yeah, what he said, but why didn't you tell me about your nightmares, Rae? About your mixed feelings on moving? Marketing?" The hurt is clear in Haley's voice, and she has every right to feel that way. I should have trusted her with it. She's always been there for me, so there is no reason why I should have hidden it from her.

"You're right. I should have told you, Hales. Everything has been so confusing lately, and I didn't want to seem like a failure. Hell, Dad, I begged you for weeks to approve of the big move, and now I'm possibly flaking on it. The sad part is I didn't even realize some of my feelings until the other day when Hudson talked with me about them."

"Back up, who is Hudson?"

"Calm down, old man. He's just a guy."

"A guy she went on a blind date with. The *same* guy she was just out having coffee with," Haley supplies, smirking at me—payback for not confiding in her, I guess.

"Rae?"

I sigh. "Yes, he's a guy. Yes, I went on a date with him Friday. Yes, we met for coffee this morning, but it was a *business* coffee date. He owns Jacked Up, the shop that fixed my car. He was looking to load up on the clientele and asked for a few marketing tips, so I put together a small folder of ideas and gave it to him this morning. Happy?" I begin inching my way toward the hallway that leads to our bedrooms and bathroom, purposely leaving out my upcoming date.

My dad huffs and concedes through gritted teeth. "Fine. You're an adult now. Scurry along. We're going for wings."

I groan because I know that means we're heading to Clyde's. "Give me fifteen minutes."

"WHAT'S THIS? Family dinner and no one invited me? That's messed up, Uncle Ted," Perry teases my dad, taking a seat on the stool next to me and giving me a nudge. "Yo! What up, Waitress Rae? I'll take a Dr. Pepper, please."

I shove him hard. "I'm not working today, you jackass."

Waitress Rae is his favorite thing to call me when he visits me at work. He says it's like he's talking to a whole new person when I'm there and he likes having "two versions" of me to choose from. He's insane.

I love my cousin Perry like a brother. He's like a best friend to me and practically lived at our house when we were kids since his mom, my dad's sister, was in and out of the picture constantly. I love my Aunt Tessa, but she wasn't the best mom. She had a habit of stepping out on her husband for months at a time. For some odd reason, Uncle Walker never left her. He always stayed and let her do whatever the hell she wanted. Because of this, he worked long hours to make sure all the bills were paid and that Perry had everything he ever needed. This resulted in Perry spending a lot of time at our house since his parents were rarely home.

Surprisingly enough, Perry has a great relationship with his dad. You'd think it would be strained because Walker was never home, but I think all it did was bring them closer. They clung to one another, and their relationship was solid. The one he had with his mother was almost nonexistent, though, especially since no one really knows where she is now.

As soon as Perry and I graduated college, Walker divorced Tessa—and when I say as soon as, I mean the moment we all gathered around for pictures, she was served the papers. After that, she bailed, and we haven't heard from her in about three months.

You'd think since Tessa is my dad's sister, the relationship between Walker and my dad would be stretched thin, but that couldn't be less true. They're best friends, and Dad talks to Tessa about as much as everyone else does, which is hardly ever.

"Whatevs, girl. So, what's up with my favorite people?" Perry beams around the table.

"Oh, you know, just enjoying lunch with my favorite two people in the world—that is until some punk-ass kid came and interrupted everything."

Perry clutches his chest in mock pain. "You wound me, Hales. 'Tis okay, though. I know you really love me."

"Barely," she grumbles.

She's such a liar. The only thing Haley loves more than me, Dad, *and* Perry? Giving Perry shit.

"Anyway, Uncle Ted, what goes on? How's the big city?"

"Boring, big, exhausting, never-ending," my dad answers on a sigh.

"Why don't you just retire? You're like, what, sixty, right?"

Dad pops Perry in the shoulder. "You little shit. I'll have

you know I'm only forty-five, a year younger than your dad, thank you very much."

"Still old."

"Hi Mr. Kamden, Rae, Haley," Clarissa says in her fakest sweet voice. Why she's over here, I have no idea. She's not the one serving us today. We all ignore her, but she doesn't seem to care as she leans into the table, propping her elbows up so her breasts look bigger. "Hi, Perry."

Ah, she's here to flirt.

In an obvious attempt to avoid any contact whatsoever with her, Perry shifts my way and dips his head at her. "Hey."

Clarissa, who is a twenty-four-year-old woman, pouts at his brushoff. Then she gives him her best *come hither* look and straightens, puffing her chest out at him. "Whatever. See you later, Perry," she says, sashaying away.

"God, that girl *kills* me. She's so pushy and fake and weird," Perry complains, adding in a shiver for dramatic effect.

"Try working with her," I gripe.

"Is she still...you know...*working extra?*" Haley asks.

"Unfortunately."

"Working extra is great! What could be so bad about that?" Dad asks, not understanding what we're hinting at.

Haley, Perry, and I exchange looks and all burst into laughter.

"Uncle T, she works extra in the back seats of cars," Perry explains in the politest way possible.

The look on my dad's face and the loud groan that accompanies it bring on the second round of laughter.

For a moment, I'm happy. My nightmare doesn't exist, and my rapidly growing feelings for Hudson aren't weighing on me. Briefly, all my fears fade away.

CHAPTER 11

HUDSON

I MAY NOT KNOW a lot about graphic design, but I do know that the deal the kid just gave me on the website is a damn good one.

"Well, what did he say?" Tucker asks. The blond-haired bastard is sitting—quite relaxed, I might add—in the chair across from my desk with his feet propped up. I push them off in order to take back *some* sort of authority.

Since they've been at Jacked Up as long as I have, I called him and Gaige into my office this morning to talk with them about my meeting with Rae. They were both on board one hundred percent.

"Eight hundred bucks," I tell him, taking up the same pose Tucker was just in. "That's with a new website, printed business cards, and a new logo. I'm meeting with him at noon to go over some details."

"Hot damn!" Gaige yells. "That's a good deal. I know Horton paid at least a grand for that shitty-ass website we have now."

I nod. "I know. I can't believe we managed to get hooked up with this guy. We owe Rae big time."

Gaige and Tucker exchange a look.

"I think we'll let *you* pay up on that," Tucker says, winking at me.

"Whatever. How'd it go Saturday, Gaige?" I say, switching gears because I know if I don't, they won't drop the Rae thing at all.

"Good." Gaige oversees the short four-hour shift Saturday mornings. "How was your date Friday?"

Of course it didn't work.

"You fuckers," I moan, looking down at my folded hands, refusing to make eye contact. "It was good—no, it was *great*. I like her a lot. We're...uh...we kind of have a date Wednesday."

"Really?" Gaige asks in disbelief.

I nod and can feel Tucker's gaze on me.

"You need to go for it," he says, his voice a whisper.

"What about Joey?" I volley back, looking back up at him.

"I'm pretty sure your kid isn't the one who's going to be dating her," Gaige replies.

"You know what I mean," I push out through gritted teeth.

"We do. Like you said: what about Joey? I'm sure the kid isn't going to care. If anything, she's gonna embrace it. I know it. Trust me on this. It's not going to be bad," Tucker reasons. "I know you have to be careful with your daughter, I get that, but I think it's the right move to make."

I hope he's right because I do really like Rae, and I know she likes me too. I can see it every time our gazes lock. It's just... it's been *so* long since I've had a crush on someone, since I've dated anyone, and I'm nervous to pursue this.

It's not just because of Joey, though Tucker is right; I *do* have to be careful with her. She's only seven and can get easily attached, which is what terrifies me the most because I don't want to break my kid's heart if things go south—something that is totally possible.

It's more than that. What if I'm not good enough? What if

Joey isn't good enough? What if the whole single father thing is a big-ass no for Rae? Do I want to put myself out there and try? Because, if I'm being completely honest, that scares me more than anything else.

"Stop it. I know what you're thinking and I get why you're afraid. You don't really have the life of most twenty-four-year-olds. I get that, but don't write everything off so fast. Have your date Wednesday then decide where to go from there. You *have* to at least try. Don't put that negativity in your head."

I look hard at Tucker. He's right. I can't be sure until I at least put myself out there. "You're right."

He shrugs smugly. "I know."

"Get the hell out of my office and go work or something."

"Dude, stop playing at being a boss," Gaige says. "It doesn't work with us."

He's right too, but I'm not admitting they were both right in a five-minute span. They'd never let that shit go either. I swear, my two best friends are a bunch of immature asshole sometimes, but I wouldn't trade them for anything.

I glance at the clock once they finally shuffle out of my office. I have about an hour and a half before I have to meet the website guy, so I take the time to text Rae to tell her the good news.

> **Me: So, Perry? Good dude. He**
> **gave us a sweet deal. I can't**
> **repay you enough. Looking**
> **forward to Wednesday.**
> **Rae: Me too! ;-)**

Suddenly, my phone goes crazy.

**Rae: Oh, fuck me!!! I meant :-)
I was not implying anything
with that winky face! I
promise!**

**Rae: OMG! I didn't mean
anything by the "fuck me"
either!!**

**Rae: Shit! Just ignore all of that
and pretend I never texted
you back. The next text is
going to be my real
response.**

**Rae: Oh, awesome! Can't wait
for Wednesday either. :-)**

Rae: Much better.

At this point, I'm laughing so loud and hard that someone bangs on the office door.

"Yo, what's so funny? We can hear you out here, ya know," Tucker says, opening my door. Over his shoulder, I see Gaige and Liam, another mechanic and friend, with shit-eating grins on their faces.

I'm still laughing when I hand Tucker my phone so he can read what Rae sent. Probably not the nicest thing I've ever done, but that whole exchange was too hilarious not to share. He holds it up for the guys to read along. They all burst into laughter too.

"Nice job on that one, Hudson," Liam says. "She seems fun."

"She's a spitfire, that's for sure," I agree.

Before I realize what he's doing, Tucker types something into my phone.

"Tuck, man!" I snatch the phone out of his hands. "What the fuck did you send?"

Me: ;-)

I laugh. "Okay, that was a good one."

My phone beeps right away.

"What did she say?" Tucker sounds as excited as me to get a response from her.

I flip the phone up so he can read her text.

Rae: LMAO!!

"You're welcome," he says, a satisfied grin on his face.

I shake my head and shove them all out the door. "Go work, assholes."

————

I'M JUST SNAGGING a table at our designated meeting spot when a shadow falls across the table. I look up, surprised at who I find standing there.

The guy Rae was hanging on last Monday at Clyde's is standing right in front of me, holding a binder.

Half of me hopes he's lost and not Perry. The other half is curious as hell how he knows Rae and why they seem so close with one another. Are they exes? Friends? More than friends? She seems into me, so I'm not banking on that, but this unexplainable surge of jealousy rages through me whenever I see the guy, and that's solely based on the way Rae smiles when she's around him. I want her to smile at *me* like that, not this doof.

"Hey. Hudson, right?" I nod. He takes a seat across from me and sticks his hand out. "I'm Perry."

I put on my game face and shake his hand.

"Nice to meet you, Perry. Thanks so much for meeting me today. I know this is sort of short notice, but I'm really wanting to get things going on this."

"No problem, I can understand that. I guess let's just dive in. I worked a little this morning after we hung up." He takes out a red folder and slides it my way. "I checked out your current website and logo and tried to go off that. I know it's not much, but it's a start."

I flip open the folder and am pleasantly surprised by what I find. This is exactly what I was wanting, and I didn't even know it.

As a play on the name of the shop, the lettering on Jacked Up is cracked without it being too obnoxious. It's placed over a sleek brushed metal that is also full of cracks. The name is in a bright white, the metal a dark blue with a gold inset. Along the bottom is a slogan—something we've never had.

"Nothing is too jacked up for us," I read aloud.

Perry screws his face up. "Yeah, like I said, it's just a quick draft."

"As lame as it—no offense—it's damn funny and probably corny enough to work."

"Really?"

I laugh, at his shock and at myself. I didn't want to like the dude, but I kind of do, at least for his talent. "Yeah, man. I like the entire thing. This is perfect, exactly what I was wanting. You did a damn fine job, Perry. Is this look something that can be carried over into the website and business cards?"

His mouth snaps shut then opens again. He does this once more before words manage to make it out. "Yes! Sorry." He clears his throat. "Yes, definitely. Easily, actually. I can start on something this week if you want?"

"Yes, please. I'm really diggin' this. I think it's going to help give us a little extra something. If this all goes well and you're up for it, I may have you design a few ads. Is that something you'd be interested in?"

"Oh, yeah!" he says excitedly. "Sorry, I'm kind of amped up over this. I just graduated in the spring and I have been struggling to secure a good design position somewhere, so this is kind of my first go at things. I interned at a firm for a few months but I don't think the office thing is my strong point, so I was going to try out the freelancing thing." He takes a deep breath. "Thanks for taking a chance on me, man. I appreciate it. I'm going to have to take Rae out to dinner for this one."

He laughs at his own joke, but all I can muster is a strangled chuckle because he's talking about taking the girl I'm way too interested in out to dinner.

My inner Logical Hudson tries to reason with me: *They're just close friends. Chill.*

But the more inappropriate No-Bullshit Hudson sitting in the forefront of my mind disagrees: *Nope, dude. They're fucking or they have fucked. They were way too chummy for anything else.*

And then there's the Hudson who can't keep his mouth shut: "Yeah, that Rae sure is something."

Once my voice hits my ears, I know I sound like a total prick. My tone is angry, annoyed. I have no right to be either. An odd expression passes over Perry's face but it's gone before I can read into it more.

"You're preaching to the choir. She's a handful, that's for sure."

I hate how he says it, full of love and familiarity. I want to reach over and slap the love-stricken look right off his face, and it's become clear that No-Bullshit Hudson has taken over my brain.

Somehow, I contain my violent urges and force out more

polite laughter. "So, did you have anything for me to sign? Anything I need to fill out?"

He pulls a packet of papers from the binder. "I do. I have a questionnaire you can fill out. It gives me an idea of what extra stuff you're wanting on your website, that kind of stuff. Then I have a contract for you to sign. Most designers require a down payment of sorts, and you'll see in the contract that I put down twenty-five percent for starters and then the rest when the project is complete. If you're okay with that, we can do that today so I can get started on things."

I glance over the questionnaire and contract. It all seems legit to me. "You say you're just getting started in this? This contract looks good for a newbie."

"My dad is handy with the legal jargon. Plus, my uncle is an accountant at a law firm so he has the inside scoop on what makes a good contract."

"Nice. Lucky you then." I quickly fill out what I can of the questionnaire and sign the contract. "I'm gonna be straight with you, Perry, I'm not good with the creative stuff like this. I have no idea what works and what doesn't. I know that in my profession, I hate when people try to tell me how to do my job, so I'm going to leave it all up to you. I filled in a few things I would like to see, but that's it. I'm an easygoing guy and I have a feeling you're not going to screw me over." My gut is telling me to at least trust his artistic abilities, if nothing else. "So, I'm leaving a lot of this up to you. Now, who do I make the check out to?"

I pay Perry and we wrap up our meeting with a promise of seeing something by Thursday. I'm pumped. He seems to have solid ideas for the new look, and I'm hoping it's going to be everything I'm wanting.

I'm also hoping that Logical Hudson is right, that they're just close friends, or hell, even family. Either way, I want everything done as fast as possible, because I don't know how long I can stomach working with him when he clearly has feelings for Rae, especially after that weird sudden urge to smash the guy's pretty face in.

The worst part is that I have no right at all to have any sort of urges like that. I don't own Rae. I don't even know her that well. Hell, I'm not even *really* dating her...yet. There's no reason for this, but I can't help it. I have this odd feeling of protectiveness when it comes to her. I felt it the first time we locked eyes. They looked tired and sad, and it felt like she was pleading with me for some sort of help.

I know—*I know*—that sounds crazy considering I *just* met the girl, but I swear it doesn't feel that way. She seems familiar, like I've known her for years. Even though I haven't, I feel like I *have* to get to know her.

My gut is screaming at me over it, and if there's anything I've learned about myself over the last several years, it's to trust my gut.

CHAPTER 12

RAE

I HAVE BEEN sick to my stomach all day with nerves. I'm t-minus two hours from my date with Hudson and I have about twelve different outfits—that I didn't even know I owned—strewn about my room, because I've been running in circles for the past hour in an absolute panic over what to wear.

"Pick up, pick up, pick up," I mumble into my phone. I've been alternating between calling my sister and Maura for the last five minutes. Neither are answering because they're both still at work.

I throw my phone onto my bed and take two steps to resume my pacing when there's a knock on the door. I wrap my robe a little tighter around me while I pad out into the living room and check the peephole before I open the door.

"Finally! You're not exactly who I was looking for but you'll do. Come on," I say, grabbing Perry and dragging him through the apartment.

"Right. Good to see you as well, Rae. How's life?"

I glance back to see a cute little grin smeared across his face. "Shush," I say, directing him to my room and pushing him down onto my bed. "Sit and stay," I command. "I need help. I have no idea what to wear and I have a date tonight. Help. Please?"

He rolls his eyes and sighs. "Fine. I suck at this shit, but since I love you and owe you a lot for the Jacked Up job, I'll help. Show me what you have."

I squeal a bit and start holding up clothes. He shoots down all my dresses and skirts, citing the weather as his reasoning, but I think he's just being brotherly again. I hold up a few of my more questionable tops to prove my theory, and of course I'm right, but I completely love him for it.

After four of my more modest tops, I'm just as frustrated as I was before he showed up. "You're no help, Perry! You're shooting everything down!"

"That's because you're showing me complete shit. Everything looks like club outfits so far. You're not going to a club, are you?"

He's right. Every outfit I've shown him so far has been way more appropriate for a club, not dinner at someone's apartment. "No, I'm going to his place for dinner."

"See? You're going about this all wrong then. If he invited you over for dinner, then he probably wants to do more than just rub all over each other on his couch, which is what wearing those clothes will lead to. Trust me, I'm a guy, and that's probably the only thing I'd be thinking about if a girl wore that shit to my place."

"Fine. Help me pick something casual and cute then."

He gets up and begins flipping through my closet like he owns the place. I'm so lucky this guy loves me like he does because I know there's no one else he'd do this for.

He walks back over to me, holding out a pair of dark gray skinny jeans and a dark purple short-sleeved top. The top has a lacy overlay and dips low enough in the front to say I'm interested, but not *too* interested.

"I think he'll appreciate this one."

"Yeah, I think Hudson will love it."

"Hudson? As in Jacked Up Hudson? The Hudson whose website I submitted for approval today?" Perry asks, slightly panicked.

I gulp audibly. "Yes..."

"What in the hell, Rae? Why didn't you tell me that's who it was? Why didn't you mention you were dating him when you texted me about the job?"

I shrug. "I don't know. I didn't think it was that big a deal."

"Not a big deal? Of course it is!" he hisses. "He probably thinks I'm too stupid to get work on my own or that I begged you to throw me a bone. Dammit, Rae, I don't want your charity cases, especially because you're dating the guy!"

I stand there, just staring at him. Is he insane? Totally out of his fucking mind? That's not even remotely why I suggested Perry help Hudson out. I wasn't "throwing him bone". I was trying to recommend a worthy client to my talented cousin.

But...I understand where he's coming from. He's scared, just like I am. He wants to do this on his own, prove to himself that he can do it and not fail. He doesn't want to have to rely on everyone else like his mother did his entire life. He doesn't want people to give him handouts or not think for one second he didn't work his hardest to achieve something on his own. He's always been that way, and you'd never guess it from the easygoing smile he always wears.

"Perry," I say gently. I pull him until he's facing me and place my hands on his shoulders. I look him directly in the eyes, so he knows I'm being serious. "What you just said? It's not even close to being accurate. You know me, and I would never do that. I *only* referred you for your mad design skills. I knew you'd be able to give Jacked Up the makeover it deserves. And Hudson? This is kind of like our first date, because the first one

—which was a blind date—didn't really count. He has *no idea* at all that you're my cousin, so whatever he said to you, whatever deal you two worked out, it's all on you and your talent. It has *nothing* at all to do with me." I grab his face between my hands. "Got it?"

He closes his eyes briefly. When he opens them back up, the storm brewing inside them is tamed. Typical Perry.

"Got it." He winces. "I'm sorry, Rae." He wraps me up his arms and hugs me tightly. "I didn't mean to overreact. It's just... well, you know. I'm sorry."

I pat his back. "Can't...breathe..." I manage to choke out. He chuckles and lets me go. "We good?"

He nods. "Always."

"Good. Now get the fuck out because I have a date to get ready for and I only have an hour to make some serious magic happen," I say, pushing him out the door.

"Pft, yeah right. You're always beautiful. No magic there, just good genes." He winks at me.

"True. Now go."

He ducks out of my room and down the hall. He's opening the door when I realize something. "Perry?" I burst through my bedroom door as he turns around. "Why'd you stop by?"

"Just had a feeling you were needing me." He smiles easily, but I can tell something's up. He's avoiding eye contact, and that's a dead giveaway when it comes to Perry and me. He knows how I feel about that shit.

I nod and blow him a kiss, pretending everything is okay because that's what he wants. I'll let him have it...for now. "Love you."

He returns the words and gesture as he closes the door, leaving me staring after him. He's been acting off lately, and I'm not sure what's going on. We usually talk about anything and everything; me saying Perry is my best friend is not an exaggeration. We grew up like brother and sister, only with a different bond. We're as close as twins some days. He means the world to me, and I'm worried about him.

The last time Perry started to act like this, he ended up in therapy. It took a month to finally get him to break down and agree to attend at least ten sessions. He claimed himself "cured" after two months and has been fine ever since—until now.

I shake off my thoughts, knowing there's not much that can be done tonight, and start getting ready for my date with Hudson.

After putting on my jeans and shirt, I add a small spritz of curling cream and hairspray to make sure my naturally curly mane doesn't turn into a complete train wreck throughout the night. I finish up my beauty routine by applying a little more mascara than normal and some lip gloss with a faint sheen to it. The outfit gets completed with a long antique-looking silver necklace filled with several different charms, and my black leather boots that always make me feel like a badass when I wear them.

This date is either going to rock my world or be the death of me.

With one final glance in the mirror, I grab my small bag and jacket and hit the road.

―――

I DON'T THINK I took a breath the entire drive to Hudson's apartment—that's the only explanation I have for the dizziness I'm feeling as I stand here staring at his door.

You can do this, Rae. Just press the damn doorbell. It won't bite you. It can't because it's an inanimate object. Just press the button!

As I'm reaching out to the press the doorbell, the door is

yanked open. I scream and stumble backward. I brace myself for the fall that's probably going to bruise my ass, but it never comes. Hudson grabs me before I hit the ground.

I'm staring into his stormy eyes when something along the lines of my "my hero" comes flying out of my mouth. I can only hope Hudson didn't hear me.

He laughs. *Shit. He probably heard me.*

"Yeah, I heard you. Why do you think my doorbell will bite?" *Fuck!* "I can still hear you, Rae. You might want to rein those thoughts in before you start talking about how ridiculously hot I am."

Of course saying something like that is just an invitation to check him out. Who am I to deny him?

He's right—he does look ridiculously hot in jeans and a plain gray thermal that brings out the green in his eyes. His hair is the perfect sort of messy it always is and that ever-present five o'clock shadow is gracing his tanned face.

He smiles, and since I'm so close to him, I can finally see flaw I hadn't noticed before. His bottom front tooth has a small chip in it, and the one next to it is a bit crooked. He isn't so perfect after all, but truthfully, it doesn't take away from his beauty—it adds to it.

Hudson sets me upright. "So, do you want to come in?"

I straighten my top and grab my swaying necklace—a nervous habit of mine. "Sure."

The first thing I notice when we walk inside is how small it is. It's even smaller than the apartment I share with Haley. You can see everything but the bedroom and bathroom—which are down a narrow hallway—just by standing at the door. Despite all that, it's cute and cozy, very homey.

The second thing I notice is how clean it is. It's spotless, reminding me of one of those "for show only" apartments.

There are a few simple paintings hung about and a big

black sofa with red throw pillows sitting opposite a huge TV that takes up almost the entire front wall. You can tell the place lacks that special feminine touch, but it's still lived-in. It's warm, inviting, and friendly, and I can easily see Hudson spending his nights here.

"Now that you have sufficiently checked out my humble abode from the front door, would you like the grand tour?" Hudson teases.

"I'm not sure that will be necessary," I deadpan.

"Good point." He sweeps his arm dramatically over the room. "Welcome. This is my home away from mother's. I know it's not much, but it's getting me by until the repairs on the house get done."

"It's cute. It fits you."

He clutches his chest. "Cute? You mean manly. That *must* be what you mean. We're pretending you said manly."

I laugh. "Yes, manly indeed."

Suddenly, a medium-sized black Lab comes barreling out of what I assume is the bedroom. The dog lets out one solid bark and stands itself up on my legs, begging to be pet.

"Rocky, down!"

I reach out and ruffle the hair behind the dog's ears. "It's okay, Hudson. Rocky's just curious about the hot chick in your apartment. He's not used to you bringing home such attractive dates," I say, shooting Hudson a look, just asking him to tell me differently.

That stupid sexy smirk takes over his face again. "He's definitely not."

"Good answer." I continue to get to know Rocky while Hudson heads into the kitchen.

"You want something to drink, Rae? I have Dr. Pepper, tea, apple juice, beer—no root—and water."

As weird as I think it is for a grown, single man to have apple juice, I ask for it anyway. "Apple juice is fine."

"Coming right up," he says happily.

A minute later, he brings the cup of juice into the living room, taking a seat on the couch. I stand up from petting Rocky and sit down next to him.

"Rae, I have a confession to make."

My face drops. *Oh crap, here it comes. He's married or some shit. I knew it was too good to be true!*

"I can't cook."

I don't remember the last time I had such an urge to punch someone, other than Clarissa on her bitchy days. I take a deep breath, exhaling sharply, and do something I don't often manage to do: I think before I speak.

Now, I'm going to be candid here. Just because I think before I speak does not mean that whatever comes out of my mouth is going to be some profound, eloquent shit. More often than not, it won't be. That's not who I am, and I'm mostly okay with that.

"Asshat!" I shriek as that *stupid* sexy smirk covers his face again. "You had me worried for a minute. I thought you were going to tell me you were married or something, which would be rude since I totally proposed to you the other night, and since this is a *date*."

I can tell he's trying to hold in the laughter caused by my outburst. "Sorry, no, I'm not married. I think you'd secretly enjoy the sneaking around, though."

"No way."

"Anyway, I called some pizzas in at about five 'til. I have pepperoni, sausage, and black olives on one and plain cheese on the other. I wasn't sure what you like."

"I hate pizza," I tell him with a straight face. "No, fuck. I can't even say that in a joking manner. It feels wrong. I *love* pizza. I could live off it."

"Thank God. This date was about to be over as quick as it began."

"Glad I saved it." I wink. "So, other than us devouring two pizzas—because I fully plan on having at least five pieces to myself—what did you have in mind for tonight?"

"Movie?"

"Ah, keeping it simple and classy. I can dig it. What movie?"

He eyes me warily. "Well, I was hoping to let you pick. That way, if you pick something horrible, I can find an excuse to get you to leave before the pizza arrives so there's more for me while I drown my sorrows over what could have been."

"I can see ending this date quickly is a thing for you. You that scared?"

"Nervous is more like it. I mean, what if you suck, Rae?"

I snort out a laugh. "What if *you* suck, Hudson?"

"I don't think I do."

"Well I don't think *I* do either."

"Pick a movie and we'll see."

I think for a second. "*Step Brothers.*"

"Did we just become best friends?"

My chest swells. *No! No way did he just quote my favorite movie to me!*

"Yep!"

"Wanna go do karate in the garage?"

"Yep!"

Hudson shakes his head, a huge grin plastered on his face. "I think it's my turn to propose to you. I can't believe you just did that with me!"

"Right now, I'd probably say yes. I love that movie. I think I've watched it at least fifty times."

The doorbell rings, interrupting us.

"Well tonight will make fifty-one then," he replies, walking to answer it.

His face transforms when he looks into the peephole then he swings open the door with a vibrant smile. "Gaige! What up, man? I didn't know you were working tonight."

Standing in the doorway is one of the guys who was at Clyde's the night I saw Hudson there. If it wasn't obvious at the bar, it's obvious now—Gaige is gorgeous. I know that's an odd description to use on a guy, but it's true. Lit up by the hazy yellow porch light, he's still so good-looking with his smooth features and dark hair that's impeccably styled. Even in his pizza delivery uniform, you can tell he has solid muscle on him. It's not overwhelming, though, and it fits his tall frame perfectly. I can't recall what color his eyes were from the bar, but from where I'm seated they seem dark under his bushy eyebrows.

His eyes find mine over Hudson's shoulder and he nods my way before turning back to his friend. "Yeah, I wasn't supposed to but picked up a shift at the last minute. You know how that is. I saw your name pop up on the deliveries and snagged it. I also threw in a little discount."

"Thanks, man. You didn't have to, but I appreciate it," Hudson says, setting the pizzas down on the end of the entertainment center.

He digs his wallet from his back pocket and hands some money over to Gaige. His voice is low so I can't make out what he's saying, but I can hear Gaige mumble "fucker" to him as he shakes his head with a scowl.

"Night, Rae. You two kids have fun," Gaige calls over Hudson's shoulder before he walks away.

Hudson grabs the pizzas and places them on the coffee

table. He heads into the kitchen, returning quickly with plates and napkins.

"So, how do you know Gaige?" I ask, being nosy as hell.

"Next to Tucker, he's the best friend I have. I've known him since we were seventeen and he started working at Jacked Up. He still works there for me and delivers pizza part-time at Harold's for extra money," Hudson explains as he sets up our plates and opens the pizza boxes.

I can see the love in Hudson's eyes when he talks about Gaige. It's sweet to see that he cares about his friends like that, a refreshing change from the men I've previously dated.

My most recent ex, Jared, was not one to share his feelings —with anyone. We were together for almost a year before I called it quits. He wanted all the physical attachments without the actual feelings. It worked for a while because—let's be honest—everyone has an itch they want scratched, so I can't say it was a total wash. I did like him a lot—more than he liked me, obviously. After several months of it, though, I felt like he was never going to reciprocate my feelings, so I broke things off about six months ago. It was an easy decision to make, and the way he just simply walked away clued me in to how little we were both invested.

Hudson shows emotion, and it doesn't seem like he's afraid to do so. If he's that open and honest about his relationships with his friends, I can only imagine how he is in an actual relationship. So far, he's a catch—one I'm certain I want to hold on to.

CHAPTER 13

HUDSON

I DON'T THINK I've ever been so grateful for a bathroom break in my entire life, because I desperately needed this moment to breathe.

I can't decide if it's cool or weird that we have the same favorite band *and* movie. I also can't decide if I should be worried that we get along as well as we do, that this date is going almost *too* well. We click—so well that I'm certain I'm going to mess it up with the simplest thing.

I very well could. If she found out about me being a father, it could send her running for the hills. I'm not trying to hide my kid, because I'm not ashamed of being a father to a seven-year-old, but I'm not ready to tell Rae just yet. This is only our second date. What if she wants to meet her? I'm not ready for that. Joey isn't ready for that. Joey doesn't even know about Rae.

And then something major hits me.

I'm on a date. An actual fucking date.

I haven't dated in...too long, not since that one random chick who walked out on the date as soon as I mentioned being a father two or so years ago. It could be why I won't tell Rae about Joey yet.

Then again, it could be because I haven't been involved in anything serious since I was with Jess, Joey's mom, and that relationship was rocky at best. It wasn't real, never was. It was held together by a thin thread that snapped and had to be tied back together over and over until we finally ran out of string.

Don't get me wrong, it wasn't all bad. I did get Joey out of the deal, and she's worth all the troubles in the world, but maybe I'm so nervous because I don't know *how* to date. Am I supposed to kiss her? Hold her hand? Suggest making out on the couch?

Okay, the last one is just wishful thinking, but whatever.

Just be yourself, Hudson. You can do this.

"You ready to quote the most amazing movie ever for the next hour and a half or what?" Rae asks, walking down the hall, putting a stop to my pacing.

Note to self: feel free to put another point in the "Rae is a Fucking Godsend" column on my imaginary list about how awesome she is.

Why are you still talking to yourself! T Swift that shit and shake it off, dude!

I follow my own advice. "The question is, are *you* ready? I know this movie forward and back so I *will* judge you if you miss a line."

"Bring it." There's no teasing in her voice.

We spend nearly two hours sitting on the floor, chowing down pizza, and quoting the movie—or at least that's what I will tell anyone that asks, because I so didn't do that.

Did I eat some pizza? Sure. As much I normally would have? No. Did I quote the movie? You can't watch *Step Brothers* and *not* quote it. Was it up to my usual standards? Nope, not even close.

The reason? The incredibly beautiful girl sitting next to

me. Every time she laughed, my heart skipped. Every time her lips moved along with the words, my heart skipped. Every time she tried to look over my way nonchalantly, *my fucking heart skipped.*

I am so completely screwed when it comes to this girl.

The room goes dark as the credits scroll.

"You suck," Rae tells me.

"Excuse me?"

"Oh, you heard me. You. Suck. You didn't even quote half the movie! I'm judging you, Hudson. Hard." She's eyeing me with what I'm sure she thinks is a fierce look. Spoiler alert: it's not. She kind of looks like an old lady squinting at her bingo cards.

"Hey! I couldn't concentrate because every time something even *remotely* funny happened, someone sitting next to me would snort like a damn pig. It was incredibly distracting." She *was* distracting, but not for the reasons I'm giving her.

"Yeah, right. My snorting is dead sexy and you know it. Admit it, you're incredibly turned on right now."

"True."

I swear to all things holy, the look that crosses her face is one that can never be replicated because she was not expecting that answer in a million years.

She laughs and shakes her head. "Yeah, definitely wasn't expecting that."

I shrug. "Guess we're even on that lack-of-filter thing."

"For some reason, I highly doubt that."

"You're probably right." Face, meet throw pillow. "Okay, I deserved that."

"So much." She grows quiet, staring down at the pillow now in her lap. I study her, watching as she picks at the fuzzies. God, she's so beautiful. And smart, and funny. She's...

Rae jerks her head up with a grin. "Have any ice cream?"

"Of course, but first, on the count of three, say your favorite flavor of ice cream."

"One..."

"Two..." I count. Something hits me. "Pause. No proposing this time if our favorites are the same, because I'm positive I would empty my bank account and fly us to Vegas in a heartbeat if you did."

"Deal," she agrees. "Three!"

"Cookies and cream!" we yell simultaneously.

"Holy shit!" she shouts, clamping her hand over her mouth.

"Don't do it! Don't you dare do it! I will kick you out of this apartment with no ice cream!" I threaten.

Her hand is still clamped over her mouth and she's shaking her head back and forth like she can't believe this is happening. I know how she's feeling, because I can barely believe it myself.

I lean in closely and slowly peel her hand away from her face.

"Do. Not. Do. It," I whisper soft and slow, keeping my eyes locked with hers. "I'm going to take your hand and we're going to go get some ice cream now. You're not going to propose and I'm not going to propose, because I have this sneaking suspicion neither one of us can afford that Vegas vacay right now."

I stand and hold my hand out. Rae looks up at me with big eyes and places her hand in mine. It's so small compared to mine, so cute and feminine.

I could get used to holding this hand.

We make our way to the tiny kitchen where Rae posts up beside the fridge. I grab two bowls and some spoons and begin scooping out the ice cream.

"So, Hudson..." Rae starts.

I look up and smirk at her. "So, Rae."

She tries mimicking my smirk and fails miserably, but it's still cute as hell. "Tell me about yourself."

"Because that's not completely cliché."

She rolls her eyes. "Fine. Tell me three things then: your favorite thing about yourself, what your favorite memory is from your childhood, and if you could meet anyone—living, dead, or fictional—who it would be. Go."

I'm a little thrown by the questions. They weren't exactly what I was expecting, because if I had just told her about myself, I wouldn't have touched on any of that. Granted, they aren't completely out there, but the answers to the questions have potential to be...revealing.

I finish scooping out the ice cream and we sit down at the small two-person kitchen table I have. Rae's waiting patiently, taking small bites of her ice cream. I take one and let it melt in my mouth, thinking on how to answer.

"The first answer is easy. I have a killer set of abs."

"Oh, I don't doubt that," she says, her cheeks turning a violent shade of red.

"Smart woman," I tease. "Really, I'd have to say...my ability to adjust is my favorite thing about myself. I've been thrown some...curveballs, and I've managed to catch them every time. Quite impressive if you ask me."

"There's a story or two there," she says, curiosity laced into her words.

"There is." I nod and leave it at that.

She accepts the answer as is and takes another bite of her ice cream. "Next."

"Probably the summer before I turned seventeen. Things were simple then. We took a week-long vacation in Herring Cove."

Rae's eyes just about pop right out of her head because it's well known that Herring Cove is a swank place. We're talking thousands of dollars *just* for the townhome we stayed in. Crazy, yes, but so beautiful.

"That's...that's..." she stammers.

I laugh. "I know. It was amazing. My parents saved up for a long time for that one week of pure bliss. We passed up Christmas, birthdays, and Mother's and Father's Day for two years just for that short vacation. It was worth every penny too."

"Why is it your favorite memory though?"

"We were happy. Everyone was alive and smiling. It's the last good time I had with my family and Jess—my high school sweetheart—and I'm so thankful I got it." That was the summer before shit hit the fan, the summer before Joey happened.

Rae's quiet, and I wonder if I broke some weird rule about mentioning an ex on a date.

"You said alive. Your dad?" she inquires, a frown creasing her brows.

I put my spoon down and nod. "Heart attack. Two and a half years ago."

She reaches over and places her delicate hand on top of mine. "I'm so sorry, Hudson."

I can feel her words down to my bones, the sincerity seeping into me.

"Thank you. It sucks you'll never to get to meet him. You two would have gotten along famously. He's not too good with the filter thing either."

"If he was anything like you, I'm sure he was a cool dude." She gives a gentle smile. "Okay, time to answer question three now."

"That one is hard. I really have no idea. Living, dead, or fictional, huh? I think I may have to go with Crowley from *Supernatural* just so I can high-five him for all his brilliant one-liners. Cheesy, I know."

She's gaping at me, and I know it's because I just came off as a huge dork.

"Okay, now you're scaring me, Rae. Do you not know what *Supernatural* is?"

She scoffs. "How dare you insult my knowledge of amazing television! I'm just a little surprised you watch it. It's one of my favorite shows. I watch it religiously."

"We're still not proposing, right?" I jokingly ask.

"Nope, sorry," she says, scrunching her nose up. She pushes her empty bowl away from her and leans forward, practically humming with excitement. "Okay, now you do me."

I give it a second because I know what she just said is going to sink into that crazy head of hers eventually.

Her eyes go wide and her pale face turns a bright shade of red. *Ah, there it is.*

"Yeah, *so* not what I meant. What I *really* meant was, 'Please, Hudson, give me questions to answer. Do so quickly because I obviously have no control of what comes out of my mouth.' So, let's just pretend that's what came out, okay?"

I laugh. "Deal. So, do I have to come up with new questions? I kind of suck at this shit."

Rae shakes her head. "Nah. Okay, first answer." She clears her throat. "Believe it or not, and as embarrassing as it can be at times, I actually *like* that I don't have a filter half the time. I feel very...honest," she confesses, shrugging. "Silly, I know, but it's true."

"No, I kind of get it. I mean, I'm sure it has put you in weird situations or gotten you into trouble a time or two, but I get it."

"Phew! Glad I'm not a total freak."

"I wouldn't go that far," I tease.

She laughs it off, and I love that she laughs it off.

"Moving on before you completely shatter my ego," she says. "I would have to say my sixth birthday party is my favorite memory. All my friends were there: my mom, cousin, aunt, uncle, everyone. My mom, Erin, painted me this beautiful ocean sunrise scene. She was so talented. The painting was flawless, so detailed it looked real, like you could step into the canvas. I used to stare at it every night until I fell asleep and would pretend I was out floating in the ocean. It was a comfort for many years. The only thing that comes close to giving me that feeling now is sitting out at Lake Quannapowitt at night."

The way she describes the painting makes me sad. There is longing and pain in her voice. Something big happened.

"Damn, Rae," I say on a loud swallow. "I have to ask, though—you said 'was'...what happened?"

"Oh, the painting was...destroyed. I don't have it anymore," she answers, avoiding my real question.

We let our mutual avoidance of the past hang between us until I clear my throat.

"What are your cousins like?"

"*Cousin*," she corrects. "I just have one. And what do you mean? He's a cousin—well, more like a brother in my case, but I'm sure most cousins are the same."

"I wouldn't know. Neither of my parents have siblings, so I don't have cousins. Always wanted one, though. I've heard they cause trouble."

She laughs. "Oh, do they ever. We get along like siblings, so it makes it even more interesting."

"So, third and final question, what's your answer?"

Rae perks up significantly at this. "This one is easy. Colleen Hoover."

I raise my brows, confusion covering my face. "Who?"

Her face drops. "What."

It comes out as more of threat than a question. Truth bomb: I'm not even close to scared. "You heard me, lady."

"Ugh! She's only the world's most amazing Instagram

video-maker ever! She's hilarious! A genius! And don't even get me started on her books. They. Are. Flawless. And Will Cooper? Be still my beating heart! That man is a god. Sorry dude, but you have some serious competition when it comes to him."

No-Bullshit Hudson: *Who the fuck is this "Will Cooper" guy and how in the hell do I kill him?*

Logical Hudson: *Wait...she said books. Dude, he's fake. Down boy.*

"Oh, come on. The guy can't be *that* great. He's fake."

"Do you write poetry, Hudson? Do you stand up on a stage and pour your heart out to strangers for a girl? Did you give everything up to take care of someone else when they couldn't take care of themselves? Will Cooper did all that and more. That's why he's amazing."

I do my best keep a straight face even though I'm internally freaking out because she just hit way too close to home and she has no idea. I don't write poetry or perform on a stage, but I'll be damned if I didn't give up everything in my life for Joey, and it's something I'd do again in a heartbeat.

"Then why do you not want to meet this Will Cooper character instead?"

"Because the panties *would* come off if that were to happen," she says with clear mischief in her eyes. "Honestly though, he's the brainchild of Colleen so I feel like it's her that I need to hug for him. Plus, she has a kickass Texas accent I'm dying to hear in person." She shrugs like it's the only answer.

"So, let me get this straight, you love her for her accent and Instagram videos?"

"And her words. She gives good word."

"Fair enough."

"Are you a reader, Hudson?"

"Only at night. I'm more of a music person."

"Ah, yes—our mutual love of Transit. You ever see them live?"

I scoff. "We live thirty minutes—at most—outside of Boston. Of course I've seen them live."

"I haven't," Rae confesses shyly.

"No!" I gasp.

She shakes her head. "It's true. I've never seen them. I've always had to work when they play."

"We're fixing that. There's no way you can live a full, meaningful life if you haven't seen a live show of theirs. It's... amazing. The lead singer is so theatrical. I love it."

"You're on," she replies, her eyes lighting up. Then they quickly dim. "However, I'm probably gonna have to bounce. I have a hot date with Maura tomorrow before work and I've agreed to come in a few hours early."

I'm a little disappointed by this, not because I was expecting her to stay over or anything, but because I'm enjoying spending time with her so much.

I frown. She frowns back.

"What? Were you hoping for a sleepover? I know my unquestionably amazing ability to quote *Step Brothers* is a huge turn-on, but I don't put out on the first date, Hudson."

"Well...technically it's our second," I tease.

"Don't push it, mister. It's *so* not happening."

"Oh, sugar, if I wanted you to have a sleepover with me, you would," I say, winking to let her know I am teasing back.

Her mouth drops open.

"Did you just fucking *wink* at me?" she says incredulously.

"Uh...yes?" It comes out as a question because I'm not sure that's the right answer.

"Winking isn't really a thing, you know. They do that in movies and romance novels, not real life."

"I'm sorry?" Again, not sure if it's the right answer.

"It's okay, but only because you look a little cute when you do it. Now, you gonna walk me out or what?"

I laugh and grab our bowls off the table, rinsing them out while she collects her things.

I meet her at the door, slipping on my shoes. "After you, my lady."

"Thank you, kind sir. Such a gentleman." She *almost* sounds like a real lady.

I lead her out the door and find her car in the parking lot. She spins my way once we stop in front of her red sedan. Sticking her hands in her coat pockets, she rocks back on her heels. I mirror her pose.

"I had a lot of fun tonight, Hudson. Thank you for dinner and ice cream."

"So did I. It's not often I get nights like these. I usually spend most evenings at my mom's with Joey so this little break from my routine has been nice. Thank you for that. Can we, uh, can we do this again sometime? Soon?"

She nods and takes a small step forward that may or may not have been intentional.

Of their own accord, my hands reach out and place themselves on her waist. My muscles move on their own and pull her close to me. A small gasp leaves her lips and she grabs my biceps. I swear I feel her squeeze them, so I squeeze back, pulling her in closer.

I rest my forehead on hers and stare into her eyes. Even though it's dark out and our bodies are casting shadows upon one another, her eyes are bright. Her small chest is moving a mile a minute, pressing tightly against mine. Our breaths mingle together as we continue to stare, our heartbeats falling into similar rhythms.

Then carefully, oh so slowly, I lean in, placing a gentle kiss on her cheek. I continue to kiss a path along her jaw to her ear, lingering a little too long just under her lobe.

"Goodnight, Rae," I whisper.

Letting her go, I turn around, shove my hands in my pockets, and race back inside my apartment, fighting with myself the entire way.

I *almost* turn back—twice.

CHAPTER 14

RAE

MY KNEES STOP WORKING like knees should and I have to catch myself on my car.

What in the actual fuck just happened?

I just experienced the most intimate and sensual kiss I've *ever* received in my entire life, and it was on the fucking cheek!

Truth be told, I'm not even mad he didn't kiss me for real, because that kiss? That was *incredible*.

Do I want to feel his lips on mine? Of course—who in their right mind wouldn't?—but I'm okay with waiting, especially if his cheek-kisses do *that* to me.

This man...he's doing something to me, and I don't mind one bit.

———

"HEY, YOU'RE BACK!"

I scream. "Holy fuck! You scared the shit out of me, Hales!"

I flip a light on. She's curled up on the couch in those damn lime green sweats again with all the lights off, reading on her e-reader.

"Sorry, Rae," she says in a way that tells me she really isn't. "How'd it go? Did you get you some D?"

I laugh and flop down happily on the other end of the couch. "You really think I'm going to put out on our first real date?"

She shrugs. "I would."

"True, but that's not me. I did get kissed, though."

"WHAT!" she screeches. "Details!"

I recount the best kiss I've ever experienced, and Haley has this look on her face that says I'm officially crazy.

"He kissed you on the *cheek* and you're *happy* about this?"

"Extremely."

"You're fucking high!" She's suddenly off the couch, waving her arms around manically.

I laugh hard because she totally just quoted *Step Brothers* unintentionally.

"Why are you laughing? Is this a joke, Rae?" she says in a motherly tone, her hands finding her hips.

"I'm sorry, I'm sorry. You just quoted *Step Brothers* and it's funny because that's the movie we watched tonight." Her face screws up. "Hey lady! Don't knock it until you've actually stayed awake through it."

"Whatever. That's not even the point of this. The cheek, Rae! You're happy about a cheek-kiss on what is kind of your third date. You two should have already rounded third base by now! Your next date is home, Rae. HOME PLATE!"

She's way off track. That's not even close to what this is about. Everything about Hudson is...*more*.

"Haley," I say seriously, looking her directly in the eyes because she knows my eye thing too. "It's more than that. So much more. I know we've only been on one real date, but I can tell he's something special, and I like him a lot. So, I'm perfectly okay with a cheek-kiss."

A look of understanding falls over her face. She sits back down.

"Wow."

"Yeah, wow."

She looks at me with worry. "Please be careful, Rae. That's all I'm going to say. Well, that and keep an open mind. I know how you can get."

I nod and get up. "I'm heading to bed. I have a date with our favorite blonde-haired babe tomorrow. Night, Hales."

"Night, Rae-Rae."

I make my way into my bedroom and close the door behind me. Taking off my shoes, I throw myself onto the bed with my clothes still on and a smile plastered on my face.

I know Haley is right, that I need to keep an open mind but be cautious. I can't blame her for being worried.

My feelings...they're escalating at a rapid rate, and I can't seem to stop it. Every time I see Hudson, everything clicks. He gives me this weird inner peace I had no idea I was missing. Well, I had an inkling of an idea, but I guess I never knew it was so bad until I found what was missing.

Is it crazy how he makes me feel even though I've only known him for less than a month? Yes, that's just nuts, but I can't explain it even if I tried. It feels like he...belongs, in my present, my future, my heart...everything. He feels *right* in my world.

My eyes grow heavy with sleep and I'm almost pulled under the blanket of sleep when something runs through my head.

Who's Joey?

———

"SO, how's it going with Tanner?"

Maura sighs. I can't decide if it was the cheeseburger she just took a bite of or thinking of Tanner that caused it. We're currently sitting at Vern's, a local diner with the best root beer floats ever, having cheeseburgers and gossiping.

"He's amazing," she says around a mouthful of food.

"Really?" I hate that I'm so skeptical of the guy, he just seems like a total sleazeball.

"Really, really. He's so damn sweet, Rae. He's funny and goofy and incredibly hot," she says, fanning herself. "Like really hot. He has an eight-pack. Like, a legit eight-pack."

"Of beer? I thought those only came in six- or twelve-packs. Weird."

She throws a fry at me. "Har, har. Very funny, you brat." Naturally, I eat the fry she just threw. "I mean it. I know he comes off a just another 'bro' but he's not."

"You mean that." It's not a question, because her tone is serious in a way I wasn't expecting. She just nods. "Well...good. I'm glad."

And I am. I was worried the Tanner I've seen is the same Tanner she gets when no one is around. I had hoped not, but if I'm being honest, it wouldn't have surprised me in the least if he were.

"We have another date this weekend," she says quietly.

At first, I don't understand her sudden shyness. Then, it hits me. This weekend is a *Maura plays at perfect daughter with her parents in the city* weekend. That means if they have a date this weekend, Tanner's going to meet the evil parents.

Evil isn't an exaggeration on my part. Maura's parents are assholes. The girl didn't even get lucky enough to have one of them be just a part-time asshole. Instead she has two full-time horrendous parents and one cool as hell aunt that used to have to sneak the poor girl off for a day at the mall, which she needed more than anything. Her parents mentally tear her down, calling her names, questioning and correcting every little thing she does. It's disgusting. The things they've said to her baffle me.

I have no idea how Maura is the way she is—strong, confident, carefree. There's no way I would've been able to put up with those two like she did all those years—or one weekend a month like she does now.

"No. No fucking way."

She nods. "Way."

I clear my throat. "Don't you think that's…?"

I'm not trying to be a bitch or judge her because I have no room to do that—not when I'm in so deep so quickly with Hudson. I'm just genuinely concerned for her. Her parents are crazy for Cocoa Puffs and they will eat Tanner alive.

"I slept with him, Rae." She covers her hands with her face, hiding from the words she just spoke.

I laugh. "Ha! Good one. Payback for the eight-pack joke."

A look of unease spreads on her face and her eyes flit about the diner. That can only mean one of two things: she's fucking with me, or she's embarrassed about it—and if she's embarrassed, she really did sleep with Tanner.

Even though Maura's been dating this past year for the first time, she's still—*was still*—a virgin. On top of her parents being the captains of the crazy train, she was very sheltered.

She came close to something serious and having sex with her last boyfriend, Aaron, but discovered his ass— literally— mid-cheat.

So, I'm a little shocked she had sex with Tanner so soon. They've only really been together for a little over a week, but who am I to judge her? No one.

"Well, was it good?" I ask with a smile.

She beams. "It was awkward at first for me, and it hurt, but

I liked it. He was so sweet about the whole thing, but you think I'm a total slut, don't you?"

"What? No! Everyone has needs, Maura. There's no right or wrong amount of time to wait to sleep with someone. Only *you* know when you're ready, and I trust your judgment."

She exhales strongly and meets my serious stare with her own. "I *really* like him, Rae. Like, *really* like him."

I get it, I really do, because I like Hudson—like, *really* like him—and I know it's way more than I probably should, but it's not something that can be helped.

"How long is he home for?" I ask. We know he'll eventually leave and Maura seems attached, so I kind of worry.

"Just another few weeks or so. He had a lot of leave time saved up and used it all at once. Lucky me."

I wince. "That's it? Then what happens?"

"Then he goes back to his base."

"And?"

"And hopefully we continue our relationship long distance, or we split. I'm hoping for the first option, though. We haven't talked about it much."

"I hope so."

"It'll all work out. If it's meant to be, it will happen," Maura says confidently.

"Word."

"Your confidence in me is inspiring. Thank you."

I laugh because oddly enough, she means what she just said. My "word" *is* my word. It's my agreement of all agreements, at least with Maura.

"And what about you? Didn't you have a date last night? Are you two engaged yet? When's the wedding? Dibs on maid of honor!"

I smile. She has no idea how close she just hit with what went on last night.

"No, we're not. We've decided to wait until at least the third date for any more proposals. It was getting way out of hand."

"And?" she prompts, dragging the word out.

"It was fan-freakin'-tastic. Completely perfect. He's completely perfect. We watched *Step Brothers*, ate pizza, had ice cream, and then wild monkey sex right there on the kitchen table."

"SHUT UP! YOU DID NOT!"

"You're right. We didn't. Your slut title is still safe."

"Bitch," she says, sticking her tongue out at me.

"You still love me. But seriously, it was easily the best date I've ever been on. He was sweet, funny, inquisitive, sexy as sin —the whole package."

"Good. It's about damn time you were happy. I think you've found your match in Hudson."

I hope so.

I toss the fry I've been holding for the past few minutes back down onto my plate and push it away. "All right, I'm officially stuffed," I say, slouching down and resting my hands on my slightly soft stomach. "What's next? You said you wanted to hit up Jane's on Main. Want to head there now?"

"Please. I need to find me some new boots to go with my new sweater dress."

"Let's get going then. I'm want to try to sneak in a few hours with the Winchesters before work tonight."

Maura rolls her eyes. "I don't see the appeal in those two."

"Watch your tongue, woman! I'll make you walk to the store," I say, shooting daggers at her.

She shrugs, unfazed by my threat.

Turns out we both walk anyway, deciding we need the exercise after devouring those burgers, fries, and floats.

"Hey girls!" Jane, the tall brunette boutique owner calls out when we walk in.

"Hey Jane!" we say in unison.

We may come here a little too much. Okay, fine, probably over half of our wardrobes come from here. In fact, we're here so often, it's safe to say Jane is like our unofficial fairy godmother. Sure, she's only a couple years older than us, but we go to her for everything. This is our spot whenever something happens in our lives and we need to cope with things. Sometimes we walk in looking for something specific, and sometimes we come to walk around and chitchat with Jane since she gives the best advice.

This visit is a mix of the two.

"Looking for anything specific today, Maura?" Jane knows what's up; she gets that Maura's the fashion-lover out of the two of us.

"Boots. I need cute boots. Rocker chic. Have anything?"

Jane throws her a look saying she should know better than to question her. "Follow me."

We follow her over to a rack full of adorable boots. Maura squeals and starts grabbing some to try on. I walk away and browse through the vintage tees and funky cardigans.

"So, this weekend, are you nervous at all?" I ask loudly so Maura can hear me, not caring if Jane hears us. I know she'd never breathe a word of any of it.

"Are you kidding? Hell fucking yes I'm nervous! You've met my parents. They're crazy as hell! I think they *may* respect Tanner for his service, but I doubt that's going to be enough. I kind of feel bad for him, but he's the one who insists on meeting them since he'll be gone soon."

"Really? That surprises me. Tanner doesn't seem to be the 'meet the parents' type of guy."

"You know, I didn't expect that at first either. He's this

good-time guy who is kind of an asshole and he seems sleazy—even I can't deny that—but he's not. Like I said before, I think it's just a front he puts on around everyone else. That guy is nothing but a total sweetheart to me and perfect boyfriend material."

"Well, good, but I cannot even imagine how your parents are going to react. This is the first guy you've ever introduced them to. You didn't even take what's-his-nuts home for the weekend."

"Reminder not necessary. That's part of the reason I'm freaking out. How about these?" she asks, appearing at the end of the aisle, modeling the boots for me.

"Hmm. What color is the dress?"

"Teal?"

"Why is that a question?"

"Because I suck at naming colors. Just go with teal."

"Then I like. Very cute, and they'd look good with a summer dress."

"Rae?"

"Hmm?"

"Did you just...give me fashion advice?" she asks, surprise coloring her voice.

I shrug. "Hey, I'm not *that* bad at putting an outfit together. I manage to look pretty damn decent most days."

"Yeah, yeah, fair enough. All right, I'm sold. Jane! Ring this bitch up, please!"

I shake my head and laugh. I grab the light pink crocheted half-cardigan I've been eyeing and follow Maura to the front.

"These are perfect for you, Maurie!" Jane exclaims.

"Right? I scored big this time," Maura replies, just as excited.

"How are things going, ladies? Any fun news?"

Maura and I both sigh.

"I think we're both smitten," I tell Jane. "Like for reals smitten. And Maura here is a sex fiend now."

"Rae Kamden!" Maura punches me in the arm. "You are such a brat. It was *one* time!"

Jane just laughs us off. "You two are such a handful. If I didn't adore you girls so much, I'd *almost* feel bad for your fellas."

"Hell, I adore us and I *do* feel bad for them." I lean in close to the counter. "Especially Tanner. Dude had no idea what he got himself into with this one," I mock-whisper, jerking my head in Maura's direction a few times.

"You are so not my best friend anymore. You're evil."

I roll my eyes. "Liar."

Maura huffs, mumbling something incoherent to herself.

"You two...I swear. Makes me wish my best friend were still around, and that I had a guy, because judging by those smiles, you found yourselves some good men."

"I know I did," Maura says on a sigh.

Jane gives me a look, waiting on me to fess up. I try to play it cool and shrug. "Hudson's okay so far. He has a great ass so I'm not complaining."

"Oh, whatever! You were practically drooling over your date last night."

"She's right, Rae. I can see it in your eyes. This one is different. He's good for you."

I shift my eyes away and try to divert the attention from me because I know she's right.

Hudson is different. Every time I think about him, my heart races and I get those stupid flutters in my stomach. A part of me wants them—craves them, even—but the other part is terrified of them, and rightly so. Relationships can suck. I'm already so in like with Hudson that I know if this one tanks—even this early—it's going to hurt, and I'm not okay with that.

"He has friends, ya know. Tucker and Gaige. I can hook you up," I tell Jane.

"Nah, I don't have time for dating. Anyway, girls, anything else for you today?"

Meet Jane, master attention-diverter. I give her a look, letting her know she didn't fool me. She gives me back a minimal shrug. I know we'll get her to break one day.

"That's all I need this trip. I'm sure I'll be back next week for some therapy shopping after this weekend," Maura says.

Jane winces. "Yeah...good luck with that."

"Thanks. I'm going to need it."

After Jane hooks us up with our usual frequent shopper discount and we say our goodbyes, we hoof it back to Vern's for our cars.

"You're working tonight, right?" Maura asks, opening her car door.

"Unfortunately. I'm on the schedule until Sunday."

"Blech! See you tonight then. I'll be the hot girl buzzing about."

With a wink and an air kiss, she's gone.

CHAPTER 15

HUDSON

"IS it weird of me to come here after last night?"

"Nah, man," Tuck reassures me for the millionth time. "Chicks dig that shit. Plus, it's guys' night. We do this almost every Thursday. We just changed venues this time."

I nod. "Right, right."

"It's cool, dude. I showed up at a girl's work the day after our first date one time," Gaige says. "I mean, yeah sure, she put a restraining order on my ass pretty quick, but it was only for thirty days. You're good."

Tucker and I exchange a look, then stare at Gaige in bewilderment because this is the first we've heard of this.

Gaige rolls his eyes. "Laugh, you fuckers. It was a joke. Ha ha. Funny."

"That was the worst joke ever," Tucker tells him.

"Oh, Tuck, you wound me. I can always count on you to knock me down a few pegs. Thank you," Gaige replies sarcastically, clutching his chest.

"You're both cracked in the head. I feel bad for your future wives and children."

"Don't worry." Tucker grins. "We feel equally as bad for yours."

I bump his shoulder. "Asshole."

"Hey boys, what can I get for ya?"

We turn toward the voice that does not belong to Rae to find a lanky blonde. She's only spoken eight words to me and her voice is already annoying as fuck. I can hear the fakeness dripping from it.

"We have some specials on *tap* tonight. Any takers?" Annoying Voice Girl asks, putting a strange emphasis on tap. She puffs her chest out and inches in way too close to me.

"Uh, *just* Dr. Pepper for me," I tell her with plenty of emphasis on "just", scooting away and farther into the dark corner.

She notices my shift in direction and turns her attention to Gaige. Poor dude.

While she's busy hitting on my two best buds, I scan the bar, hoping to catch a glimpse of Rae.

I spot her and watch as she effortlessly moves around behind the bar with a big bulky man, shelling out drinks left and right. They're smiling easily at one another, moving around together so swiftly. I can tell from here that they're familiar with each other.

Then, a shorter, smaller man leans over the counter and kisses the guy standing next to Rae. He then holds his fist out to Rae. She bumps it, of course. They laugh and continue to sling around drinks.

I didn't even notice before, but there's a dark-haired guy sitting in front of Rae. Even from the back, I can tell that it's Perry.

She smiles at him, and my heart cracks a little.

That smile? The one she just gave a guy that isn't me? It was easily the most beautiful smile I've ever seen, and it wasn't *my* smile.

She leans across the bar and Perry whispers something to her. She laughs. That wasn't *my* laugh either.

I look away from them before my jealousy gets the better of me.

"You saw that too, huh?" Tucker asks.

I shrug.

"I'm sure it's nothing. He's probably just a friend," Gaige tries to reason.

While I was watching Rae, they were watching me, and while they were trying to talk me away from inching closer and closer to the edge of a damn cliff, none of us were watching Perry.

"Hey, Hudson! Fancy running into you here."

Fuck. Me.

Perry's standing at the end of our table and I'm fighting the urge to either hug the guy because the website and graphics he sent me this morning were fucking amazing, or to punch him. That whispering in her ear shit still has my blood boiling. I have no idea what's going on between the two of them, and no idea how they know each other, but damn if it doesn't piss me right the fuck off.

I peek over at the bar and finally make eye contact with Rae.

She smiles. It's *my* smile.

I feel like I can breathe for the first time in minutes.

"Hey Perry, didn't expect to see you here," I say with an edge to my voice. He doesn't know me well enough to know what I really meant, but Tucker does and I get a good kick to the shin for it. "Tucker, Gaige, this is Perry, the website dude. Perry, these are my employees."

"Just your employees? Well fuck you too, man," Tucker says in jest. He extends a hand to Perry, who shakes it. "Tucker.

Please excuse this asshole. I'm *way* more than an employee to this dude. We're totes besties."

"*Totes besties?* The fuck? God, you two are douchebags. Gaige. I'm the attractive, funny, and very, very best friend of Hudson here."

You know how on that show *How I Met Your Mother* Barney and Marshall fought for nine seasons over who was Ted's best friend? Welcome to my life for the last seven years.

"You wanna join us for some burgers? This place is pretty damn good," I offer. I almost feel like a dick for secretly hoping he'll say no and leave.

I like the guy as my designer and all, but I'm not sure I can be around him and Rae.

"Sure. Just let me go tell my girl. I saw who your waitress was and you don't want that shit skanking up your table, trust me."

His girl? Rae?

Yes. Of course it's Rae.

I watch as she laughs again from behind the bar and then says something to the bartender, who looks over at our table then smiles back at Rae and nods. Then she's following Perry over to our table, holding my stare the entire way.

Internally, I'm panicking, because I have no clue what I'm going to say to her. I didn't text her all day, which was probably a dumbass move on my end, but only because she said she was spending girl time with Maura. Now I'm rethinking that because what if I should have contacted her, told her how much I loved our date?

Because holy hell was it everything I could have hoped for. It took everything I had not to wrap my hands up in her silky locks and smash my lips against hers for hours.

"Hey Rae, good to see you again."

"Tucker, always a pleasure." She turns to me. "Long time,

no see. Or text. Or call. Or anything." She winks, and I know I'm off the hook.

"Hey, Gaige, do phones work both ways?" I ask with a smirk, still holding eye contact with Rae.

"Yes, I do believe so, Hudson." I can hear the smile in his voice.

"Huh, fancy that."

Rae bumps my shoulder. "Touché."

"I see you all have already met," Perry says, taking a seat. "I feel a bit out of the loop then. I only know Hudson."

"Quick rundown: Tucker sucks at video games, Gaige is quiet, and Hudson is a total smartass and proposes on the first date. You're all caught up. Congrats," Rae tells Perry, giving him a pat on the back.

"Proposing, huh? You're moving a bit fast there, bud."

"To be fair, Tuck, she was technically the first one to propose, on the group date. Did you forget already, Rae?"

She lifts her hand to her forehead. "Oh my," she mocks. "How could I possibly forget? Hey, you know what, thanks for ditching me on the first date by the way. I had such high hopes for us, Tucker."

He chuckles. "After I ditched, I realized my mistake in leaving you with this tool. My deepest apologies. Can I make it up to you?"

"Hey, fucker, find your own girl to date!"

"Already have the boys after you, huh Rae?" Perry nods in satisfaction. "Nice."

Rae flips her hair in a mocking gesture. "As if we didn't all know that would happen."

Perry fist-bumps her.

"You're all so weird," Gaige mumbles.

"I doubt any of us would deny that. So, what do you boys

want? I'm taking over so you don't have to endure the painful company of Clarissa all night. She's, uh, *clingy*."

"And crazy," Perry adds.

Rae nods toward Perry. "That's saying something coming from him."

He shrugs. "True enough."

We take turns ordering burgers, wings, and fries, and before I know it, Rae is capping her pen and sticking her pad into her back pocket.

"Sweet deal, dudes. I'll be back later. Holler if you need anything."

"Yo, Tuck, where's Tanner tonight?" Gaige asks once it's just the four of us guys left. "I'm not missing him—no offense or anything—but he's been tagging along for weeks now and then all of a sudden he's not here. What gives?"

Tucker looks to Perry. "Brother," he says in explanation. "I don't know where he's at tonight. He's been out with Maura every night she's not at work so I'm surprised he isn't here since she is."

"Wait, Maura? As in Rae's best friend Maura?" Perry asks. We all nod. Perry looks at Tucker. "She's dating your brother?"

Again, Tucker nods.

His eyes light up and he grins. It reminds me of how he looks when he's talking about Rae. I don't know how to take that. "Holy crap. Poor Tanner."

"Wasn't expecting you to say that," Tuck tells him. "My brother is...well, he's a damn asshole. I love him to death because he's my brother, but he doesn't rank high on, well, just about anyone's list."

"Well since she's besties with my girl, I've known Maura my entire life. I know how off her rocker she can be. She used to be shy and quiet but she's...let's say *blossomed* in the past few years. Girl will give you whiplash."

Again with his "my girl" shit. Who is this guy to her?

"I know on our little double date she and Rae seemed to have quite a few similarities. It was comical and slightly unnerving."

"They have their moments. They're different, but also kind of the same. It's weird. I love them both dearly though—but that info doesn't leave this table."

His joke gets lost on me because I'm too busy trying not to strangle him for using "love" and "Rae" in same sentence. Luckily, Tucker and Gaige keep up the conversation while I count the ways I could hide his body.

"Be right back, dudes," Perry suddenly says, getting up from the table and heading toward the bar.

As soon as he's gone, Tucker turns to me.

"So?"

"So what?"

"Who is he? I can't figure it out. He talks like he knows her better than anyone else does. Maybe he's an ex," Tucker ponders.

"Maybe he's family, you dumbasses," Gaige mutters.

"I don't know, man. That thought briefly crossed my mind, but I'm not sure. They seem close, almost too close, ya know? Like they *know know* each other."

"What, is Logical Hudson taking the day off or some shit?" Gaige asks.

"Logical Hudson was the one that thought of the family thing, for your information, but then, ya know, No-Bullshit Hudson chimed in. Fucker wins every time."

"Amen. I've met the dude. He's kind of a dick," Tucker comments.

"All right, so, exes? Close friends? What?" I ask.

"Close friends."

"I'm still going with family."

"Exes," I say.

"Well, that's settled then," Tucker snarks. "I mean, why don't you just ask her?"

I think on it and eventually shrug. "I don't feel like I have that right yet. We're just getting to know one another. I haven't even told her about Joey yet. It's all too new and I don't want to come off as a possessive jerk, or whatever you want to call it."

"From the five minutes she spent over here earlier, I don't think Rae would take it that way at all," Gaige offers.

"I don't think I can take that chance just yet. I like her too much."

At the same time, we all take a drink of our sodas, taking a moment to process everything.

"How's Joey doing? We gonna have a movie night soon?"

"I think you're way too excited to watch old Disney movies with a seven-year-old," Gaige says to Tucker. He turns back to me. "But really, when's the next movie night?"

I love that they love Joey almost as much as I do.

"Joey's great. Probably a little peeved since I've spent the last two nights away from Mom's, but we'll just have to do movie night soon to make up for it. Next Saturday or Sunday?"

They look to one another. "Sunday," they say at the same time.

"Sunday it is. My apartment or Mom's?"

"Mom's," they answer, again at the same time.

"I can grab some pizza if you want so Mom doesn't have to cook dinner," Gaige offers.

"You just want her to make extra desserts."

"Can you blame the dude? Your mom makes the best fucking cherry pie ever. You were a lucky little shit growing up," Tucker says.

"True. You two need to watch your mouths this time. There were two weeks of Joey saying 'shit' and 'asshole' after the last movie night." Both the jerks snicker. "Oh, you think that shit is funny? You do realize that every time I said 'Joey, don't say shit!' or 'Joey, don't say asshole!' that kid made me pay *fifty cents* to the cuss jar? You know how expensive that got? You both owe me at least five bucks!"

At this point in my rant, they're both laughing so hard, neither one of them is making a sound.

"I think... I think..." Tucker starts, gasping for air and holding his stomach.

"Oh yeah? I think, I think you're both dicks," I mock grumpily.

"I think that just made me love that kid even more. Genius!"

I just shake my head, because he's right. My kid is damn smart for a seven-year-old.

"All right, all right," Perry says, sitting back down at the table. "What'd I miss?"

"Looks like we're buying dinner. Hudson's broke," Gaige supplies.

Perry laughs politely while Tucker and Gaige are back to their hysterics. I roll my eyes and turn my attention to the rest of the bar as Rae comes out of the back carrying a huge tray stacked full of food.

I don't pay much attention to anything she says as she passes the plates out because I'm too busy watching her. She moves like she's...air—which sounds weird as shit, but I don't know how else to describe it. It's fluid and flawless and smooth. She breezes when she walks, her steps light and quick, yet steady and calculated.

Then, something happens. Something so stupid and small and unimportant that there's no reason my chest should be constricting, my breaths seizing, my entire world stopping.

She brushes against my arm, and I feel her everywhere.

Our eyes connect, and I'm hit with the same thing I have been hit with over and over when it comes to Rae: familiarity.

I don't understand it either. I've never met her before, because trust me, I'd remember. With the way my body and mind react when I'm around her, there's no way in hell I'd ever be able to forget.

And I damn sure wouldn't want to, not with the way she's looking at me right now as if I'm the only thing that matters.

It should feel wrong, because it's *way* too soon for feelings between us. We've only recently met, don't really know one another, so why are we so engrossed? Why can't we look away? Why do we have this magnetism between? And why do I want to say to hell with all the rules and put my heart out there right this minute?

Because of the way she looks at me. Because of the way she makes my heart race. Because of...her.

She's all I can see, and I'm perfectly okay with that.

WHACK!

"Fuck me, Tuck! That—"

"Nah, I'll pass."

"—hurt, you asshole." I rub arm where he just slammed his stupid meaty fist into me and glare. I use all my energy to focus in on not flipping the asshole off, because even though he completely deserves it, I *am* somewhat of a gentleman.

I turn back to Rae just in time to see her scurry off like she's sprinting in the Olympics or some shit.

Now I *do* flip Tucker off.

"I see you," he says, grinning.

"I see you, too."

Feeling his eyes on me, I glance over at Perry. I'm assuming he witnessed the...exchange between Rae and me because he's staring at me, and I can't tell if it's a friendly stare or a *back away while you still can* stare.

Then, the shadows that were laced in his eyes disappear and I swear I watch a small amount of weight lift off his shoulders because he's suddenly sitting straighter. He nods twice then turns his attention to his food, ending whatever the fuck just happened.

I peek over at Tucker because I have no clue what that was all about. He shrugs and takes a sip of his soda, leaving me to try to decipher that all on my own.

But, I'm confused. I have no idea if I just received some sort of warning for retribution later for the staring contest with Rae, or if it was permission.

I'll hope for the latter and prepare for the former.

CHAPTER 16

RAE

MY BODY IS STILL on fire from the point-two seconds I spent touching Hudson. I can feel him on me still, like his hands are all over me, touching me in the most intimate of places. I'm pulsating with excitement.

Which is utterly ridiculous considering all I did was brush up against his arm.

"Did he..." Maura starts from beside me.

"He did," I manage around a loud gulp, trying to calm my rapid breaths.

I just witnessed my best friend, my cousin, my protector of all protectors other than my dad, give his approval to the guy I'm kind of going crazy over.

"Y'all are so gonna get married," Benny says from my other side.

"Shut it, Ben."

He holds his hands up in innocence. "Hey, I just call 'em like I see 'em."

Maura makes a surprised noise. "I've never seen Perry be so...accepting so quickly. It's..."

"It is."

Benny's warm hand falls on my shoulder as he says, "Good luck, kiddo. I think you're gonna need it."

Gee, thanks for all the help, bud.

"You're welcome," he calls over his shoulder.

"Let's not think too much into all this," I say to Maura with false bravado. Her brows furrow because she knows me better than to believe I'm not freaking out over this. Luckily, she ignores it...for now.

"So, where's Tanner tonight? Isn't he usually with the guys?" I ask, changing the subject.

I swear to all things holy, Maura melts at the mention of his name.

"He's meeting up with a buddy that just got home from deployment. Guess he's having some trouble adjusting and has some family around this area so Tanner's visiting him."

"That's cool of him." He scores some major good guy points in my book for that.

"Yeah, they were really good friends growing up and ended up joining different branches. Kind of neat if you ask me. Sucks the guy is having such a hard time after deployment. I can't imagine."

"Has Tanner ever been deployed?"

"He did a nine-month tour in Germany, but wasn't in a combat zone or anything. I'd probably worry myself sick if that happened now. I feel terrible for Tucker, knowing his brother could be deployed at any time."

I shrug. "That's the military, Maura. Deployment happens. It's not always a bad thing, though."

"I know, I know, I just...can't wrap my head around it. Brave. They are all brave—Tucker and his family included."

"Word," I tell her.

"All right, I need to go refill drinks, and I know you, so go take your minute out back to have your freak out. I'll cover your tables for you if I need to." She pats my arm and walks off.

I take my cue and head toward the kitchen, making my way out to the alley. Funny enough, it's not even an alley. It's just a small, enclosed space around back. It's usually used as a smoke break area for Benny, Cookin' Curt, and Clyde himself, but a few people on the wait staff use it too cool down when things become hectic on the floor.

I push through the door, letting it close behind me, and walk over to the tall brown fence on the opposite side. I lean my back against it and press my palms flat to the surface. Closing my eyes, I take a long, deep breath and simply stand there. I take a few seconds to just breathe, absorbing my surroundings. I get a chance to listen to the crickets, a sound I find soothing, because Clyde has this place locked down when it comes to sound leaking outside. Everything is contained inside when the doors are closed, giving us an illusion of peace out back.

It's a weird feeling when you find someone who makes you suddenly feel all these crazy things at once. You're excited, overjoyed, overwhelmed, and nervous as hell all in one.

There are billions of people in this world and you find the *one* person who jumbles you up inside like this. You find them and you freak out over them and then you find this inner calm you've been searching for all your life and you realize you only have that because of that person.

Then you freak out some more.

And then you step outside of a burger joint and try to get your shit together and pretend you don't smell the dumpster that desperately needs to be rolled away.

Can I do this? Can I let Hudson in? I'm scared in a way I never have been before. Letting him in would mean dates, which I can do. Kissing, which I can do. It would mean family, which I can *probably* do, but there's a chance they would scare him away—I've met them, I should know.

But then there's the whole talking about things, not skating around truths, and being entirely open with someone. You relinquish control over yourself, your emotions, when you let someone in, and that's what scares me the most.

For the most part, I've felt like I had a good grip on my life. Then I graduated college and I felt lost. Then I felt okay. Then I met Hudson and confused as hell again.

I was *so* sure I had talked myself into it, that I was ready to leave this town, to get a big girl job in the city. Then Hudson told me it was okay to feel like I don't have to do those things, told me I could stay here forever and still have all those things.

He makes me feel...worthy. Full. I feel like he knows something about me that's hidden deep within and he pulls at that. He helps center me.

It's all I have right now, and I'm going to cling to it while I can.

My concentration is broken when Clarissa comes barreling through the door on her cell phone, screeching at someone. I feel sorry for the poor bastard on the other end. She gives me a glare and rolls her eyes like *I'm* intruding on her space or some shit.

Guess break time is over. I push off the wall and head back inside.

I scan the dining area as soon as I walk through the hall. Everyone seems good, so I hit the bar to see if Benny needs me to run drinks for him.

"You okay, little one?" he asks, giving me a look that tells me he knows I just had a minor freak out.

I give him a thumbs-up. "Need me to run any drinks?" He nods, sliding a glass filled with thick dark liquid my way. "Guinness? Gross," I shudder.

He laughs. "Just run it to table twelve. You don't have to drink it."

"I'm gonna at least plug my nose. This shit stinks."

Benny just shakes his head at me. I grab the drink and am ready to head onto the floor guns blazing when I come face to face with Hudson.

Being the smartass I am, I hook my thumb over my shoulder in the direction of the restrooms. "You already forget? Bathroom is that way. Or did you need me to wait five minutes while you muster up the courage to ask me?" I smirk at him.

He folds his arms over his chest. "Goddamn do you have a smart mouth or what? I love it."

You're welcome.

"I didn't say thank you, but now I feel like I should have."

I mentally slap myself in the bed. *Of course I said that out loud.*

"So, I was wondering..." he starts.

"Wonder away, stud."

His lips twitch at my interruption. "Can I give you a ride home? Or would that be weird?"

He's in luck because I caught a ride with Haley tonight. She was going out with some moms from daycare and wanted an early out in case they all "sucked more than a vacuum." Yeah, those were her exact words.

"I guess," I tease.

"Wow. Don't sound too excited about it or anything."

And now he's played with fire...

"Oh, Hudson, *of course* you can drive me home! You are just *soooo* sweet!" I yell at the top of my lungs. We get some stares, but most of the patrons know me well enough to ignore me.

He throws his head back in loud laughter. Benny looks to

me, his eyebrow quirked up in question. I lift a shoulder in a *What can you do?* sort of way.

"That fuckin' mouth," I hear Hudson mumble in an amused voice as he walks away.

"Poor guy. He has no clue what he's getting into with you," Jaret, Benny's partner, says from his perch at the bar.

"Nope, and I don't really have it in me to feel bad for the guy." I smirk, grabbing the beer once again and walking out onto the floor.

After I drop off the beer for Benny, I pull my phone out to text Haley.

> **Me: You're off the hook. Found a ride home.**

She responds immediately.

> **Hales: You so suck, dude. These women are boring! I just want to take my e-reader out and read. Is that bad? Ya know what? Fuck it. I'm gonna read on my phone and pretend I'm texting.**
> **Hales: Wait...who's taking you home?**

Shit. I knew that was coming.

> **Me: Hudson...**

**Hales: Just wrap that shit, sis.
Love you! Be careful!**

And for some reason, people trust her with their children. That's terrifying.

**Me: Love you too! Enjoy your
book!
Hales: OMG, SHUT UP! I'M
READING! RUDE!**

Pocketing my phone, I roll my eyes. She's such a dork sometimes.

The next thirty minutes fly by as I make my way around the bar to check in on all my tables. I know I need to go check on Hudson's table, but I'm nervous. He makes me that way. Being near him gives me weird jitters.

Okay, fine, I'm also procrastinating because they're one of my last tables and that means I'm one step closer to being in a small, enclosed space with him alone.

But...my bed *is* calling my name, so it's time to put my big girl panties on.

"Ah, there's my girl," Perry says, pulling lightly on my ponytail. I smack his hand away as I slide up close next to him, pushing him until he's only halfway on his chair, and then sit beside him.

Resting my elbows on the table, I blow out a tired puff of air. "Are you dudes done yet? I'm ready to get out of here and you're holding me up."

"Shit, really? I didn't realize we were your last table," Gaige says as politely as one can while still using the word *shit*.

"No, I still have two other tables, but I can pass those off on

Maura and bounce out early. This dude"—I point at Hudson —"wants to take me home. As you can see, he's old, so he probably has a bedtime he has to stick to. You should all respect your elders and scoot scoot."

"Did you just call me old?" Hudson asks in a shocked voice.

I nod solemnly. "I can totally see your gray hairs from here." Not true. He doesn't have a single gray hair on his head. Not a wrinkle or any sign of aging. He looks young and happy... and handsome as hell.

He scoffs. "I'm only twenty-four!"

"Must be your air of maturity." That isn't a lie; there is something about him that makes him seems older, more mature, like he had to grow up fast or something.

"Hudson, I think I love your girl. She gives you as much shit as I do," Tucker says with admiration in his voice.

I throw him a wink. "I told you dudes I'm a catch. You missed out big time, Tucker."

"And she's full of herself. I feel like you're a female version of this weird Gaige/Hudson hybrid. It's creepy...and kind of hot."

"Don't compare me to that asshole!" Gaige says defensively.

"Yeah, that's rude as shit, man. I am way better-looking than him," Hudson says.

I blink rapidly. "You guys are exhausting." And so damn entertaining, but I'm not stroking egos tonight, so I leave that part out. "All right, unless you boys need anything else, I'm going to go check on my other tables. But really, let's pack this shit up, huh? We have a senior citizen we need to take care of."

———

THE RIDE to my apartment is quiet. We haven't said much beyond me giving him directions. Both our elbows are resting together, barely grazing one another, on the center console of Hudson's small SUV. Every time we hit a bump, they rub together even more. It's strange how attractive it is, how good his arm feels rubbing against mine. His freakin' *arm*. Like that's supposed to be sexy or something.

I study him as he drives. He has his left arm extended, resting easily on the steering wheel. He looks comfortable but alert. *Even his driving is sexy.*

He's in his usual attire: plain shirt—this time a light green one—and jeans, an outfit that's so simple and somehow so damn good-looking. His black hair is messy, and his face is covered in about two days' worth of stubble. So effortless, so handsome, *so fucking hot.*

I think he can feel my stare because his chest starts rising and falling in fast spurts and he's swallowed roughly ten times since I've looked over at him. I can see tiny beads of sweat forming on his neck.

Suddenly, his tongue glides out, wetting his bottom lip swiftly. My eyes track every second of it. I inhale sharply and notice he's really sweating now.

He reaches out and flicks the AC on. It's September. In Massachusetts. AC is *not* needed.

"Left or right?" he asks, his voice thicker than normal.

I swallow loudly. "Right. Then left. 180E."

He nods once then the car grows quiet again, leaving just breathing to fill the space.

I'm not certain where this sudden sexual tension is coming from, not sure if it's because we're in a confined space together for the first time since our car ride after the blind date, or if it's because of how connected we are.

Hudson parks in front of my building. We unclick our seatbelts and just sit there, staring up at the apartments.

Then we start talking at the same time.

"Do you want to come up?"

"Can I see you again?"

We laugh. He motions for me to talk first.

"Uh, would you like to come up? I mean it's only fair that I show you my place since I've seen yours."

He smiles. "I'd like that."

We climb out of the car and Hudson follows me up the stairs. I stop at my door and look to him. He seems to read my mind.

"Rae, you're just giving me a tour. That's all this is. I know that. Relax. I'm not expecting anything. Promise."

I nod and unlock my door. He trails me inside, walking so close I can feel the heat coming off him. Flipping on the light switch, I glance around the room, checking to make sure there aren't any stray bras or underwear lying about. We may be women, who are usually way more organized than men, but we aren't saints. We Kamden ladies are a messy duo.

"Welcome to my digs. This is the living room." I point to the couch. "That's where I fell in love with Will Cooper."

"Lucky bastard," Hudson says with that smirk of his.

"I agree."

We spend the next few minutes walking through my small apartment. I point out but don't show him the bedrooms; I feel like that would be too tempting right now.

He notices.

"What, not going to show me your bedroom? Afraid I'll talk you straight into bed, Rae?" he teases.

"So terrified," I retort in a falsely snappy tone. He has no idea how close to right he is. "You're not even close."

"Then what is it? Do you have some embarrassing secret you're hiding?" The smirk is in full force now.

"No," I say a little too quickly, my hand flying to the door-knob in case he tries to open it. His eyes track my movements.

Hudson inches in closely, holding my stare. He places his hand on top of the one I have on the doorknob and I can feel his breath on my face. His eyes are churning their usual green-blue color, captivating me more than ever before. "You have me all kinds of curious now, Rae." His voice is quiet, sexy, and dangerous to my nervous system. "You gonna show me what's in the room?"

Before I know what's happening, the door is opening and I'm tumbling backward into my room. Hudson swiftly catches me with an arm around my waist, righting me before I can hit the ground.

"You're always falling for me," he whispers.

I gulp and nod, rendered speechless.

Then I hear it, the one thing I *knew* was coming: Hudson is laughing. I can feel his entire body shaking against mine. I'm bury my face against his chest, so embarrassed that I can't even fully appreciate how good it feels to have him this close to me. He wraps his other arm around me, holding me to him but continuing to laugh.

"Stop it," I growl. He laughs harder.

"It's just...I didn't expect this. I thought it would be something like dirty clothes or maybe stuffed animals to the max. But this? This is just too good. Someone's obsessed," Hudson teases.

I manage to snake my way out of his hold and step away, crossing my arms over my chest. "You are so rude."

"Come on, Rae. It's creepy, but cute as hell. You *love* the Winchesters, like *love* them, and Cass. It's adorable."

I drop my face in my hands, groaning loudly. I don't want

to look around my room right now. Yes, it's covered in nothing but *Supernatural* stuff. Posters galore, a couple throws, and even those tiny little bobble-head things. It's embarrassing as hell but—hello—it's *Supernatural*. It's okay to love it a little more than a lot.

I hear Hudson shuffle his way to me. He tugs on my wrists, trying to pry my hands from the face. He succeeds, but I refuse to look at him. "Come on, silly girl. I'll leave you alone now. I won't speak another word of your Winchester fever."

Hudson pulls me out of the room, my face still red, and leads me back into the living room. Now we're standing in front of the couch, just looking at one another.

"So, now that things are awkward, care for a drink? I have beer—heavy on the root. No Dr. Pepper, sorry," I ask, trying to get the attention off me.

"Am I that transparent?"

I shrug, walking into the kitchen. "I'm a waitress. I notice stuff like that."

"Bet I can guess your drink of choice," he calls from the living room.

"Doubt it!"

"Mountain Dew." I walk back out holding his drink in one hand and mine behind my back so he can't see.

"That's it? That's your big guess?"

He takes his soda and sits on the couch, shaking his head. "Not just any Mountain Dew, but Mountain Dew Code Red from the bottle only. No fountain or can soda for you."

What the hell...?

I pull the bottle of Code Red from behind my back and slowly sit down next to him, leaving enough room between us so that we're not touching, but easily could be.

"How in the hell did you know that? Are you inside my brain?"

He laughs. "You had a bottle in your purse the day your car broke down and again last night at my apartment. Then when I offered you a drink, you turned down soda in favor of apple juice. Not many grown-ups do that."

Hudson watching and paying attention to all things me? Catching on to little things like that? Total turn-on.

"I'm impressed. Not many people know that about me. Haley doesn't even remember half the time."

"Haley?"

"I haven't told you about Hales?" Hudson shakes his head. "She's my older, completely crazy sister. We share the apartment, so if you're ever over here and you see a bra or two on the floor, they're hers."

His eyes widen, and I realize I just indirectly invited him over here again. I wait for the nerves to set in, for my head to start weaving all these insane scenarios that leave me broken.

They never come, which surprises me. Maybe it's because the moment he stepped inside my apartment, I didn't feel intimidated by whatever it is we have anymore.

I'm ready to accept it...whatever it is.

"I have to be honest, if you're calling someone crazy, I'm terrified to meet them."

I laugh. "She's me on speed, but I love her. Surprisingly enough, she runs a daycare." His eyes bug out. "I know, I know. Can you imagine?"

Hudson shakes his head. "I'm really trying not to. No offense."

"None taken. Besides, kids aren't my thing."

Now, I'm pretty observant. I notice a lot of stuff other people don't. Hudson tensing up at my confession? I noticed, but what does it mean? It's *way* too soon to be talking kids and marriage—other than our joke proposals, of course.

"You don't like kids?" he asks after taking a long drink of his soda.

"Well...I like them...when they aren't mine and I can give them back to their parents. They aren't something I *have* to have to feel like my life is complete. If I can avoid it, I will. I don't think I'll ever actively try for children."

"Why?"

"I think it stems from my—" I pause, narrowing my eyes at him. "Wait, why are you so curious?"

His grin is hesitant this time. "Just trying to get to know you better is all."

"Let's just say I didn't have the best mother-daughter relationship and I don't think I'm mom material. I resent my mother too much. I don't want that with my own kid."

I watch as he takes another big drink. I never thought watching a guy drinking a soda would be hot, but this totally is. The way his throat moves is so sexy. And his mouth? Perfect. His lips...they look so soft. *I bet they feel just as soft as they look.*

I somehow manage to drag my gaze from his mouth to see his brows slightly scrunched.

"Sorry about your mom. I, uh, I actually like kids. I think they're fun. A little messy and wild, but still fun. If it makes you feel any better, from what I know of you, I think you'd be fine with children. I don't think you could screw them up *that* bad." He tacks on that last bit with a wink.

"You're a kid person? That's surprising."

He gets this faraway look on his face and smiles. "Trust me, it was for me too."

Was?

Hudson clears his throat. "I think I need to get going. I have an early morning at the shop tomorrow. We received a rush job before closing tonight and they need it done by nine when the shop opens. It should be quick, but I'm still going to have to go in at six." He stands and shakes his empty soda can at me. "Trash?"

"Tsk, tsk. We recycle. There's a box in the kitchen."

"Be right back."

I watch him walk away. It's a nice walk, a strong, confident walk.

Fuck it, who am I kidding? The man has the nicest ass I've ever seen. Those jeans fit well.

"Thank you," he says.

I blink and look up at him, confusion lining my face. "For the soda," he says. Then he gives me that fucking smirk again. "And for the compliment."

"What compliment?"

"My ass, your eyes. Thank you." He's still smirking.

I cover my face in mortification. "You're welcome," I utter through my hands.

He laughs, holding his out. "Walk me to the door?"

I accept it with ease.

I can see myself doing a lot of that with Hudson—simply accepting things with him. Anything. Everything. It all feels so right, so fresh and exciting. *I like it. I like him.*

We walk to the door, our hands still clasped.

"So, before you rudely interrupted me earlier," he jokes, "I was going to ask you if you wanted to go out again sometime. Ya know, if you aren't too tired of me yet."

"Gee, I don't know, Hudson. I have a few other dates lined up for this week so I'm not sure if I'll have the time. I can give you a call, though. Oh wait, I forgot you don't know how to use a phone."

"Just for that smartass comment, I'll be texting you daily from now on. You'll get at least five texts from me, all completely random questions. Be prepared."

"You don't scare me, mister."

He just laughs and tugs me closer into him. He's quick and kissing me right at the corner of my mouth before I know what he's doing. His lips linger for all of two seconds before he pulls back and stares into my eyes.

That look? The one he's giving me right now? It's saying *I want you.*

My breath catches from the intensity I see in them. Hudson notices. His hand, the one that isn't still holding mine, moves deliberately upward.

Then it stops and Hudson reaches out, placing his hand on my chest just above my breasts. My chest is heaving at this point. *Up, down. Up, down. Updownupdownupdown.* I know he can feel my rapid heartbeat. Hell, he can probably *see* it— that's how hard and fast it's going right now.

He mutters something but I can't hear it over the pressure in my head.

His hand is traveling now...slowly...ever so slowly. I close my eyes and do my best to control my breathing as his hand creeps higher and higher, gently moving my heavy hair off my neck. Then it stops, cradling my neck with just the right amount of pressure.

I can feel him move in closer, feel his breath on my face. His lips connect at the corner of my mouth again, moving toward my ear, barely grazing my cheeks.

"Goodnight, Rae," he whispers.

And then he's gone, rushing out the door before I can utter another word.

Again? Are you fucking kidding me?

I begin pacing my apartment. I have never been so sexually frustrated from simple cheek-kisses in my entire life!

Does my breath stink? I check. Nope, smells breathy. Maybe he's a psycho that gets off on baiting women because I swear it seems he has an MO or some shit.

I pull my phone out to call the one person I know will know what's going on.

"Miss me already?"

"Perry!" I shout. I can hear him wince.

"Ow. Yes?"

"I have a problem..." I spend the next five minutes telling him about my dates with Hudson and how he's left me hanging with a cheek-kiss every damn time.

"Hmm...I don't know, Rae."

"I don't either. I know he likes me and this was date two-point-five so I just don't understand. I mean, there's no way he doesn't know I want him to kiss me."

"Maybe he's waiting for you to make the first move? Or maybe waiting for lucky date number three?" Perry tries to reason.

I shrug even though he can't see me. "Maybe. I don't know. This dating shit sucks."

"Tell me about it. Why do you think I don't ever do it?"

"Thanks for the warning," I mumble.

I hear Perry quietly talking to someone in the background. I'm not certain who exactly it is, but I know it's a girl. He chuckles at something she says.

"Are you fucking flirting while I'm in the middle of a crisis? You're a terrible person, Perry Hartman!"

"I love you, sweet girl," he says, laying the charm on thick.

I huff even though I can't help but smile at the idiot. "Love you too. Wear a condom."

"Always. Night dear."

"Later gator." I hang up, still as confused as I was before I called him.

I pace my apartment for about ten more minutes until I decide to call it a night.

I'm crawling into bed when I hear the front door open. Then I hear giggling. I can tell it's Haley.

"Hales?" I call out.

"Shh...be quiet," she says to whomever made her giggle. "Rae! Don't come out. I've brought home a man!"

Is she drunk? "Are you drunk?"

"No. Yes. Kind of. We went to Clyde's and I ended up having a good time after all. And I met a man. A really sexy man. He's going to take care of me," she yells dramatically. I hear more giggling and footsteps as they go into Haley's room.

I just roll my eyes and put my pillow over my head.

I'm almost asleep so I barely hear my phone vibrate on my bedside table. Grabbing it, I check the screen. It's Hudson. I put in my headphones, just in case Haley decides now is a good time to start having sex.

> **FMK: What's your favorite**
> **color?**

I smile. He wasn't kidding about the random texts.

> **Me: If we're going to do this,**
> **then you have to answer**
> **every question you ask.**
> **Deal?**

He takes a minute to respond.

> **FMK: Deal. Dark blue. Your**
> **turn.**
> **Me: Orange.**

FMK What's your middle
name?

Me: Rae Bethany Kamden.
Yours?

FMK: Hudson Michael Tamell.
Why the name Rae? No
offense or anything, it's just
different.

Me: I don't know. Ask my dad,
he picked it. I hate it.

FMK: Really? I like it. I have a
thing for girls with boy
names. It's unique. And
Hudson was my mom's
maiden name. Guess she
wanted some connection to
her life pre-Rocky Tamell.

He likes my name. That causes me to blush...a lot. *Fuck, I
feel like I'm a damn teenager again.*

Me: Rocky? As in your dog? You
named your dog after
your dad?

FMK: Yes? Is that too weird?

Me: Does that count as a
question?

FMK: *rolls eyes* Sure.

Me: No, I think it's kind of
sweet. He's always there
with you.

FMK: Favorite Transit song?

This is too easy.

> **Me: "All Your Heart"**
> **FMK: Nice. Mine is "Please,**
> **Head North"**
> **Me: Of course it is. That's my**
> **second favorite song of**
> **theirs.**
> **FMK: HA! Okay, last question**
> **and this one is extremely**
> **important. Get ready…**
> **What are you wearing?**

I die. Laughter bubbles up and out so fast I can't keep it all down. At this point, I don't even care if I'm being too loud.

> **Me: No laughing! I'm wearing**
> **PJs with little cupids on**
> **them and a matching shirt**
> **that says LOVE.**
> **FMK: You have on Valentine's**
> **Day jammies in September?**
> **That's hot. Flannel pants**
> **and a tee. I'm a simple guy.**
> **Me: That's hot.**

It really is.

> **FMK: That was number five.**
> **Sweet dreams, Rae.**
> **Me: Goodnight, Hudson. x**

I turn on "Please, Head North" by Transit and rearrange myself on my bed until I'm comfortable.

These last few days have been good—great, even—full of laughter and fun. My favorite part though? My nightmare is gone...for now. I'm sure having a full night of sleep has helped in the happy department, but I know that's not all it is.

It's Hudson.

He's made me smile more since I met him than I have in the past few years. He's sweet, witty, and kind of sort of perfect so far—and it doesn't hurt that he's super freakin' hot either.

But that's not even what I like most about him. It's his heart. I have never in my life met a guy that shows their love the way Hudson does. I don't know if he even realizes he's doing it, but he does. I can see it in his eyes so clearly. The love he has for his friends and family when he talks about them is...well, remarkable.

As my eyes drift shut, I realize my heart may be in a little deeper with Hudson than I realize.

And that I'm okay with it.

CHAPTER 17

HUDSON

I SPEND the next week alternating my time between Joey, my apartment, and Rae.

Joey's been busy running back and forth to a school play of *The Wizard of Oz*. I've had the chance to sit in on a few rehearsals, and nothing is more adorable than watching a bunch of seven-year-olds "act". Plus, Joey makes a great Cowardly Lion.

Every moment spent at my apartment is focused on getting this Pembrooke shit moving along. The amount of time it's taking is ridiculous. I would have turned my mom's friend down so I could stay with Joey more often if I knew it was going to take a month and a half, but I couldn't let my mom down, couldn't leave her hanging.

I miss my kid though. I'm tired of babysitting this apartment. Not going to lie, it's been nice to have a few extra hours of "me" time that I didn't have before, but I'm starting to feel guilty for thinking that and it's starting to eat away at me.

I do my best to push those thoughts out of my head because Logical Hudson knows it's all just silly parent guilt.

Out of the corner of my eye, I notice the little notification light on my phone blinking. I rush to check it, hoping it's Rae. No luck; it's Tucker.

> **Tucker: Yo. What goes on tonight?**
> **Me: Getting ready to head back to my mom's and chill with Joey.**
> **Tucker: Huh, figured you'd be at C's hitting on your little lady friend again.**

Rae. A goofy grin spreads across my face just thinking about her.

That mouth of hers continues to amaze me at every turn. Every time we met for coffee, texted our random five questions, or had dinner this past week—which was a lot—she's said something weird that did nothing but give me a semi in public. Everything about her is a turn-on. I feel like a total dick because I still haven't kissed her, but I don't deserve to yet since I haven't been one hundred percent honest with her about the fact that I'm a dad, even though I almost tried to tell her last week, and that was ruined when she told me she didn't think she was mom material. If I'm being honest, her confession has kept me guarded—another reason I haven't kissed her.

Even without having kissed her, I can see myself falling for her, and it's scary as shit.

But, it can't be helped, and I can't be blamed. Rae's witty, smart, sassy, and beautiful as hell. Hell, just a text conversation is fun with her, something I've been lacking a lot of in the last several years—not with Joey, but with life in general. I have to "dad" all the time and don't have time for adult fun.

One thing I have noticed though? We've barely brushed the surface of the more serious topics like her job hunt and wanting to move, or Joey. I can feel her pull back every time we get serious about any of it, and I so do I. We're both scared, because I think it's clear we have the potential to destroy one another.

I sigh and text Tuck back.

Me: Nah, it's Joe's turn tonight.
Tucker: Damn you and your
**   responsible ass. Tell the**
**   little shit hi for me.**
Me: Will do, man.

I put my phone back in my pocket and grab my shoes. I'm shoving my right one on when the doorbell starts going crazy.

"Hudson! Why aren't you answering your phone?" my mom says in a panic, pushing through the door with Joey in tow as soon as I twist the handle.

I frown. "I didn't get any calls from you. Why? What's going on? Is something wrong with Joey?" I ask, now thoroughly panicking, grabbing Joey and checking for any signs of damage.

Joey's wearing a panicked look, probably freaked out by my reaction.

I'm not looking at her, but I can *feel* my mom roll her eyes. "No, you goob. If it were anything bad, I would have gone to the hospital. Joey's fine."

I let Joey go, straightening and looking my mom over now. "Is it you then? What's wrong?"

Again with the eye roll. "Same answer," she says dryly. "It's Marcy, the neighbor. Her husband fell off the ladder from the roof. He was rushed to the hospital and Marcy has no one there for her with all her kids being off at college."

"Say no more. Go. I was just headed over there anyway. Please let Marcy know I'm sorry."

She gives me a quick hug, kisses Joey, and then she's gone.

I look to Joey.

"Guess it's just you and me, kiddo."

I get an eye roll. *From a seven-year-old.*

"Not cool, dude," I say in the most parental voice I have.

I swear I get the most adorable pair of blue eyes turned on me. "Sorry," Joey whispers before looking down at the floor.

I sigh because how in the hell can you stay mad at that? You can't.

Squatting down so I'm eye level, I say, "Hey, it's okay. Just remember for next time, okay?"

I get a nod...and a sniffle. After a few hugs and reassuring words—because I hardly ever get on Joey's case about anything —I suggest a movie.

"Wanna watch *The Lion King?*"

A shrug. "I guess."

"Okay, bug. We'll watch that and order some pizza. Maybe Gaige will be working and he can deliver it to us. How's that sound?"

"Do we still have ice cream?"

I get a flashback of the last person to ask me about ice cream. *Rae.* I wish she were here for this.

The smallest flair of panic races through me because that's a heavy thought. Then I realize that yes, I do want Rae here, for all these small moments and all the big ones too.

I just have to gather the courage to tell her about Joey...then possibly watch her walk away because of it.

"You're asking me, The King of Ice Cream, if I have any? Where's your faith in me, bug?"

"Good point," Joey says with a serious expression and pat on my arm. "Ice cream first, okay?"

I pretend to think on it for a few seconds, but really, I'd never deny this kid anything. "Deal."

We fist-bump.

"I'll go get Rocky and you go get the ice cream."

"Please?" I encourage.

"With cherries on top!"

Now I'm confused. "Of the ice cream or the please?"

I get a *duh* look. "Both."

———

ABOUT TWO HOURS later there's another knock at the door. I assume it's my mom because I'm not expecting anyone else so I fling the door open.

It's Rae.

SHIT! It's Rae!

Out of reflex, I close the door so she can only see my face. Her brows pinch together in an instant.

My breathing becomes labored and I can't seem to hear anything because of the pounding in my head. She's talking, I can see her mouth moving, but I can't hear a damn thing she's saying.

Fuck, fuck, fuck! Deep breath in...and out. In, out. In, out.

I do this several times until I'm able to focus. I blink, really looking at her for the first time. She has on a pair of those weird half-pants thing girls wear and a t-shirt. Her dark brown hair is pulled back in a bun and she just looks...well, confused right now.

I make sure to drink the sight of her in, afraid this may be the last time she wants to see me because of what's about to happen.

"Hudson," she says. This time I can hear her just fine. "Are you okay?"

"I...uh...well..." I stammer. I swallow loudly. "I kind of have something to tell you."

She looks worried now. I would be too. She scrunches her brows even more. "Kind of or you do? Which one, Hudson?"

I can tell she's getting irritated. I can't blame her; I'm acting like a total fucking tool right now.

"I do. I *definitely* do." I glance back inside at Joey, making sure everything is okay. When I see *The Lion King* 2 still has a firm grip on the kid's attention, I turn back to Rae. "Can we talk outside maybe?"

"Um, I'd kind of rather not. I'd rather you just tell me what the fuck is going on?" It's not a question, but it comes out as one.

My eyes widen and my entire body tenses, because I know —oh, boy, do I know—what's coming next.

"Daddy, your friend said a bad word. Tell her she has to pay up," Joey says, sticking her hand out from behind me. "It's fifty cents, you know."

Rae gasps, her hand flying to her chest. Her eyes are bigger than I've ever seen and her face is losing its color rapidly.

"Did she just... She... Daddy? Are you..." she starts. And restarts and restarts and restarts.

Then, she goes blank. I wave my hand in front of her face. Nada, nothing, zip. She doesn't move or even blink.

"Joey, honey, back up, please. Daddy needs to bring his friend inside. I think she's having an attack of some sort," I tell my daughter, who is still standing directly behind me.

"Like when those ninjas attacked us at the dog park? That was insane!"

I smile because that was a fun day. Running around and

pretending to fight ninjas with my kid was the highlight of my week.

"Kind of, only the ninjas are all in her head. You gonna help me get them out?" I ask, grabbing Rae and walking her inside. She's doing nothing else but moving her feet. It's a miracle she's still upright at this point. "Let's sit her down here," I tell Joey, who's holding Rae's other side.

We gently push Rae down onto the couch, right in the middle. Joey sits on one side; I sit on the other.

I'd be lying if I said I wasn't worried right now. I'm not just worried about Rae, who I know will snap out of it once the shock wears off, I'm worried for whatever future we have—or had. I mean, she plainly expressed her feelings about children last week. And Joey? Well, she's my whole world. She's it for me. If Rae can't accept that—the hand life has dealt me—I'll walk away in an instant.

"Dad? Can I poke her? Ya know, just to make sure she's okay. I sawed it in a movie once. They were pokin' a dead guy with a stick. Should I get a stick?" Joey says.

"First, what kind of stuff does Nana let you watch? Second, it's 'saw', not 'sawed'. Third, you can try, but no sticks." I shrug, because I'm kind of curious to see if it'll work.

Leave it to my fucking kid to poke Rae all right...smack dab in the middle of her forehead.

To my surprise, it works.

Rae flinches. "Did...did you just poke me? On the forehead?"

Joey looks to me, her eyes taking up about half her face. I nod at her, letting her know everything's okay. She looks Rae right in the eyes.

"I did. You're not dead," Joey tells her.

"Well, that's good to know," Rae deadpans. She exhales

loudly and turns to face me. I give her my trademark smirk. "Nope, don't even try. You have a lot of explaining to do."

I wince because she doesn't sound even a little bit happy.

"Bug, can you go play with Rocky in my room for a bit? Daddy needs to talk with his friend."

"No way. Not until you introduce me," Rae says.

"Sorry. Rae, this is my daughter, Joey. Joey, this is my... friend, Rae."

"Your girlfriend? The one you smile about with Nana all the time?"

Another wince, because it's kind of embarrassing that my kid is giving away all my secrets.

"Girlfriend?" Rae asks with a small smile. "Don't you think *this*"—she gestures to show she's referring to our current Joey situation—"would be something your *girlfriend,* or at least the person you've seen or talked to every day for the past week, should know about?"

"Rae...I'm...I'm sorry." My voice is pleading, begging her to understand.

She ignores me and turns to Joey. "How old are you?"

"Seven. How old are you?" Joey asks her.

"Twenty-two," Rae tells her. She looks back at me. "That means..."

"Seventeen," I confirm. A look of pity crosses her face, and fuck do I hate it.

I don't ever want to be pitied for the best thing to ever happen to me. Having Joey, no matter how young, was one of the greatest moments in my life. I would never trade it for anything else.

"I'm a first grader, you know," Joey tells Rae proudly.

"Oh, really? What's two plus two then?" Rae bounces back, a small smile playing on her lips.

My bug gives her a look like she's crazy. "Four," she says

slowly, like Rae is the one learning something. "I also know what twelve times twelve is. It's one hundred and forty-four."

Rae's hand comes up and she covers her smile before she regains composure. "Wow. You're smart. You sure you're only seven?"

I can't believe this woman says she's horrible with kids. She seems to have taken to Joey right away. Granted, they just met and haven't interacted much, but kids are great judges of character, so Joey talking with Rae is a good sign.

Joey nods vigorously. "Yep! Daddy, can I go play with Rocky now?" I nod. As she's passing by us, she pats me on the arm. "Your friend is cool. I like her."

I catch Rae's stare. "I do too, bug. I do too."

Rae's shoulders drop as soon as Joey walks out of the room. I gulp because I know it's coming—she's pissed. I get that. I do. I kept something big from her. I didn't necessarily mean to, but it happened.

"Hudson."

"Rae."

"What in the actual...f...rench toast!" she catches herself. "This is huge. Why would you keep this from me?"

"I didn't really mean to. It's kind of hard to explain. I—"

"Try," she interrupts.

I sigh. I know that no matter which way I explain it, I'm going to sound like a total douchebag. "No judging, okay?"

"Have I judged you yet, Hudson? That's not fair." I can feel the heat radiating off her, and it's not the fun kind.

"Right." I clear my throat and hope she can understand what I'm about to tell her. "So, as you now know, I have a seven-year-old daughter. She's amazing, the light of my life, my entire reason for breathing."

"Why do you not live together?"

"Oh, we do. Remember that house in Pembrooke I told you

about? There were electrical issues with it and the wiring had to be almost completely redone. My mom has a friend who needed someone to watch over his rental while he found someone new to sublet it to and she volunteered my services. She knows being a single parent is hard enough already, and moving into a new house is going to make it even harder. She wanted me to have a little bit of freedom before everything changes. So, I stay here a few nights a week to watch the place," I explain. I pause to make sure she's catching everything. She motions for me to continue.

"When I met you, I had no idea this would turn into a relationship of any kind. Hell, I wasn't even supposed to go on that blind date with you, but I did, and I'm glad. I like you, Rae, like *really, really* like you. I selfishly liked having that freedom, getting the chance to get to know someone and not just being the single dad for a change. It was nice to just be Hudson—to just be twenty-four for a while. It's not like I was never going to tell you. In fact, I was going to last Thursday when I drove you home, but then you made that little confession." She purses her lips and tilts her head, trying to remember. "How kids aren't for you, that you're not mom material—what am I supposed to do with that? I have a kid, and she's definitely for me, Rae."

She sits there, staring at my coffee table, her eyebrows still bunched together. "I don't know. I still don't get why you just didn't tell me."

"I didn't know how. I haven't had to before. You're the first person I've been on a date with in three years, Rae. I was with Joey's mom before that, so she was obviously already clued in to the situation."

"How long were you with her then?"

"Since I was sixteen until I was twenty-one." I can see the wheels spinning. "Yes, Jess, my high school sweetheart, is Joey's mom, and before you ask, no, she's not in the picture anymore."

Her demeanor doesn't change with that confession, and I get the distinct impression that even if Jess were in the picture, Rae wouldn't care. It makes me feel like this, despite what she's said about not being mom material, is something she just might be able to handle.

"That's it? No more surprise children running around? Just Joey?"

I chuckle. "Just Joey."

The only noise in the apartment is coming from Joey, who is currently in my bedroom playing with Rocky. She throws a toy and Rocky takes off after it. You can hear his tail smacking against the wall and her giggles floating through the air.

"She's gorgeous," Rae tells me. "I don't know why you hid her from me."

"I didn't *hide* her, Rae. I just didn't let you meet her. She's a kid. They get easily attached. What if we ended up not liking one another? What if it didn't work out after I introduced you? I have to be careful with that sort of stuff. I knew last weekend, just after two dates, that it would be safe to let Joey meet you, but then Thursday night happened and I got scared to mention anything. So, I didn't. I figured I'd see where we were next week and then go from there." I pause and take a deep breath. "And I also wanted to know about Perry, but I had to find the courage to ask about that too. I figured you'd tell me all that when you were ready though."

Another look of confusion crosses her face. "Perry?"

"Yeah. I was wondering how long you used to date and if there was anything still there between you two. You seem close for exes, is all. Made me wonder if there was something still... lingering between you and hesitate to put myself into this any further."

"Perry? The same Perry that did your website and ate with

you guys last week?" she asks, brows raised, a smile forming at the corners of her mouth.

I give her a small, uncertain nod.

"Hudson," she says, bringing a hand up to her mouth. "Perry isn't my ex. He's my cousin."

CHAPTER 18

RAE

HUDSON THINKS Perry is my ex! This is rich!

My chest is on fire and I'm hardly making a sound because I'm laughing so hard.

Wait...if he thinks Perry is my ex, that means he thinks we had sex! *Ew! GROSS!*

I sober up because poor Hudson has his mouth hanging open. I reach over and gently close it for him. "What did I tell you about those flies, Hudson?"

"I just... I don't get it. I mean...you two seem so close. I don't...I don't understand."

"We *are* close. Next to Maura, he's my best friend. My right-hand man. The best guy I know."

Hudson drops his head into his hands and groans. "Gaige was right. He said you were probably family but No-Bullshit Hudson was in full swing so I was having none of that."

"No-Bullshit Hudson?" I question with a smirk.

He gives me side-eye. "Don't laugh," he says, trying to fight a smile of his own. "He's my inner asshole that tries to tell it to me straight. He rarely makes an appearance. Logical Hudson is usually the one milling about." His head drops back into his hands. "Ugh! I cannot believe I thought he was your ex!"

"Why didn't you just ask me about him? I'm shocked I haven't mentioned him before, but I can see where I may have forgotten. I've been a little wrapped up in...well, you lately."

"I didn't want to ruin anything by sounding jealous. Plus, there was Joey. I guess I felt you were entitled to your past as much as I am mine. I didn't tell you about her, so why should you have to disclose your past—and nonexistent, apparently— relationship with Perry," he confesses. "And I really don't remember you mentioning him. I mean, you said you had a cousin, but you never mentioned a name. I guess you not mentioning his name is only fair though. It made me worry a little. It was like karma for springing Joey on you."

"You're right. Paybacks suck, huh?" I say.

Hudson sighs loudly. "I am so sorry, Rae."

I know he's not just talking about the Perry thing, but also about Joey. I don't know what to say because it's kind of not okay. I know we've only been seeing one another for a couple weeks, but he should have said something. I mean, this is *huge*. I don't know what to do with it all either. I've never dated anyone with a child, and I've never seen myself doing so either.

"I know you are, Hudson. Right now though, I'm not sure what to do. I like you, like *really, really* like you," I tell him, repeating the words he spoke earlier because they *are* true. "I just don't know how to feel about anything else. Like you, I don't want to hurt your daughter. I just know children have always been a hard no for me."

His head drops, and his shoulders sink as if they are carrying too much weight.

God, I hate how sad he looks. I hate that it makes my chest constrict and my body ache. That has to be a sign, right? That Hudson isn't just some person? That I can't walk away from this because of something I've always perceived a certain way?

It has to be.

I take a deep breath and let it out. "But for you, I'm willing to try."

Hudson slowly lifts his head, locking his eyes onto mine. "Are you...are you sure? I don't want you to push yourself into this, to regret this decision, because it's huge, Rae. You *have* to be sure."

"I am."

He takes my hands and kisses my cheek quickly. "Thank you. You have no idea what that means to me."

"Can I ask you a question?"

"Anything," he says, his face hard and serious.

"What's with the cuss jar?"

His eyes crinkle at the corners with laughter. "My parents used to have one for me when I was a kid. Figured I'd carry on the tradition. You should see the thing. It's so full between Tucker, Gaige, and me."

That tugs on my heartstrings. It's so sweet that he carried that on from his childhood.

"Um, Daddy? I'm bored," Joey says, suddenly appearing from around the corner. "Can we watch another movie, please? This time with Rae."

Hudson turns toward Joey, who's now standing at the end of the couch. "No way, bug. It's past your bedtime."

"But we have a guest! It would be rude to go to sleep now," she says so matter-of-factly.

I can see the exact moment Hudson gives in to his daughter. It's obvious he loves his little girl. "Fine, fine, you win, but just a few episodes of *Adventure Time*."

"Deal. Can I sit there?" she asks, pointing to the small spot between Hudson and me.

Hudson looks to me for approval, and I nod. "Of course! Come here, kiddo," I tell her, scooting over and patting the spot beside me.

"I'm parched. You girls want anything?" Hudson asks, heading toward the small kitchen.

"Apple juice, please, Daddy," Joey requests.

"That makes sense now. Same for me, please."

Left alone with Joey, I study the small child sitting next to me. If I were to ever see Hudson and Joey out together, there would never be a doubt in my mind that she is his daughter. She has shiny jet-black hair just like her father, and hers is cut into a cute shoulder-length bob. Her skin is the same tanned tone as Hudson's. She even has his nose. The only difference is her eyes. While Hudson's are a beautiful, captivating mix of blue and green, hers are all bright blue.

She's adorable.

"You're pretty. I like your hair," Joey suddenly announces.

"Thank you. I was just thinking the same thing about yours. You look a lot like your daddy."

She giggles. "All the people we meet say that, even Nana. She's at the hospital tonight. Mr. Matthews fell off the roof."

"Oh, that's terrible! I sure hope he'll be all right."

"He's old but he's tough. That's what Nana told me in the car ride here."

I smother a laugh. A child's lack of filter has always been my favorite thing, usually the only part I can relate to.

"Okay ladies, I come bearing apple juices," Hudson says, setting down the cups. Joey dives for her cup and downs half the glass. "Whoa, slow down, dude. That's all you're getting before bed so you better savor it."

"Fine," Joey says, her bottom lip coming out in a pout.

Hudson reaches for the remote and turns on the flat screen. He looks to Joey. "Do you know what time it is?"

"ADVENTURE TIME!" she shouts.

They fist-bump. My heart melts.

We spend the next hour—because it turns out the episodes

are only about ten minutes long and every time Joey said, "One more, please," Hudson gave in—watching a show about an awkward kid and his stretchy yellow dog.

Though the night started rocky, this is the easily the best night I've ever had.

After about six episodes, Hudson finally reaches up and clicks off the television. "All right, kiddo, bedtime. Go potty and brush your teeth, please."

"Will you read to me after?"

He winks at her. "You got it." She tries to wink back, fails miserably, and scurries off to the bathroom.

I watch Hudson watch her. The love on his face is evident and breathtaking. He looks so happy being with his daughter that I have to fight back the tears threatening to spill over.

"You scared off yet?"

"Nah. She's adorable. She looks and acts just like you."

He rolls his eyes. "I know. Scares the crap out of me."

"DAWWY! FIFWY CWENTS! CWAP COUNTS!" Joey yells from the bathroom, apparently with a mouth full of toothpaste.

We laugh.

"Sorry," Hudson whispers to me. "She's still working on that whole manners thing."

"Again, adorable. Do you ever charge her for saying bad words?"

He laughs and shakes his head. "No. It's actually for her college fund. Between Tucker and Gaige, she's sitting quite comfortably right about now, and I'm sure after tomorrow she'll have at least twenty more bucks."

"Tomorrow?" I ask, curious.

"Movie night with Joey, something we do every month or so."

"You, Gaige, and Tucker?"

He nods. "And my mom. We all sit around, eat junk food, and watch whatever movies Joey wants. She usually makes it through two before she passes out."

I laugh because I can just picture Gaige and Tucker during that whole thing. "That sounds like a lot of fun."

"It is. You should come."

Panic zings through me. Is that something I'm ready for? Meeting his mom? Being in his life? *Fuck.* I don't know if I should...but I want to.

"You can say no, Rae. I won't be mad," Hudson offers, mistaking my silence for me saying no.

"I'd love to."

He squints and tilts his head like he can't believe what he's hearing. "Really?"

"Yeah, I think it'd be fun."

Hudson claps his hands once and rubs them together. "Great!" He walks into the kitchen and then right back out. He hands me a piece of paper. "Here's my mom's address. Is five okay?"

"Perfect."

"Perfect," he echoes.

Just then, Joey runs out of the bathroom in some *Adventure Time* jammies. "Ready, Daddy!"

"Dude, what did I say about running in the apartment?" Hudson's hands fly to his hips. I get the feeling this is his "dad stance" that he breaks out when he means serious business.

Can't say I don't like it. It's doing wonders for his ass right about now.

Joey's small shoulders drop and she hangs her head. "Don't," she says quietly.

"Right. And why is that?"

She lifts her head and scrunches her nose up. "'Cause you said so?"

"Good enough for me." Hudson shrugs. "Come on, let's get you tucked in."

He steers her toward his bedroom but she wiggles from his grasp, turning back to me. "Come on, Rae! Dad reads the best stories!"

I look to Hudson; I'm not sure how to answer her.

"Yeah, come on. We're reading *Harry Potter and the Sorcerer's Stone*, and I'm apparently really good at it."

I shrug and follow them to the bedroom. I stop in the doorway and watch as Hudson tucks Joey into his bed. Rocky jumps up there too, circling for a spot until he's comfortable. They all curl up close together—Joey under the blankets, Hudson lying on top of them, and Rocky on Joey's legs.

"Okay dude, you ready?"

"Ready Freddy!"

Hudson's deep voice fills the room and Joey becomes entranced. She was right; he's good. He uses different voices for each character and sometimes uses his hands to make a point. Entertaining doesn't begin to cover it.

I take a moment to glance around Hudson's bedroom. It's simple, as plain as the rest of the apartment. I don't even see a dresser. The only thing giving it life is the striped blue bedspread and the photographs of Joey and her drawings tacked to the walls.

"Okay, that's it for tonight."

"But Dad! Things are happening! Important things!"

Hudson chuckles. "As great an argument as that is, you need sleep if you want to have movie night tomorrow."

"Movie night! Okay, hurry up and kiss me then. I need sleep!"

Hudson tucks the blankets tighter around Joey, careful not to disturb Rocky, and gives her a kiss on the forehead. She puts her little hands on his head and kisses his forehead right back.

I can feel my chest tighten for the millionth time tonight. If there was ever a perfect moment between a father and daughter, it was that.

"Goodnight, bug. Sleep good, have good dreams—no weird ones," he tells her gently, backing away from the bed.

"Mmkay. Goodnight, Daddy. I love you."

"I love you most."

"I love you mostest."

His smile lights up the room and my heart stops.

In the future, if I'm ever asked when exactly it was that I fell in love with Hudson Tamell, I'll tell them right now. In this exact moment, I fall in love with his smile, his voice, and the way he loves his daughter all at once. Because this moment? It's perfect.

"Goodnight, Rae. You're my fourth favorite person in the whole world."

I not sure if that was a compliment or not, but I go with it anyway. "Thank you. You're mine, too. Goodnight, Joey."

He flips the light off and leaves the door cracked open. I look to Hudson for an explanation of Joey's ranking as we walk to the kitchen. "I'm assuming you come after me, my mother, and Rocky," he whispers.

"Makes sense."

"Did you want to stay a little longer? Or did you need to be going? Also, what are you doing here? No offense or anything, but I thought you had to work tonight," he questions, leaning against one of the counters.

Laughing quietly, I hop up on the counter opposite him. This was all something I told him earlier when I opened the door. Guess he was too busy freaking out over me discovering Joey to listen. Can't blame him, because I clearly checked out for a moment too.

"I was cut early. We were dead. I figured I'd come surprise you. Guess that one worked out well, huh?"

He reaches up and cups the back of his neck, giving me a small grimace. "Yeah, sorry again about that, Rae. I really didn't intend to keep it from you. And sorry about the Perry thing."

I realize then that I'm not even mad any more. I feel like I should be, but I'm not. Hudson had his reasons, and they are valid.

"You know what? It's okay. I get it. I'd want to protect that little girl, too. She's something, Hudson. You've done really well with her on your own."

"I can't take all the credit. My mom has been a great help. My father was as well when he was still alive. He loved the shit out of that kid. I'm just mad he didn't get more time with her because we were both stubborn."

Something clicks. "Joey's the reason you got in a fight and you moved out."

He nods solemnly. "Yeah. Missed out on a lot of good years because of it too."

"I'm sorry, Hudson. That has to be hard."

"It was—still kind of is—but I'm glad they had what they had together. It was better than nothing."

"My optimist," I mutter. He catches it and smirks.

"Yours, huh? I like that," he says, stalking closer to me. When he reaches me, he steps between my legs and cradles my head between his hands, getting all up in my personal space. "Rae..."

"Hudson." My voice comes out thick and husky, nothing like I've ever heard before.

"Can I... May I kiss you?"

My head barely moves up before his lips meet mine and my entire world implodes.

He's gentle at first, testing my response. I press into him, letting him know I'm fully okay with what's happening. His kiss grows firmer. His lips are soft, way softer than they look, and they taste good.

He glides his tongue along my bottom lip and I open for him on a moan. Taking his chance, he dives right in. Our tongues mesh together, playing along one another perfectly. I pull him in closer with my legs then place my hands on his stomach, sliding them up unhurriedly and then back down. I mentally take note that he doesn't really have "abs" like he said, but more of definition. It's nice. *Really* nice.

I'm sure it's only seconds that pass, but it feels like minutes before our kiss slows. He backs only inches away, brushing small, soft kisses along my lips.

Then, he pulls back all the way, staring me directly in the eyes, our breaths coming in heavily and mingling together. His eyes are glowing, the blue standing out even more against the green.

"Wow," he says on an exhale.

"Wow," I repeat.

"That was...intense. Amazing. Perfect."

I smile and shrug. "It was okay."

He laughs breathily. "That mouth of yours is dangerous." He leans in, nipping at my bottom lip. "I like it. It was my first favorite thing about you."

"Your *first* favorite thing? What else made the list?" I ask, hooking my legs back around his and pulling him closer to me again.

"Your eyes. They speak, telling me things you don't," he says seriously. *I can say the same about yours, Hudson.*

He continues, "And your laugh. It's intoxicating. Then your sense of humor, your love for Maura, your intelligence. Oh, and your ass. It's *very* nice."

I snort out a laugh. "Thank you."

"That too. That's number eight and nine. I love that you're not afraid to be yourself. Your confidence is such a turn-on. The fact that you can accept a compliment is so...refreshing. I can't stand when women argue with one. It's annoying and petty. I love that you're not like that."

His mouth is on mine again and we're back to where we just were, tangled up as much as we can be for our positions. We clutch one another, using our hands to tamely explore. Small gasps slip through, but no other sounds escape. Our lips and tongues are fused together, tasting every single dark corner of each other's mouths.

Hudson pulls away again, and this time he rests his forehead against mine.

I simply smile, because really, how can you respond to what just happened? We continue staring at each other in silence. It's a moment I'll never forget. Hudson looks so...peaceful, and I helped with that.

"This is going to sound like the shittiest thing I've ever said in my entire life, but I kind of need you to leave."

My shoulders slump before I can catch them.

He dips down to meet my gaze. "I mean no offense by that. Quite the opposite. You see, I'm extremely turned on right now, and my daughter is in the other room. I can't let anything else happen tonight, but I really, *really* want it to. So, I'm being proactive. You have no idea how sorry I am."

"Oh, you thought I was going to just rip my clothes off and sleep with you? Shame on you, Hudson. I'm not that kind of girl." I feign offense because that's all I can muster now. My heart is beating wildly and I want nothing more than to do just what I said.

Then I lean in closer to him, getting right up next to his ear. "Or am I?" I whisper.

He shudders. I laugh and push him away, hopping down off the counter.

"I'll see myself out," I say with a smirk, walking out of the kitchen and leaving Hudson lightly banging his head against his kitchen cabinet, muttering to himself.

That night, I sleep fitfully—and not from my nightmare.

CHAPTER 19

HUDSON

"YOU'RE SAYING she just showed up unannounced and Joey was there? Just, 'BAM! Here's my seven-year-old daughter. Surprise!' and that was it?" Tucker asks, disbelief lacing his voice.

"Yep," I say, popping my P for emphasis.

"Damn." He whistles, leaning back into the recliner in my mom's living room.

Gaige, Tucker, and I are all waiting for my mom to get back from the store with Joey so we can get started on movie night. They are bound to walk in the door any moment, and so is Rae.

"That's rough, Hudson. How'd it go?" Gaige asks from beside me.

"It...went. She was a little pissed at first. Then she was unexpectedly okay with it."

"Like *really* okay? Or just 'woman' okay?" Tuckers questions.

"*Really* okay," I answer. He gives me a look, basically telling me he calls bullshit on that. I shake my head. "No, man, I mean it. She was fine. A little upset at first, but then okay. I don't know what changed, but she just stopped being mad. I think I may have Joey to thank for that. Kid is a miracle worker."

"Anyone in their right mind would fall in love with her. She's impossible to resist."

I nod at Gaige's explanation. "I know. I'm totally fucked for when she's older. I give in to her now over everything. It can only get worse from here."

Tucker snorts. "Wimp."

"Oh, like you don't do the exact same, *Uncle Tuck?*" He shakes his head. "Bullshit. You're so wrapped around her little finger it isn't even funny."

"Whatever," he mumbles. "Does she know about Jess?"

"Kind of? I mean she knows she's Joey's mother and she's not in the picture, but that's about it. We didn't go into detail about it. The subject kind of dropped after I brought up Perry."

"Oh, yeah? Family?" Gaige questions.

"Exes?" Tucker throws out.

I look back and forth between the two of them, purely for dramatic effect, because at this point they're both literally sitting on the edges of their seats.

"Cousins," I finally say.

"NAILED IT!" Gaige shouts. "Pay up, asshole!" he says to Tucker, who is already digging in his wallet. He slips Gaige a twenty.

"You two had a fucking bet over that shit? Assholes," I say with a headshake.

"Yoohoo! We're home!" my mom calls, opening the front door.

Gaige is the first to his feet to help her carry stuff in—or get a hug from Joey. I'm not sure which.

"Uncle G!" Joey squeals. I assume Gaige picked her up and is swinging her around. It's kind of their thing.

"My little bug! How are you, kiddo? Being bad and eating lots of sugar, I hope."

I hear Joey giggle. "Noooo. I've been extra, extra good."

"Well good. I was afraid I'd have to tickle you all night for being bad."

"That's no punishment. I like your tickles."

"You're terrible at keeping secrets, dorko," Gaige teases.

I smile at their exchange. Gaige is a natural with kids, but he kind of has to be. He has four siblings at home he takes care of so he's had a lot of practice with them.

"Is Uncle Tuck here, too?"

"I'm in here, dude!" Tucker calls to her.

I listen as her feet hit the floor and she comes running down the hall, barely skidding to a stop before I can see her. *Little shit.* She tiptoes casually into the living room, *almost* making it all the way to Tucker, going slowly before she runs at the last moment, launching herself into his arms.

"Uncle Tuck, did you bring me anything?"

"Joey!" I scold. "It's not polite to ask things like that."

"Sorry," she mumbles.

"It's okay, Joe. I brought you this," Tucker says, reaching into his pocket. He pulls out a small porcelain ladybug painted a bright green and hands it gently to her.

It's something so tiny and simple, but she loves it. He brings her a different "bug" every time he sees her. It's *their* thing. It's also the reason we call her bug. She's sort of had a fascination with ladybugs since she was four.

"Cool! This one is the best yet!"

"What, no hug? No 'thank you'?" Tucker teases her.

She throws her little arms around his neck and squeezes him tight. "Thank you so much, Uncle Tuck."

I watch with a smile on my face as Tucker closes his eyes

and hugs my little girl right back with just as much ferocity. It tugs at my heart.

I love that my best friends love my daughter like their own. I love that they accept her and her weirdness. I love that they accept me and my dad status, even though it's a game-killer sometimes for two single dudes.

I catch Tucker's eyes as he opens them back up. *I see you,* I mouth.

I see you, too, he mouths back.

"Don't worry, assholes, I helped Ma out," Gaige announces as he walks back to the living room.

"Seventy-five cents, Uncle G!"

"Seventy-five! I thought it was fifty?" Gaige argues with Joey, but still digs in his pockets for a dollar and holds it out to her.

"Inflation," Joey says with a shrug, taking the dollar and running out of the room to put her money away.

Tucker and I laugh. Gaige just stares after her.

"Dude, what kind of kid are you raising?" he asks, sounding awestruck.

I shrug. "A smart one."

"Touché."

The doorbell chimes and I freeze.

Rae is here. *Rae. Is. Here.*

"Breathe, man. The worst that can happen is she falls in love with me," Tucker says.

"Asshole," I mutter with a smile. I get up and head to the front door, only to discover my mother standing in the doorway.

"Rae, it's so great to finally meet you. I've heard wonderful things from both Hudson and Joey. Please, come in," my mother tells her, stepping aside to let her walk in.

The air leaves my lungs because holy hell is she gorgeous... and all she's wearing is a damn t-shirt and jeans.

I think I just fell in love with everything else about her.

"Thank you for allowing me to crash your movie night, Mrs. Tamell. I didn't know what to bring so I grabbed some M&Ms," Rae says, holding out a huge bag of the chocolate candies.

"Oh, you didn't have to do that, darling, but thank you. They won't go uneaten, that's for sure. And please, call me Eleanor. Actually, that's way too formal. Call me Elle," my mother tells her, taking the bag of candy. "I'll go put these with the other snacks. Make yourself at home, please."

As my mom walks by me, she fist-bumps me because she's that cool.

"Did she just..." Rae starts.

I stuff my hands in my back pocket and lift a shoulder. "Yeah, she's cool like that."

We laugh lightly, still standing about five feet apart. All I want to do is walk over there and kiss her, because what I had of her last night was not enough. But, I don't know how appropriate that would be in my mother's house with Joey right around the corner.

Rae licks her lips subconsciously. I watch with want, every cell in my body tingling, itching to grab hold of her and never let go.

I give in.

"Oh, fuck it. Come here," I practically growl, stalking closer to her. I pull her into me, push my hands into her soft brown hair, and possess her mouth with mine.

I kiss her hard but briefly.

"Wow," she says once I pull away. "Hello to you too."

"Hi," I whisper.

"Hi," she repeats on a small giggle. "Oh, shit." Her hand covers her mouth, her brows furrowing. "What have you done to me? I haven't giggled since I was a kid."

I feel the corners of my lips tip up. "I have that effect," I say with false confidence, because honestly, I have no fucking clue.

"I...I kind of like it," she confesses.

"Me too."

"You two just gonna make out in the hallway or actually come socialize with everyone?" Tucker asks from behind me.

"Tucker," Rae says, stepping away from me. "Did you miss me that much?"

"Oh, of course. You're all I've been thinking about." He winks. "But only because this asshole"—he points to me—"won't stop talking about you. Ever. Actually, I kind of find you annoying now."

She just laughs. "And by annoying you mean more attractive. I get it, Tuck, but I'm kind of taken. Sorry, dude," Rae says, walking past Tucker and giving him a small pat on the arm.

The look on Tucker's face is priceless as he watches her walk away into the house like she's lived here all her life.

"Dude," he says, turning back to me. Now his face is serious. "Marry her. Please."

I laugh and shake my head. "I would if I could, man. I would if I could."

CHAPTER 20

RAE

"DID YOU NEED ANY HELP, ELLE?"

Hudson's mother is bouncing back and forth around the kitchen, wearing the most *Stepford Wives* apron I've ever seen. She resembles Hudson in the face, but it's very clear he must take after his father the most. Elle's hair is a lot lighter than his, and her eyes are a bright green. I guess that's where he got his weird combo.

"Oh no, dear. You sit. You're a guest," she says, pulling out a barstool for me. I take the seat. "Tell me about yourself, Rae."

I smother a laugh, thinking back to when I said the exact same thing to Hudson.

"Well, I graduated college back in June. Right now, I'm working at Clyde's as a waitress and occasional bartender. Other than that, I'm working on finding a job in the city for marketing."

"Marketing, huh? Hudson told me about you helping the shop. He said he's already had a few hits off the ads and new website. Thank you for that. That little shop means the world to him."

"I can tell. His face lights up when he talks about it, almost as much as it does when he talks about Joey."

The corners of Elle's mouth dip down and her eyes shift around the room. She must like what she sees—or rather doesn't see. She clears her throat, turning her gaze back on me.

"How do you feel about that, Rae? About Joey?" she asks in a low voice.

Rae Kamden, meet Mama Bear Elle. She looks tough. Smile through it girl, you've got this.

"Honestly, Elle? I don't think kids are really my thing." Her shoulders tense just as Hudson's did last night. I continue, "But that stems from my own personal demons, I think. I'm smart enough to separate the two, or at least I hope I am. I like Joey and I like Hudson—a lot. I'm willing to try anything when it comes to him. So, I'm going to give it a go and do my best. I can't say I won't mess up with Joey, or with Hudson, but I'll try my hardest not to."

Elle nods, thinking over everything I just said. "I admire your honesty, Rae, and I appreciate that you're willing to try. I know it can't be easy for you to do all this, especially since I just found out this morning that my son sprung this on you last night. Not his best move, honestly," she says, a small smile playing at her lips. It's eerily similar to Hudson's. "Thank you for taking a chance on them, and for understanding him. Just, please, if you feel it getting to be too much, get out before everyone gets hurt. It will be easier in the long run."

I nod my head in agreement because it really is only fair to everyone. "I promise."

She gives me a full smile this time. "Great. Let's go get this movie night started then. I'll grab the pizzas that are warming in the oven if you want to grab the drinks."

I do as she asks, also grabbing some napkins and paper plates. We walk into the living room to find Tucker, Gaige, Hudson, and Joey all having a silent contest of some sort.

"You boys hungry?" Elle asks, setting down the pizzas. Joey

animatedly motions to herself. "Sorry, sorry. Are you boys and *Joey* hungry?"

They all nod.

"Who's winning?" I ask while handing out the plates and napkins.

"I am!" Joey says proudly. The guys laugh and she groans, realizing she just spoke. "Aw man."

"You owe us each twenty-five cents. Pay up, sucker," Gaige says.

"Puh-lease," I say, rolling my eyes. "Joey, you may as well keep those quarters. I'm sure these boys will be owing you by the end of the night."

Joey sticks her tongue out at Gaige.

"Okay, before we all start this excellent and well-deserved movie night by watching..." Hudson starts, turning to Joey for an answer.

"*Monsters, Inc.!*"

"Nice one, kiddo." She beams. "Before the feature presentation of *Monsters, Inc.*, I have an announcement." He pauses dramatically and turns to his daughter with a huge grin. "Joey, how would you like to move out of Nana's and live with me in our own home?"

Joey jumps off the couch excitedly. "Finally!" she shouts and then turns to Elle. "No offends, Nana, but I miss my daddy and Rocky so much!"

Elle barely manages to smother a laugh at Joey's incorrect use of 'offense'.

"No *offense* taken, baby girl."

"How about I let you and Nana decorate next weekend? You'll still have to spend next Sunday and possibly Monday night here, and we have to get your school bus schedule figured out Monday morning when the address change goes through."

"YES!" she yells, punching the air. "Woo to the hoo! Thank

you, Daddy!" She launches herself into his arms and he hugs her tightly, soaking in her happiness.

They look so happy together, so ready for this next step. It makes my heart swell.

He looks at Tucker and Gaige, who are sitting on the loveseat. "You two are going to help me move in what little I have on Saturday. We'll say you were at work so you'll get paid for it."

"Sweet, dude. Thanks," Gaige says.

"How do you know I didn't already have plans?" Tucker fusses.

Hudson glares at him. "Simple. You cancel them."

I catch Tucker mouth *asshole* to him. I know that if Joey weren't all wrapped up in her daddy's arms right now, she'd have caught it too.

"Okay, movie time!" Elle announces, turning the TV on.

We all grab a few slices of pizza and get comfy. Elle takes the recliner and Gaige and Tucker remain on the loveseat, leaving Hudson and me on the couch with Joey between us.

We're about halfway through the movie when I feel the first touch. Hudson has his arm stretched across the back of the couch, gently twirling my hair around his fingers. It feels so soothing, so natural.

I check my peripheral to find him watching me. He must see me do it because he chuckles softly. Joey shushes him. She means serious business when she watches movies. There's to be no talking and hardly any moving. It's comical to watch three grown men try to sit still for an hour and a half and get scolded by a seven-year-old when they can't. We had to pause the movie three times so she could tell Tucker to stop talking. We all wisely kept our laughter to ourselves.

Joey only allows for a short break to grab drinks, desserts, and use the bathroom. Then we're back to movie-watching. This time around it's *Monsters University*.

"Can I sit on your lap, Rae?" Joey asks sweetly right before the opening credits begin.

I nod, not even thinking on it for single second, which is unusual for me.

Joey climbs up on my lap and makes herself comfortable, wrapping a blanket around her. I look to Hudson because I can *feel* his gaze on me. The look in his eyes makes my chest heavy because it's so full of love. I'd be lying if I said I didn't want that look to be directed at me too. He scoots closer to us and slowly wraps his hand around mine.

It's the last thing I remember before falling into a peaceful sleep.

———

"THEY LOOK SO CONTENT," I barely hear Elle say. I have no idea who she's talking to because my eyes are still closed.

I feel something heavy on my lap shift around. It takes me a few seconds to remember it's Joey; we must have fallen asleep during the movie.

I'm about to open my eyes when I hear Hudson speak. "Ma, this isn't good," he says, worry filling his voice.

I do the most asshole thing I've ever done in my entire life: I pretend to keep sleeping because I can tell that whatever he's about to say next is big.

"You're in love," Elle states, the shock in her voice clear. "How? You two haven't been together long at all. Are you sure?"

If I've learned anything about Hudson over the past few weeks, it's that he likes eye contact. So, I assume he pierces his mother with his beautiful blue-green gaze, because I can hear her sharp intake of breath.

"Holy shit, Hudson," she breathes out.

Holy shit is right! If I didn't have Joey on my lap right now, I'd be jumping for joy—or running out the door. Maybe.

How in the world is it possible to fall in love this fast?

"When you know, you know. Isn't that what you used to always say to me?" She must nod. "I know, Ma. I'm sure of it. It feels soon, but it also feels right. Right trumps soon."

"Damn," Elle says softly.

Tucker and Gaige must be gone, because I don't hear them chime in at all.

Joey shifts. "I heard that, Nana. Seventy-five cents," she says, her throat scratchy from sleep. She pokes me in the forehead. "She got ninjas in her head again, Daddy?"

I decide it's time to "wake up" now. I shift and open my eyes slowly, scrunching my eyebrows. "You poke hard."

"You looked dead again," Joey reasons.

Instinct apparently kicks in and I tickle her. Her laughter makes my heart sing, and it brings me a joy I never knew I was missing—never knew I wanted. I laugh with her because it's impossible not to.

"I was sleeping, silly," I tell her through our giggles.

She gets smart enough to try to tickle me back. She succeeds. We're both now rolling around the couch, barely breathing from laughing so hard.

"Okay, okay. I give, I give," I gasp out.

She stops immediately and bounces off the couch. She stands in front of me and crosses her arms over her chest, giving me a smug grin. "That's what I thought. I win."

I look to Elle and Hudson for help. They both just laugh.

"All right, girls. As much as I hate to break up your bonding, it's bedtime. You have school tomorrow, bug."

"Ugh," she groans. "I HATE school!"

"You little fibber. School is your 'most favoritest thing in the whole wide world ever' as I recall," Hudson tells her, now in his "dad stance".

"Fine," she drags out. "Only if Rae will tuck me in, though. I like her more than you right now because she's not making me go to school."

I smother a laugh. Hudson glares at me.

"You turned my kid against me? That's messed up, Rae," he says, slowly approaching me. "You know what happens when that happens, don't you?" He has that stupid smirk on his face again.

I burrow myself into the couch as far as I can go, but it's no use. His hands are on my sides in an instant and he recruits Joey for help.

"White flag! White flag!" I yell. "Elle, your son is a monster!"

"You're on your own with those two. I'm going to bed. Night, Joey. Night, Hudson. Make sure you clean up after your weirdo friends. Great meeting you, Rae." And she's gone.

"That's so messed up, Rae. You tried to turn my own mother against me too. That didn't help your case at all," Hudson threatens, tickling me even more.

"Please," I gasp, barely able to breathe through my laughter. "Plea—"

Hudson backs off and Joey follows his lead.

"You good?" he says, extending his hand to help me sit up.

I manage a nod. "Holy wow. You're good at that."

He points to Joey. "I've had a few years of practice. Speaking of...scoot, kiddo. We still have to tuck you in."

Joey lets out another sigh and trudges upstairs. I stand and start picking up our trash and cups.

"You don't have to do that. I can take care of it."

I shrug. "It's no big deal." I hand him an empty cup. "Here, you can help."

"Jerk," he mumbles. I throw a napkin at him. "Rude, too."

I huff. "Whatever, you crybaby. Keep it up, I'll turn this whole family and your friends against you with my wicked ways," I say, waggling my eyebrows.

"Evil woman," he teases with a grin.

We pick up the rest of the trash and dishes and dump them off in the kitchen before heading for the stairs.

Hudson starts walking up them. I pause, partially to enjoy the view because this man has one hell of an ass, and partially because I know how big this next moment is. I'm about to tuck his child in for bed. A kid. *His* kid. I'm nervous, because what if I do it wrong? What if I make the blankets too tight and she hates me forever? What if I forget to check for monsters or some shit? What if I'm just overreacting?

Monsters? Really, Rae. Just walk up the damn stairs.

But I can't. My own mother hardly ever tucked me in, and when she did, it was so awkward that I dreaded it. My dad was almost always the one to do it, and he was amazing at it. I'm scared I'm going to be as bad as my mom at it, just as awkward.

Hudson's halfway up the stairs before he realizes I'm not following him. He turns back to me. "You still coming?"

I screw my face up at him, letting him know I'm not so sure this is a good idea. He's back down the stairs and holding my hands in the blink of an eye.

"It's okay, Rae. It's just tucking her in for bed."

"*Just?* It's the first kid I've ever tucked in."

He chuckles. "You'll do fine. You can't mess it up. Stop worrying."

Hudson tugs me up the first step. And then another. And another. He walks backward the entire way up to make sure I'm still doing okay.

We pause at the top step while I work on breathing.

"You ready?"

I nod. Still holding his hand, I follow him to Joey's room. He stops and peeks inside, smiling at his daughter.

"She's amazing," I whisper to him.

He turns his smile on me and pushes the door open. He walks over to her bed and sits down next to her. Hudson motions for me to do the same so I do, taking a seat on the other side of the small bed.

"You ready, bug?" Joey nods. "Did you brush?" She nods again. "Go potty? Change into your jammies?"

"Yep," she says proudly.

"Good job, but I have some bad news. I forgot the book."

"That's okay," she says, patting his hand. "I just need Rae to tuck me in tight tonight."

"She's a bit nervous, so go easy on her," Hudson tells her. He leans in close and pretends to whisper to her. "It's her first time tucking anyone in."

Joey's eyes go big. "No way. You've never tucked *anyone* in? *Ever?*"

"Nope, never," I tell her.

"Wow," she says in wonder. "Even *I've* done that, and you're *way* older than me."

"Joey!" Hudson scolds.

"But you're old! And she hasn't tucked anyone in *ever*. That's crazy, Daddy! I tuck you in all the time when you're sick!"

I smile because even though she called me old, she was cute about it.

"Well when you put it that way, I guess I've tucked my sister in before when she was sick."

She gasps. "You have a sister? Cool! I've always wanted a sister."

My eyes snap to Hudson's. He's watching me closely.

"They're okay." I shrug. "Annoying sometimes and they are horrible about doing the dishes, but I like mine just fine."

"Wow," she says with wonder.

"All right, chatterbox, bedtime. You're not going to want to get out of bed in the morning and I'm taking you to school."

She kicks her legs in excitement and barely, *just barely*, holds in a squeal.

The way she loves her father is so pure, so beautiful. My chest tightens again, something that's been happening a lot when I'm around these two.

"Goodnight, bug. I love you," Hudson says, kissing her on the head. "Sleep tight."

Joey returns his sentiments and Hudson exits the room, leaving me alone with Joey.

"So," I start. "Goodnight, kiddo. Sleep well." I have no idea what to do next so I just pat her on the head.

She giggles. "You're supposed to give me kisses, silly."

Kisses? I gulp loudly and lean down, pressing my lips against her forehead.

And then I can't breathe.

I can't breathe because tiny arms are now wrapped firmly around my neck like a constrictor.

She's hugging me. Holy crap! She's freakin' hugging me! I mentally high-five myself for the good job I've done.

"Goodnight, Rae." She lets me go and I get up, ready to head to the door. "You forgot to tuck the blankies!" she calls.

Damn. So close.

I turn back and tuck them in tight for her. She wiggles loose just a little and closes her eyes, ready to fall into slumber.

I grab hold of the door and turn out the light.

Then I hear it. The sweetest words ever spoken to me. The

words that seal my place in Hudson's life. The words that change my entire world.

"I love you, Rae."

Tears fill my eyes and I find it hard to swallow.

"I love you too, Joey," I say honestly. In this moment, I realize I do. Not only do I love Hudson, I love his daughter, too.

I'm so fucking screwed.

CHAPTER 21

HUDSON

CALL ME THE GRINCH, because I swear my heart just grew three sizes listening to those two.

She loves my daughter.

I don't know if this is the craziest thing to ever happen or the most amazing. If I wasn't in love with Rae before, I am now.

"Hey," Rae whispers, her voice scratchy. "Were you out here eavesdropping?" I nod because I can't seem to form words right now. "That's rude, you know," she teases, leaning back against the wall opposite me.

I shrug and take the two short steps to reach her. I cage her in, my arms around her head, and lean in close. "That was one of the most beautiful moments I've ever had the pleasure of hearing. I'll never forget that, Rae."

I can hear her swallow thickly. "It was for me, too. Beautiful, I mean."

I brush my lips across hers once, twice, three times. "You're amazing," I mutter.

She shivers and pushes me back slightly. "I...I need to go. Long day tomorrow," she says, her voice shaking.

I nod and grab her hand, leading her downstairs.

"Hey, Rae," I say once we're outside by her car.

"Hey, Hudson."

Suddenly, I'm nervous. "Um... Uh... Do you want to maybe come have dinner at my new house next Sunday? Just the two of us?"

She smiles. "I'd like that."

Rae reaches up and tries getting away with a chaste kiss on the cheek. She laughs when I back her up against her car. I'm a lot faster than she is, so I capture her mouth with mine, running my tongue against her lips, begging her to open for me. She complies and leans into me.

I press against her harder, knowing she can feel *me* at this point. Testing the waters, I gently grind my hips into hers. She moans, and it's the best fucking moan I have ever heard. So, I do it again. She moans again and runs her hands down my chest and under my shirt. She starts gradually raising it up, feeling my bare skin. Her cold hands scarcely register, and I'm so hot right now that my body warms them almost instantly. I take her lead and slide my hands down to her ass, pulling her closer into me.

I'm so completely screwed. If this is what it's like to kiss Rae *with* clothes on, I can only imagine what it would be like to kiss her *without* clothes on.

Fuuuuuck.

Now I have the image of Rae naked in my head and if I don't stop now, I won't be able to at all.

We're both gasping for air when I finally peel my mouth off hers.

"No, no, no," she whimpers. "Why? Why in the hell did you stop?"

I step away, putting a good amount of distance between us. "Because if we don't stop now, we'll both end up naked and we're outside right now. I like my mom's neighbors and all, but I don't really want to give them a show."

"Okay, okay," she says, shaking out her body. "Okay. Woo. I'm getting in my car right now and I'm going home." She opens her door but turns back to me as she's climbing in. "Thank you, Hudson. Just...thank you."

"I'm pretty sure I should be saying that to you." I grin.

She rolls her eyes at me. "You know what I mean." I do; she's talking about Joey and tonight and...well, everything.

"Thank *you*, Rae. You have no idea what tonight has meant to me. Now go before I change my stance on exhibitionism, and text me when you make it home, please."

She blows me a kiss and gets in her car.

I watch as she pulls away, taking half of my heart with her.

CHAPTER 22

RAE

"YOU HEARD HIM SAY *WHAT!*"

"What did I tell you about my eardrums, Maura? Those things are important, you know."

"Oh, never mind those," she says on the other end of the line. "They aren't important right now. Now, you hearing Hudson say he loves you, that shit is important. What did you do? What did you say?"

"Nothing. He thought I was asleep. What was I supposed to say?" I pause to chew on the sleeve of my sweatshirt for a moment. "Is this even okay, Maura?"

She's quiet, which is odd.

"Fuck. It's too soon, isn't it?"

"When you know, you know," she says, unknowingly repeating the words Hudson spoke to his mother last night.

"Hudson said the same thing," I say softly. "I'm scared, Maura."

"I'm kind of scared for you. I mean this is huge. Not only do you find out he has a kid—again, sorry I didn't tell you—but then you find out he's in love with you. That's kind of huge."

"I already told you it's okay. I get why you didn't tell me. It wasn't your place to do so, and all is forgiven," I tell her. "And I know it's huge, that's why I'm scared—well, that and because I'm totally in love with him too. And his kid. *His kid.* Me! Kids hate me! I don't get it."

"I don't think kids hate you. I think you just never met the right one. Maybe this is just how it's supposed to be."

She's probably right, but I won't tell her that.

"Okay, okay. Where do I go from here?"

"Um, sex. Obviously."

I laugh. "You damn horndog! You get down and dirty with one guy and that's all you can think about. You little minx."

"Hey! That shit is good! Can't believe I've been missing out on it for all these years, and I *still* can't believe my parents liked Tanner. I mean I knew they'd dig that he was a soldier, but holy shit! I thought they were going to ask him to move in or something. They're smitten, but that's okay, because so am I."

I can hear her smiling.

Just then, Haley comes barreling in. "Honey, I'm home!"

"Ugh." I fake disgust. "I have to go, Maura. Haley's home."

"I can hear you! Don't pretend I'm not your favorite sister, Rae!" Haley shouts from the kitchen, her usual first stop when she gets home from work.

"You're my only sister!" I shout back.

"Winning by default is still winning."

"Damn, she's good," Maura says in my ear.

"You're taking her side? That's jacked up, Maura."

"Whatever. I love you both. Text me later, woman." She hangs up.

I sigh and toss my cell on the table, lying back on the couch.

I know Maura's right about the Joey thing. This whole situation with Hudson feels...different. Right. Natural.

"What up, girl?" Haley asks, flopping down on the couch. I move my feet just in time.

"I'm in love."

"I know. Tell me what else is bothering you."

I sit up quickly and squint at Haley. "Wait, how do *you* know?"

"I'm not blind. I see the way your face lights up when you get one of those weird texts from him. Your eyes glow whenever you talk about him or his kid," she says. "I'm still surprised by that, by the way."

"Word."

"And because you're just...happier. I know you, Rae. In the twenty-two—almost twenty-three—years we've been beside one another, I've never seen you this happy. Ever."

"That's because I haven't been."

"And how are you sleeping? Still having the nightmare?" she asks, concern evident in her voice.

Something occurs to me that hasn't until now: my nightmare has stopped. I haven't had one in weeks—not since those three weeks after my car broke down. More specifically, not since the Wednesday Hudson and I had our first official date at his house.

"Holy shit." I gasp, my eyes going wide. "It stopped again."

Hudson is my miracle worker.

A slow smile forms on Haley's face. "Told ya."

I groan at her smugness and throw a pillow in her face.

———

I PULL into what I assume is Hudson's new driveway, shut my car off, and look up at the house. The first word that pops into my head is *cozy*. The brick and white siding is inviting, and when you add in the partial wraparound porch, neatly trimmed bushes, and freshly cut lawn, it screams *family*. It's just what I pictured for Hudson and Joey.

I step out of the car and smooth out my orange skirt on

unsteady legs, suddenly nervous about this date I've been looking forward to all week long. It's silly, because it's just Hudson, but I know—*I know*—this date means more than all our others have.

Hudson comes walking out of the house in a sinfully sexy pair of jeans and dark blue button-up shirt as I'm walking up the small driveway. I can already feel the sexual tension between us.

"You found it. Excellent." He smiles, taking my hand and guiding me inside. I'm hit with the smell of whatever it is he's made for dinner. It smells like Mexican, and I fucking love Mexican.

He takes my coat, leaving me in my thin white tank top. He places a small kiss on my now exposed shoulder. "You look gorgeous," he says softly in my ear.

I shiver.

"Would you like a tour?" he asks.

I just nod, because I can't speak yet.

He shows me the living room first. Everything is bright and colorful. I recognize the sofa from his old apartment and the huge flat screen that now looks smaller in the bigger room. There's a matching recliner and a small bookcase now, too.

"You did a great job decorating."

"My mom did most of it," he confesses. "She and Joey spent all day putting things together. Joey has an eye for color. She and Mom are having a 'spa night' after all their hard work."

"She's a smart kid—it looks amazing in here."

"Come see the rest then. It's even better," he says, taking my hand and guiding me through the rest of the downstairs.

There's a beautiful sunroom and small dining room, and each room is decorated in different but coordinating colors. It almost looks like a professional did it.

"Wow. This looks fantastic."

"I know. My girl has talent," he says proudly. He brings his hand up to scratch his nose, something I've noticed him do when he's unsure of how to approach whatever it is he's going to say next. "I can, uh, show you upstairs later if you'd like."

I don't know how suggestive that was supposed to sound, but it causes these tiny, unfamiliar sparks to form in my stomach. Apparently my body likes his idea.

"I...I'd like that." My voice is huskier than normal.

He gives me his stupid trademark smirk and pulls me toward the kitchen next. "For now, the feast."

The table is set and loaded down with all different kinds of Mexican dishes—two massive burritos, rolled taquitos, enchiladas, and chips and salsa. I even spy some rice, beans, and queso dip.

"Holy shit, Hudson! I love that you have all this food, like *really* love it."

He chuckles. "Come on, I'm starving." He pulls a chair out for me, leaning down and kissing me gently on the back of my neck. It's enough to cause me to break out in a sweat. He chuckles, obviously proud of himself, and takes a seat opposite me.

We dig in and, for the first several minutes, we only converse through moans and mmhmms.

"This food is phenomenal," I say, wiping my mouth between bites.

"It's from Los Amigos. Best Mexican food in the city, maybe even the whole Boston area."

"I can get behind that statement. Mexican is my favorite food, next to pizza, of course.

He winks. "I know."

I shake my head at his winking, knowing he only did it because he knows I find it weird.

"Did you hear back from Carter's?" he asks, referring to the marketing company that contacted me for a phone interview yesterday.

"Nah, not yet. I'm still crossing my fingers though."

"It'll come through. I have faith in you. What about the apartment hunt?"

"Nope." I take a drink of my water, doing my best to avoid his gaze.

"My, my, Rae. If I didn't know any better, I'd say you weren't so sure about moving anymore."

My stupid, stupid lips betray me, curling upward at the corners.

"HA! I'm right! Has someone caught your eye?"

I give a noncommittal shrug. "Meh."

"Rae Bethany Kamden, did you just 'meh' me?"

"I did indeed, Hudson Michael Tamell."

The look on his face is priceless, causing me to burst into laughter.

Abruptly, my laugh comes to an end. The heat in Hudson's eyes mixed with the smirk on his face stops me dead. I gulp, terrified and excited to know what's going through his head.

He leans onto the table, folding his hands and lowering his eyes into slits. "Do you remember our first encounter, Rae?" I nod. "Do you remember what you asked me?" I nod again. He gestures around him. "Well, here's dinner."

Oh. My. God. Payback sucks.

His grin is wolfish, and my body is on fire.

"Here's dinner," I repeat quietly.

He stands, grabbing a few dishes and placing them in the sink. I watch as he quickly boxes up the rest of the food. He looks so sexy when he's domestic, so natural, humble, and inviting.

Every time he twists, his jeans hug his ass and legs even more. My God is it a sight. My eyes follow his movements as he

rolls his shirtsleeves up, exposing lightly tanned and toned forearms. Never have I ever paid any attention to forearms before,
but everything about Hudson—even his forearms—is sexy and
worthy of attention.

I must get lost in my thoughts because he's suddenly
standing in front of me, extending his hand in my direction. I
have no idea what he just asked me but I place my hand in his
anyway. I'd follow him anywhere at this point.

We soundlessly climb the stairs, walking through the dimly
lit hallway, straight to the end. We stop in front of the door that
I assume leads to Hudson's bedroom.

"Rae," he says, turning toward me.

"Hudson," I answer.

We laugh lightly.

"We don't have to do anything. I know you know I was just
kidding about dinner, but I have to say it out loud just so we're
clear."

I squint up at him.

"No. You don't get to get me all hot and bothered, parading
around in those sexy-as-hell ass-hugging jeans, and think you're
going to get out of fucking me. Not happening."

Hudson's standing there with the biggest smile on his face.

I slap my free hand over my mouth.

Fuck! I just said that all out loud. Shitshitshit!

He pulls me into him, cupping my face and kissing my lips
once.

"You've left me speechless more times than I can count," he
says softly. "I love it."

We enter the bedroom and the first thing I notice is the wall
color—it's a deep, dark blue. The second is the bed—it's the
same as the one from the apartment. The setup is similar, only
now there's a long dresser with a mirror just opposite the bed,
leaving only a small space between the two.

I stand there, between the bed and the dresser, getting a feel for the room. I watch in the mirror as Hudson walks to the bedside table, flicks on a lamp. He catches me staring and holds my gaze until his body is flush against mine.

"You're breathtaking." He reaches up and pulls my hair to the side, keeping his eyes locked on mine in our reflections as he leans down and kisses my neck. He nips at me lightly and kisses away the sting. "You taste amazing."

"Shut up, you weirdo," I say, blushing harder than I have in my entire life.

His body vibrates against mine as he buries his face in my neck and laughs. Then I feel his tongue tracing a line. Up, up, up he goes, stopping just below my ear.

"You. Taste. Amazing," he says huskily, his voice full of desire.

This time I don't tell him to shut up. This time, I feel a tingle start in my toes, warming my entire body.

He kisses a path along my jaw, turning me so he can take hold of my mouth. I open for him the moment his lips part.

And then we're falling.

We land gently on the bed, me on top of him briefly before he rolls us over and scoots us upward gracefully. Our tongues are still dueling and our bodies are moving together in a melodic rhythm. My skirt is now bunched around my waist, so when Hudson rolls his hips into me, I *feel* it. Oh boy, do I feel it. He breaks our kiss to let out a heavy groan.

"Fuuuck."

I take some initiative, reaching for the buttons on his shirt. I make it as far as two before Hudson sits up and pulls it off over his head.

"I'd be all sexy and just rip it off, but clothes are kind of expensive these days," he teases.

I don't even try to form a response because I'm way too

busy admiring his body. It's so...natural. It's clear all the muscles he has are purely built from his job and not hours in the gym. They aren't perfectly sculpted and he doesn't have a six-pack, but he is toned. *Nicely* toned.

He watches as I run my hands across his chest, run my fingers through the small smattering of hair. He shivers some when I brush his nipples. I smile up at him.

"What?" He shrugs. "They're sensitive."

Knowing this fact, I go back to them, taking pleasure in the noise he lets out. He swiftly grabs my wrists, pinning my arms above my head. He gives me his signature smirk before dipping his head. He licks from just below my ear, across my collarbone —moving the strap of my tank top out of the way with his tongue—and continues until he's tracing the swell of my breasts.

My breath hitches, and I feel him smile against me.

"Hudson," I breathe out.

"Rae," he says innocently.

"I...I want to feel you against me. I need to take my shirt off, and my bra. Maybe even my skirt. Maybe even your pants. Everything. Now. Please."

He laughs heartily.

"Tsk, tsk. So impatient," he teases. I huff. "But you're lucky I haven't had sex in a very long time so I'm impatient too."

He rolls off me, pulling me up as he goes, and sits down next to me.

He pulls the strap of my tank top down, trailing kisses along my shoulder the entire way. "I'm sorry," he says, tugging at the hemline, encouraging me to pull the rest off. I comply. "But this first time is probably going to be quick."

I grab his face between my hands. "Hudson, I can guarantee you that any sex with you is going to be the best sex of my life, no matter how quick it is."

He chuckles.

"Now, take your pants off," I tell him, reaching for my skirt and slipping it off. I lean back on my elbows in my bra and panties, watching as he stands and pulls his jeans off.

The bulge in his tight gray boxer briefs leaves no question as to whether he's turned on or not.

Smirking at me, he hooks his thumbs in his underwear, ready to pull them off. "I really feel like I should be charging you for this with the way you're staring at me."

I throw the nearest pillow at him. It barely misses.

"That was rude, Rae," he says on a laugh. "I don't think I'm gonna strip for you now." He folds his arms across his chest and quirks an eyebrow at me.

"Now *that's* rude," I tell him. He doesn't move at all. I sigh. "Fine. Never trust a man to do a woman's job," I mumble, getting up on my knees and crawling over to the edge of the bed. I reach out and grab hold of his underwear. "I feel like *I* should be charging *you* for *this*."

His chest vibrates from a barely contained laugh.

Then he's naked. Completely.

Me likey.

"Nice," slips out quietly.

"Thank you." He grins then leans down and gives me a peck on the lips. "Are you one of those girls that keeps their bra on during sex? If so, that's fine, but I kind of like to see them. I mean, I *am* a guy and boobs *are* fun."

"No, that's just weird," I tell him, reaching around and unhooking the garment in question. I toss it across the room dramatically.

"Nice," he echoes, gently pushing me back down on the bed. He follows, crawling on top of me and settling between my legs.

"Your confidence is so fucking sexy," he growls in my ear,

pressing his erection right into the center of me. "I really want to taste you, but I just can't right now. I *have* to be inside you."

Straight to the point. I like it.

I nod and push up on him. "Wrap it before you tap it."

"Did you just..." He shakes his head with a smile. "Never mind. Take your panties off," he instructs.

I do as he says, watching as he scoots off the bed and pulls out a box of condoms from his bedside table.

He quickly covers himself and it's too bad, because watching him touch himself is the hottest thing I've ever witnessed. If I wasn't wet before, I am after seeing that.

"You good?" he asks, moving back between my thighs. "You can tell me to stop at any time." I respond by wrapping my legs around his waist. He chuckles. "Guess you're ready then."

I feel him try to line himself up, going a little too far up. "Fuck. I feel like a goddamn virgin," he mutters.

I giggle. Then I gasp, because he's suddenly fully inside me.

"Don't laugh, Rae. It's rude," he whispers in my ear, pulling back and slowly grinding back into me.

I moan, clutching his back and pulling him closer to me.

"Now that's what I want to hear," I hear him mutter before he claims my mouth again.

Our tongues and bodies create a perfect rhythm. In, out, in, out. We push and pull on one another, gasping between kisses. It's nothing short of magnificent.

Then Hudson stops thrusting, a smile forming on his face. He holds my stare as he traces a line down my chest, sucking a nipple into his mouth. Even though I'm not one for nipple-play, I can get behind this. He switches back and forth between my breasts, using just the right amount of pressure and teeth and tongue, even rubbing the stubble on his face against them. It's enjoyable, but I need *more*.

I wiggle and tighten my inner muscles, trying to get him to move inside me again.

He releases my nipple with a loud pop. "Fuuuck. You're killing me, woman. I'm about to blow as it is."

"I don't care. You have to move. *Please.*"

He complies. Moving up on his knees, he begins thrusting in and out and in and out. *Fast.* It feels good, so good, like he was *made* to fit inside me like this, like our bodies were made to go together. It's…indescribable. Nothing like I've ever felt before. It's as if he knows exactly what my body wants, twisting me at just the right angle, plunging at just the right depth.

And my heart? Yeah, that's going crazy. It's pounding so hard I can barely hear the gasps I know are leaving my mouth. I swear I can almost feel it jumping out of my chest. I *feel* myself falling even more in love with him, and it doesn't scare me near as much as I thought it would.

Suddenly, he slows down, grinding into me harder, moving his hips in small circles.

"Goddamn," he grunts. I can tell he's scarcely holding back his release. "Are you even fucking close?"

I nod. "Harder."

He reaches down and barely—just barely—touches my clit. That's all it takes.

I break. He follows, collapsing on top of me.

"Holy. Fucking. Shit," he says shakily in my ear. "That was…wow." He lifts up, kissing my temple. "I hate to sound so damn cliché, but was that okay?"

I grin and nod. "*So* okay."

He kisses my nose and moves off me, getting up to toss the condom in the adjoining bathroom.

"Uh," he says, walking back in the room, scratching the back of his head. "I'd offer to clean you up and all, but I think that shit is kind of weird."

I shudder. "Me too. Be right back."

As I'm about to walk out of the bathroom, I realize I don't have any jammies. I had hoped the night would lead to this, but I didn't want to seem presumptuous by packing an overnight bag.

"So," I say, walking through the doorway. "I kind of... Oh." Hudson's sitting on the bed, his boxer briefs back on. He's holding a pair of basketball shorts and a t-shirt in his hands.

"These are the only things I have that may fit you. I figured you wouldn't have anything to put on," he says, handing me the clothes.

I take them. "Thank you," I tell him, pulling the shirt over my head. I ignore the shorts since I usually sleep in a shirt and underwear anyway.

Hudson scoots back up the bed and crawls under the blankets. He pats the space beside him, giving me a small grin. "Wanna snuggle?"

I sigh and climb into his bed. "I guess, if I have to."

Hudson lies down on his back so I can put my head on his chest. I nestle in beside him, putting my leg over his.

We relax in silence for several minutes.

"This is weird," Hudson suddenly says, causing me to jump.

He shakes with laughter. I pinch his nipple. *Hard.* He's not laughing anymore.

"What's weird?" I ask.

"This, how natural it all feels."

He's right, it does. Everything about this feels so normal, like this is what it's meant to be like, and I really, *really* like it.

"I agree," I say on a sigh, closing my eyes, already feeling sleep tugging at me.

He kisses the top of my head and reaches over to turn the lamp off.

My breathing evens out and I'm almost asleep, barely hanging on, when Hudson speaks next.

"I fell. I totally fucking fell," he says on a whisper, kissing my head once more.

I smile, knowing exactly what he means, and slip into slumber.

CHAPTER 23

HUDSON

I WAKE up with my dick pressed against Rae's sweet, sweet ass.

I smile. *I got laid.*

Rae laughs. "I think I'm rubbing off on you. You totally said that out loud," Rae says, pushing back on me.

Oops.

"I think that means we spend too much time together or some shit like that. Maybe we need a break," I say, teasing because I don't think I could ever get enough of this girl.

"One sleepover and you're already trying to get rid of me? That hurts, Hudson."

I pull her into me and nuzzle her exposed shoulder where her shirt has slipped down. "Mmm...want me to kiss this new wound of yours?"

Nipping and kissing her neck, I roll until she's on her back so I can get to her plumped lips. They're still slightly swollen from our kisses last night. I settle gently on top of her and her eyes shine up at me, filled with happiness and laced with desire.

"Possibly. What time is it?" she asks.

I reach over and grab my phone, squinting at the bright light. "Six. I have to be in the shop by eight."

She pretends to think on it. "Yeah, sure, I guess."

I laugh and kiss her nose.

"That's not where my wound is, silly."

"You're such a damn smartass. It's cute as hell."

This time I kiss her lips. She opens instantly, deepening the kiss. I don't even give a shit about her morning breath. I don't know if it's my raging boner or because I just love this girl that damn much. Either way, I continue kissing her until we're both panting and rubbing against one another.

I peel my mouth off hers. "Was that it?"

She crinkles her nose. "Nope. Think south. *Deep south.*"

I chuckle and decide to play dirty...real dirty. I drop my voice and whisper in her ear, "Do you want me to taste you, Rae? Is that what you're trying to get at?"

I hear her gasp, feel her body quiver. She swallows loudly. "I think I just fucking came," she says, her voice thick with arousal.

That may be my favorite thing to ever come out of her mouth.

I sit up, pulling her with me, and tug her shirt off, mentally thanking the gods she's not wearing any panties. I gently lay her back down, trailing kisses from her chin, down her neck, and to her chest. I spend a minute at her breasts, sucking on each nipple before continuing my kisses all the way to her cleanly-shaven mound.

I inhale. *Mmmm, damn.*

Containing my groan, I look up at her before I go any further. She's watching me. "Well?"

"YES!" she shrieks.

I laugh and part her lips with my tongue. She moans and

presses into my face as I swirl my tongue around her folds and begin sucking lightly on her clit.

She's writhing beneath me, bucking her hips like she can't get enough, and I don't blame her—I can't get enough either. Nothing has ever been this good before. My heart is pounding against my chest and I'm trying with every ounce of restraint I possess to not come all over my bed sheets.

"Hudson..."

I chuckle around her and move downward to her opening. I push my tongue in and out quickly a few times, feeling her muscles starting to contract.

"Fuckfuck*fuck*. I'm gonna come."

She tries to pull away, so I grab her hips and hold her steady. I suck hard on her clit and her hands fly to my head in an instant, nails digging into my scalp as she bucks up. She inhales a strangled gasp and freezes for just a millisecond before falling heavily back down on the bed, gasping for air.

Don't you dare fucking blow your load now, Hudson!

I take a calming breath of my own before giving her a few gentle strokes and kissing my way back up to her mouth.

"Hi." I smirk at her.

"Hi." She reaches up, wiping my mouth with her hand, and then surprises me by kissing me right on the lips.

I groan and press into her, my dick straining against her lower stomach. She can feel me, knows I'm about to explode.

"Wanna get laid again?"

I nod vigorously, not even bothering to laugh at the way she phrases her question, and roll off her to grab the condom.

Rae parts for me as I settle between her legs. I line myself up and slip inside my little slice of heaven with ease. We both sigh, and I try not to fall apart. She wraps her arms around my neck and pulls me down for a chaste kiss. I grab her hands and bring them above her head, holding them there as I thrust into her slowly, maintaining eye contact with every push.

My chest tightens at the look on her face. Even though we haven't spoken the words out loud yet, I can see the love in her eyes. It's so intense that it's making it hard to breathe—or that could be from the sex.

It's in this moment that I realize the difference between the sex we had last night and what's happening right now. Right now, we're showing one another how we feel with our bodies. Last night was all about a release for us both—not that it didn't mean anything, I just know this is a defining moment in our relationship.

I continue my slow pace, grinding harder and harder with each thrust. Even though we've been going slow, I'm close. So fucking close. My balls tighten up.

"Rae," I gasp out.

"I know, Hudson, I know," she says, her green eyes shining brighter than I've ever seen. "I'm right there with you."

Something about the way she says it that lets me know she's not only talking about our orgasms, but about us, our feelings, our love for each other.

With our gazes locked tightly on one another, we give in... to it all.

Rae

LAST NIGHT WAS everything I thought it was going to be— awkward, sweet, fun.

This morning was everything I had hoped it would be— amazing, beautiful, meaningful.

Hudson scored major bonus points for not trying to make

me shower with him because that shit is weird to me. I also thought he was going to have some comments about me not wearing panties—because I refuse to put on my ones from yesterday after showering—with my skirt, but he's been a total gentleman...so far.

"Rae? Is that a yes? Or a no? Or maybe even a maybe?" Hudson asks.

"What?" I can feel my face heat. I didn't hear a word he just spoke, too busy living inside my own bubble.

"Your birthday weekend...me, you, Joey, the beach."

"Umm...yes?"

He squints at me. "Even though that totally came out as a question, I'm taking it as an affirmative."

Dread races through me because truth be told, I'm terrified of big bodies of water. Okay, that's a lie. I love going to Lake Q on nights I can't sleep and watching the water, and the lake seems big from the safety of the rocks. It's just...my nightmare. Even though I know it's only a dream, it keeps me far, far away from the ocean.

But I just agreed to go to one...for Hudson.

He has no idea of my fear. I've never told him about my horrible dream because I haven't had one since I started seeing him—officially—and I haven't thought about it in weeks. I never expected it to come back and bite me in the ass.

There is a small part of me that is thrilled to go to the beach because it means a weekend away from this town. There's also a tiny part of me that realizes how major it is that I'm willing to face this for Hudson, on my birthday of all days. There's a *huge* part of me that's fucking scared—with good reason—as all get out.

"Hey," Hudson says, walking over and cupping my face in his hands. "We don't have to. You just talked so fondly of the water before and I know how much you love Lake Q. I thought it would be nice to have a little mini vacay for your birthday. We won't be swimming or anything because it'll be mid-October and probably too cold, but at least we'll be going somewhere and it will only cost us gas. I have full access to my grandparents' old beach house. The new owners are awesome about letting us use it."

I grab his hands and pull them from my face. "I know. I was just worried about getting off work for a second but then remembered Clyde still owes me for working my birthday last year," I lie.

I don't know why I lie...or maybe I do.

I'm not ready to tell Hudson yet. I should be, but I'm not. I need to mentally prepare myself for all of that and right now, that's not happening.

He stares at me—hard—for a second and I hold my breath, worried he's going to see through my bullshit. He either does and lets it go or doesn't and moves on. Either is fine by me at this point.

"Okay. Two weeks. Your birthday. Talk with your boss. We can go up on Saturday morning and come back Sunday night."

I fake a smile and give him a thumbs-up.

He gives me a real smile and my heart starts to hurt, because this is *so* not going to end well.

"Well, as delicious as the coffee and cereal was—which you're welcome for because obviously my culinary skills are impeccable—I need to hit the shop," he announces.

"So eager to get rid of me," I tease, giving him a flirty smile.

He smirks, and I just know something dirty is about to leave his mouth. "I'd love nothing more than to bend you over that stool you're sitting on, and I'm probably going to be sporting a semi all day just thinking about the fact that you're not wearing any panties right now, but I gotta run."

I laugh. *So much for him being a gentleman.*

———

"PERRY!" I shout as my cousin plunks down on a stool at Clyde's.

"Well, if it isn't my ex-girlfriend. How are you, sugar? Ready for another round?" He waggles his brows at me.

I called him first thing in the morning the night after I met Joey—even before I called Maura, but we vowed to never tell her that—so I could tell him what Hudson thought we were to each other. Now he won't stop making fun of Hudson.

"Ew!" I shiver to drive my point home. "Knock that shit off. It gives me the creeps."

"But it's still funny as fuck. I cannot believe he actually thought that," Perry says, *still* laughing about it.

"True." I lean against the bar, resting my head on my hands. "So, what are you doing here? Shouldn't you be out, I don't know, looking for a job or something?"

"Hey! I'm getting close! Maybe. Why don't *you* have an interview yet?"

"Jerk."

Though I still haven't had a single firm call me back since my phone interview, I'm not as upset as I feel I should be, and I have Hudson to thank for that. He's managed to make me see Wakefield in a whole new light, making me not want to leave as much now.

"Why are you smiling?" Perry asks. He leans in across the bar. "Did you forget to take your crazy pills again this morning, Rae? Tsk, tsk," he mock-whispers.

"Ohmygod! Go bug someone else," I yell, attempting to swat him with my wipe-down rag.

He jumps down from the stool, his hands raised in the air. "I'm going, I'm going. Love you, crazy!" he shouts, turning away and heading back to his friend Colt, who is laughing at his antics.

I roll my eyes at them, knowing Perry will be getting a taste of karma momentarily, because Clarissa is their waitress today.

"Yo! How you doin', girl?" Benny calls out, walking behind the bar and getting to work.

"Hey! What up, Big Ben?" I say, giving him a high-five and returning to the task at hand: pouring beers.

We automatically fall into a pattern, working around one another for an hour or more.

"I see you've requested off three days for your birthday. Big plans?" he asks once there's a lull.

A blush creeps up my face at his suggestion. "Hudson's taking me somewhere."

"Oh yeah? Where to? Vegas? 'Cause you two need to make that shit legal real quick. I ain't ever seen two people better suited, and I've only been around you two a few times."

I laugh his comment off, ignoring the way my heart flutters. "Nah. We're waiting for our six-month anniversary for that one."

He nods. "Good plan."

Clearing my throat, I tell him, "It's the beach, Benny. Hudson's taking me to the beach."

The bear of a bartender stops midstride, almost dropping the glass he's holding.

"Shit, Rae. Are you... I mean... Wow." He whistles. "Are you sure?"

"As I'll ever be."

"You...you sure that's a good idea? I mean...the date, the place. Will you be okay?"

I love that Benny is concerned for me. It warms my heart to know he cares so much, but I need to grow up, face my fears.

"I'm scared shitless," I say on a sigh. "But...I have to do it. I mean I *really* have to. I just have this feeling this is going to be something big for me. I have see what that is, you know?"

"I get it, but hell, kid...I worry. Only if you're sure you'll be okay."

"I really don't know if I will be, but I promise to be extra careful. Deal?"

We shake on it and Benny pulls me into a brief hug. "You're brave, kiddo. I admire that. It's gonna be fine, I'm sure of it."

That makes one of us.

CHAPTER 24

RAE

"YOU REALLY DON'T NEED to be here for this, Dad."

He gives me a *don't go there* look, letting me know he's staying.

We're waiting on Hudson to arrive with Joey in tow for our weekend getaway.

I turn to my sister. "Haley, you *definitely* don't have to here."

"What? And miss Dad meeting your boyfriend? Nope, not happening." There's a twinkle in her eye because she knows something my dad doesn't—she knows about Joey. "You're going to love him, Dad. You two have *so much* in common."

I flip her off before my dad turns back to me.

"This is the same guy that fixed your car, right?" I nod. "Well, he gets bonus points for that already."

Good, because he's going to need them.

The last two weeks have been nothing short of amazing. I've spent all my free time with Hudson. I've played make-believe with Joey for countless hours and watched an insane amount of *Adventure Time.* My favorite moments have been at night when I'm wrapped in Hudson's arms, falling asleep and falling even more in love with him and Joey.

Now here I am, waiting for him to meet my father and unknowingly help me face my biggest fear. You'd think I'd be more nervous for him to meet my father, but I have it all bass-ackward. The beach terrifies me more.

The doorbell rings and we all freeze.

"I'll get it!" Haley and I shout at the same time.

We take off racing toward the door, reverting to our child-hood years and shoving one another the entire way.

She beats me—barely.

"Hudson! Hello, hello. Come on in!" Haley says, moving out of way.

He looks at me over her shoulder, fear written all over his face. Joey follows him inside.

"I'm Haley, Rae's sister." She shakes Hudson's hand.

"Nice to meet you. I've heard great things," he says with small smile, because I tell him almost daily how crazy my sister is.

Haley bends down and sticks her hand out to Joey next. "And you must be Joey. Such a pleasure to meet you."

Joey stands tall and takes Haley's hand, shaking it once before dropping it. "Hi." Then she spots me and makes a beeline into my waiting arms. "Rae! I am so excited to go to the beach! Dad says that even though we can't swim, we can still stick our feet in. Right, Daddy?"

"That's right, bug."

"Daddy?" my father says, standing in the kitchen doorway. He's rocking his "dad stance" too.

I clear my throat and set Joey down. "Dad, this is Hudson, my boyfriend. Hudson, this is my father, Ted." They exchange an awkward handshake. "And this is Joey, Hudson's daughter."

My dad looks at Joey and scrunches his nose up. Joey mimics him.

"You're short," my dad tells her.

Joey shrugs. "At least I'm not old."

Hudson, Haley, and I are frozen, unsure how my father's going to react.

Then, my Dad bursts into laughter and holds his fist out to her. Joey bumps it. "Nice job, kiddo."

"Thanks. My dad says I get my smarts from him," she says, pointing an accusing finger right at Hudson.

Hudson groans and I stifle a laugh, because *damn*. She just unknowingly threw Hudson under the bus.

"Thanks, bug," he mutters.

"So, Hudson, Rae tells me you fixed her car for her. It *is* going to last longer this time, yes?"

"DAD!" I hiss. "That's so not even kind of okay!"

Hudson gives a nervous chuckle. "I sure hope so, sir."

"Right," I interrupt before my dad can chime in with anything else. "We had better get going, huh? We have a nice little drive ahead of us and I'm sure Joey's just *dying* to get there."

"I *am* close to death. Can we go now, Daddy?" Joey says, her voice wispy and dramatic.

"We can." Hudson grabs my bag and walks over to my dad. Using his free hand, he shakes my dad's again. "It was great to meet you, Ted. I hope our next meeting is longer."

"Looking forward to it." Having just met my dad, Hudson has no idea of the meaning behind his words. My dad is going to grill his ass the next time they meet. Even though he's a nice, easygoing guy, he's *extremely* protective of Haley and me. There's no doubt Hudson will be limping away from that encounter.

"It was great meeting you finally, Hudson. You should come over for dinner sometime. I'll cook," Haley offers.

"NO!" Dad and I yell at the same time.

Haley huffs and folds her arms over her chest, stomping her foot once. "You two are so rude!"

Hudson shakes his head and laughs. "Joe, say bye. We're heading out since you're *dying* and all."

"Bye, Rae's sister. Bye, Old Guy."

We all laugh and Hudson throws an apologetic look over his shoulder to my father.

As we're walking out the door, I catch my dad's eye. He doesn't look too happy with me right now. I give him my best *I'm sorry* look and he gives me a nod in return, letting me know we'll discuss this later.

Oops?

———

WE PULL off into a gas station right on the edge of town. Hudson turns to face Joey and Rocky in the back seat.

"You need to pee?" he asks, eyeing Joey, daring her to say no.

She gets the hint and bobs her head up and down. She opens the door some before turning back to me. "Will you go with me, Rae?"

"Of course," I say, unbuckling my seatbelt and getting out of the car with her.

"I'll let Rocky out," Hudson says, meeting us around the front.

"Sounds like a plan, Stan."

Joey looks up at me with a serious expression. "His name isn't Stan. It's Hudson."

I hear Not Stan laugh as we walk away and inside the gas station. *Asshat.*

We're nearing the restrooms when a slimy guy in a shirt

that's way too small for his big gut slides in front of us, a creepy grin on his face.

"Damn, girl." He whistles appreciatively. "You're *way* too young to be a mama. You lookin' for a daddy? Because I can be yours."

I wrinkle my nose in disgust and move around him, ignoring his comment.

"Hey, lady. I'm talkin' to you. Come here."

He grabs for me and I instinctively throw Joey behind me. The man's hand connects with my wrist and my other arms flies back on its own accord. My palm connects with the side of his face and he growls, stepping toward me.

"Little bitch!" he spits my way. "Don't you ever—"

"Hey! Get the fuck away from them!"

Hudson comes barreling down the aisle and the man spins on his heel, taking off in an instant. He runs from the store, glancing back several times. Hudson rushes for me, wrapping me in his arms and hugging Joey close to him.

"You girls okay?" We both nod. "Good." He leans close to my ear. "That slap was hot as hell. You're so getting laid tonight."

I laugh lightly and shrug. "I may be little, but I'm tough. Besides, I'd do anything to protect Joey, and you. I do that for the people I love."

His eyes fill with surprise. "Did you just, uh...did you just say you love me?"

I wait for the worry to fill me but it never comes. I do love him, and Joey, and I don't give a crap who knows.

"Nah. Probably just a heat of the moment thing," I tease. "Couldn't possibly be true."

He laughs and hugs me close, kissing my temple and then straight down to my ear. I can feel him smiling against my face in every kiss. "I love you too, Rae," he whispers.

"I said it was a fluke," I say softly back to him.

"Uh-huh. Right. You *so* love me."

I push him away, laughing. "Oh, grow up, you weirdo. It was a fluke!"

"Daddy," Joey says, from beside us, "that guy cursed a lot. So did you and Rae. That's like five dollars!"

"Five? I thought it was only seventy-five cents per curse word!" he argues, trying to keep Joey's attention on anything other than what we just encountered.

"Not when it's that many," she explains.

Hudson huffs and pulls a five out of his pocket. "You're going to make me go broke, dude. Then who will pay for your groceries?"

She shrugs. "Rae will. She loves me."

Hudson looks to me, waiting for me to say that was a fluke too. I shake my head. "Nope, I meant that part."

He laughs. "Come on, goofballs. The beach is calling our names!"

I almost—*almost*—forgot where we were heading. I almost forgot about my biggest fear. Hudson did that for me—to me. *Maybe it won't be so bad after all.*

After we report the incident to the cashier, opting to not involve the police just yet, we pile back into the car. Joey's asleep before we hit the highway. I envy how children can just do that—fall asleep anywhere.

"Can I ask you something?"

"You can ask me anything since you love me and all."

I shove his arm lightly. "Shut up."

He grins, never taking his eyes off the road. "Ask your question."

"What happened with Joey's mom? Is she in Joey's life at all?"

"Up front, let me just say that I didn't leave Jess just

because, and I didn't rip Joey from her. I want to be sure that's not what you're thinking."

"Not for a second. I'm curious is all."

"At one point, she was the light of my life. She was smart, kind, and the most beautiful girl I'd ever seen. Then we got pregnant. At sixteen, Rae. Sixteen! Do you have any idea what that can do to a person? It can completely break them, and that's exactly what it did to Jess."

The sadness in his voice is so clear that it hurts. He used to love Jess, that much is obvious, but I can also hear sadness over everything he lost: his youth, the mother of his child, a normal life for Joey.

"What happened?" I inquire quietly.

He sighs. "Well, after we decided we were going to keep the baby, we told my parents first. My dad freaked out, my mother cried, and things were strained around the house for months afterward. Then it all blew up. My dad and I had a horrible fight. I moved out and in with Jess. Her parents said we had until the baby came and then we had to get our own place. So we did, and it awesome for some time. Even though we had a new baby, the freedom we had felt amazing, but it only took about a year and a half for it to all start falling apart right under my nose."

He pauses, taking a deep breath and scratching his nose, his eyes never leaving the road.

"We were eighteen. I had graduated early and was working all the time, and when I say working, I really do mean working. I spent countless hours at Jacked Up, sixty hours a week sometimes. Horton used to pay me cash under the table to help him out with personal projects. I did it to keep up with the bills because it seemed like every time I turned around, Jess was asking for more money. I didn't know jack shit about the finances so I assumed it was all going to Joey and rent and utilities. I was wrong. So very wrong."

He stops again, briefly squeezing his eyes shut.

"You don't have to continue, Hudson. I can guess what happened next."

"No, I *need* to tell you this."

I nod. He continues.

"I came home one night to find Jess sitting on the couch and Joey screaming her head off only a few feet away. I assumed she was tired and spacing out. What I didn't realize was she was as high as a kite. It took me another week to find out what she was doing with all that money I'd been giving her: drugs. She started with coke about two months after Joey was born to lose the baby weight. A friend at work got her hooked. I had no clue it was going on for two years. After all, she didn't seem off. Apparently it was only an occasional thing at first. Then it turned serious and she started shooting up. After I found out, I took Joey and left for a week. Tucker saved my ass with that," he says, a small smile slipping through.

"Tucker is a good guy."

His smile grows even bigger. "The best."

Hudson's quiet for a moment. I can see how much talking about this is affecting him. There's a tightness in his jaw and his hands are gripping the steering wheel, turning his knuckles white. I'm just not sure who he's more upset with—himself or Jess.

"So," he finally says. "Eventually I went back. Jess sought me out every day, telling me how sorry she was, promising she'd quit. I believed her. I think a part of me craved the kind of relationship my parents had and that's why I went back. Everything was great for about eight months...and then I caught her fucking around with another coworker. At that point, we hadn't been intimate in months. Maybe that was my fault, because this

was when Horton got sick and I started taking over the shop."
He sounds so sad about that last part, like he still blames
himself, which is really fucking stupid. "Anyway, I stayed.
Forgave her even. But then, a few months later, I started finding
little hints that she was back on the drugs. That was the last
straw. So, I took Joey, who was four at the time, in the middle of
the night and left. Moved back in with my parents and never
once looked back. She's reached out once in the last three years
and it was for money. That's it. I don't regret leaving for a
second."

We don't speak for miles.

I reach over and place my hand on his arm. "You were
young, afraid, and trying to make it work on your own. You
did what you thought was right at the time. You're a great
father, Hudson. Everything you went through with Jess
brought you closer to your amazing daughter. Don't ever think
you did anything wrong because at the time, it was right for
you."

The air around us shifts. I think Hudson finally telling me
about Jess somehow brought us closer together.

"Thank you," he says, emotion filling his voice.

"No problem. It's what I do," I joke, attempting to lighten
the mood. "Does Joey ever ask about Jess?"

He shakes his head. "Not anymore. She did a lot at first, but
I told her she had her Nana, who has been in her life every day
since she was four, and I guess that's always been enough for
her."

I nod. "Makes sense I guess."

"Now, can I ask you a question?"

"Anything."

"Why don't you like kids?"

Fuck.

"Anything but that?" I try. He shakes his head no. "Damn.

Points for trying." I blow out a breath. "This isn't a happy story, Hudson," I warn.

"Like mine was?"

"You got Joey out of it."

He grins. "True, but you're not getting out of this. I'm ready."

"Right. So, my mom...well, she kind of sucked. She wasn't affectionate at all. Remember that painting of the ocean I told you about?" He nods. "That's the absolute closest she ever got to showing affection. Haley remembers a different mother up until those last two years. I was too young to remember. All I know is I don't ever remember her saying 'I love you' or even hugging me."

"Shit. That does suck," Hudson chimes in.

"It gets worse. The year after my last good memory, we went to the beach for a small vacation to celebrate my mom's and my birthday—we have the same one. I guess my dad thought it might make my mom happy." I smile sadly. "My dad was all about making her happy. The sun set with her for him," I tell him, my voice cracking.

Hudson reaches out and grabs my hand, squeezing it a few times.

"Anyway, the first few days were amazing. My mom smiled often and everyone was happy, or so we thought."

Memories of that weekend crash into me and tears begin to roll. It was the best and worst weekend of my life. I'll never forget it.

I wipe at the tears and push through. "Our birthday was on the last day of the vacation. It was also the last day I saw my mother."

Hudson clears his throat. "Wha...what happened, Rae?"

"She killed herself."

CHAPTER 25

HUDSON

"OH HELL. I am *so* sorry, Rae. That's... I can't begin to imagine."

I can't put into words how her confession makes me feel. It's a mixture of sorrow for what Rae lost and intense anger at her mother. I can understand her aversion to kids now.

"Thanks. It's just hard sometimes around kids. I don't understand the whole 'a mother's love' thing. I never had any of that, you know? I don't know how to act around them, how to express myself. I clam up, terrified I'm doing it wrong, worried as hell I'm going to make them feel the way *she* made *me* feel."

"I understand, Rae, and I appreciate you trying with Joey."

Rae beams. "She makes it easy. It's impossible not to love her. While I'm glad Jess isn't around considering how she was when you last saw her, I don't understand how she doesn't care about Joey. Blows my mind."

"Word. So much word."

She laughs. "So eloquent."

I shoot her a look. "That's rich coming from you."

"Are we there yet?" Joey's scratchy voice comes from the back.

"Close, bug. About ten more minutes."

"Drive faster, Daddy."

I roll my eyes at her. "So demanding."

"Are you getting excited, Joey?" Rae asks, turning around to look at her.

"So very excited!"

"Me too," I confess. "I haven't been to the beach since the summer before Joey was born. We used to go all the time though, checking out different rentals with my grandparents to see which one they wanted to buy. Actually, I saved a random girl from drowning one year. Made me feel like a hero for weeks afterward."

Rae scrunches her brows in a way that has me asking what's going through her head.

"Oh, nothing," she answers, but something is off. I don't press it, because I know the conversation we had was draining for her.

"Hey, Daddy? I have to tell you something."

Whatever it is, she has that *I didn't mean to* tone to her voice.

"What's up, bug?"

"I was fake sleeping for a while. I heard you talkin' about Mommy. I miss her sometimes. All the kids at school talk about their moms. I tell them about Nana. Sometimes they laugh and say I don't have a mom."

I rub my chest, feeling the pain of her confession. "I'm sorry, bug."

"I'm not. I love Nana. And you know what, Dad?"

"What?"

"I don't need no mommy. I have you and Nana and Rae," Joey says proudly. "Oh, and Uncle Tuck and Uncle G, but don't tell them I almost forgot about them."

My heart doesn't hurt anymore. It soars.

She knows she doesn't need approval or love from a woman

who isn't in her life. Even at her young age, she understands the love she gets from everyone else is enough, is just as good.

"Good, Joe. That's good."

Rae's hand comes to rest on my thigh. I reach down and grab it, bringing it to my mouth. I kiss and squeeze it tightly a few times before dropping it down to rest in my lap with mine. Knowing Rae is here with me for all this comforts me in ways I'll never be able to explain to her.

"I SEE IT!" Joey suddenly shouts from the back, leaning forward as far her seatbelt allows.

"How do you know that's it?" Rae asks. "Your daddy told me the house was yellow. That doesn't look yellow to me."

"It's...it's yellow? But that's my least favorite color! I can't stay in a yellow house!" Joey shouts, tossing herself back on the seat.

I chuckle. "Relax, my little drama queen. Either you stay in a yellow house or you walk your little butt back to Wakefield."

"Fine. Yellow it is," she huffs. "But I want the big bedroom to share with Rocky. He's a bed hog."

I look to Rae, who barely hides her smiles and shrugs.

"Deal."

Rae makes a low whiplash noise and I laugh, because she's *so* right.

———

"OH MY GOSH! This place is *so* cool, Daddy!" Joey cries, running all over the house. "My room is huge! Can we live here, please?"

"You haven't even seen the beach yet and you already want to move in?"

"Ahh! I can't believe I almost forgot about the beach! We *must* go see it. Now please!"

Rae leans in and whispers, "How much sugar did you give her?"

"Probably too much. Just means she'll crash and burn later." I waggle my brows at her suggestively. She giggles and I fall in love with the twinkle in her eyes.

I've had a huge stupid grin on my face since we climbed out of the car, partly from Joey's excitement, and partly from this amazing girl I'm holding in my arms, staring out at the water with.

We get lost in one another, forgetting about everything else. I lean in and brush my lips across hers, telling her with my sweet kisses how I feel.

"Come on, you two!" Joey yells from the front porch, the door wide open.

"Ugh, should have named her Mood Killer," I grumble.

Rae laughs and pushes me toward the door. "You love it and you know it."

I hold out my fingers, pinching them close together. "Just a smidge."

Rae's quiet the entire way down to the shore, holding her breath as we walk the small path. I don't think she wants me to notice, so I pretend I don't. I'm sure being here is hard for her, considering how it ended the last time she was at the ocean. I wish she had told me about her mother before we were less than twenty minutes away, because I would have never suggested this trip in the first place. But, I also know Rae, so I know how straightforward she is. If this were something she didn't want to do, we wouldn't be here now.

As Joey dips her toes into the water for the very first time, Rae reaches for my hand, squeezing it tightly.

"Something's rolling around in that pretty little head of yours. I know you'll tell me when you're ready, but I just want you to know that I'm here for you," I tell her quietly, never taking my eyes off Joey as we stop about three feet from the water's edge.

Rae responds by squeezing my hand once.

"Don't go too far in, bug. Don't want you getting swept away," I yell to Joey. She takes two more steps. "That's good. No farther."

I picked the worst weekend ever to do this. It's cloudy and kind of cold with high winds that are creating choppy waves, so I don't want her too far out. The ocean is too unpredictable for that.

"Can I collect sticks in case we find a dead body, Dad?"

Rae bursts into laughter, helping to ease the weight she seems to be carrying around.

"Do I even want to know?" she asks.

"Nah, probably not."

"Well, can I?" Joey pushes.

"Yeah, bug. We can even get some together for Rocky so we can play fetch later. Rae and I will help," I tell her.

"You guys can use your sticks for Rocky. I'm saving mine for the dead bodies," Joey tells us seriously.

That's how we spend the rest of our day—wading in and out of the water, collecting sticks, playing with Rocky, and laughing.

———

HOURS LATER, Rae and I are wrapped around one another in bed, exhausted from our day.

"I am so stuffed!" Rae exclaims. "That seafood Alfredo was amazing. I'm still in shock you cooked. Should I be worried about food poisoning?"

"Hey! Take that back," I say, tickling her until she gasps out an apology. "That's what I thought."

"Ugh, you're so smug. It's such a turn-off."

"You mean turn-on." I smirk, and she hits me with a pillow. "Okay, settle down, spitfire."

We snuggle into "our" position—her head on my chest and one leg thrown over both of mine. It's not very comfortable for me but...anything for Rae.

We lie in silence for several minutes and I twirl her hair as she draws little patterns on my chest. Even though this is something simple that most couples do, I feel like it's extra intimate somehow. I don't know if it's because of what we shared with one another earlier or if it's from the way her fingers keep curling inward, like she's clutching on to me.

Just when her patterns slow and her breathing starts evening out, making me think she's falling asleep, she speaks.

"Hudson."

"Rae."

I feel her smile against my chest.

"Will you tell me more about you saving that little girl?"

"That hero thing totally revs your engine, doesn't it?" I tease.

Her voice dripping with sarcasm, she says, "Ridiculously so."

"There's not much to tell. Some of it is fuzzy. I was nine and, like I said before, went to about a million beaches before my grandparents fell in love with this house, so I don't even remember where it was," I tell her. "Anyway, I was out collecting seashells and thought I heard a little girl screaming, so I took off running down the beach. What I happened upon wasn't pretty. There was a woman and she was...well, just standing there staring out into the ocean as this little girl screamed and cried for help. I tried talking to the woman, yelling at her even, but nothing worked. So, I ran out into the ocean and pulled the little girl to the shore."

I peek down at Rae when she doesn't say anything. There's a hard frown on her face, a perplexed bend to her brows.

"Well, what happened next?" she asks, looking up at me.

There's sadness in her eyes. It makes me uneasy, but I continue. "The woman was gone by the time we hit the sand. Nowhere in sight. A man came rushing down the beach and snatched the little girl up. He was bawling and thanking me. I asked a million times over if the girl was okay and he just kept saying, 'She's breathing. Oh, thank god, she's breathing.' It was hard to watch and I didn't know what else to do...so I left."

Rae's quiet for so long that I begin to drift off to sleep.

"Do you know what happened to the little girl?" she asks, sounding like she's almost asleep herself.

I sigh because it's something I've wondered myself over the years. "No, but I wish I had stayed to find out."

"Me too," she says softly.

It's the last thing I hear before I give in to sleep.

CHAPTER 26

RAE

"CAN we go outside and play, please? I wanna touch the water again!" Joey's bouncing up and down, a grin splitting her face.

Hudson's been gone getting birthday donuts for about fifteen minutes and she's been bouncing off the walls for fourteen of them. I have no clue how he does this all the time, but as exhausting as she is, she's adorable as hell.

This is now the second time she's mentioned touching the water. I'm nervous to take her out there by myself, because I get this icky feeling whenever I stare at the water for too long, but it's impossible to look her in her blue eyes and tell her no. So, I don't.

"Well...since I'm the birthday girl, I say yes! Let's grab Rocky and head out there before your daddy gets back."

"Woo!" she shouts and does a little victory jig.

I try to remember how far Hudson let her wade out yesterday. I think she gets a little farther out than he permitted, but she's seems to be doing fine, so I let it go.

I stand there watching her, not touching the water myself, and let the wind whip my hair around. It's another cloudy day, so the water is choppy. It reminds me of another time, but I can't place it, so I ignore the tug my head is giving me.

Feeling a little brave, I take two steps forward, close enough that the smallest amount of water touches my toes. It's cold but still feels good. I take another step.

"Oh! You're coming in! Yay! Come out farther—come out here with me!" a tiny voice yells.

In the deepest part of my mind, I know it's Joey, but in the forefront, the part that counts, I hear and see myself when I was seven and I'm transported to another time.

It's like my nightmare, only this time I'm not the little girl in the ocean—I'm my mother. I watch as seven-year-old me struggles hard to keep her head up. I even hear her yelling for help repeatedly, but I do nothing. I try hard to move my feet, but I can't. I have no control over anything.

Then, suddenly, there's a little boy in front of me with a striking pair of blue-green eyes. He looks so familiar, but I can't seem to place him.

He begins waving his arms in front of my face frantically. He's yelling and pointing toward the water. Everything he's saying comes out mushed together, but I assume he's begging me to help the little girl.

I do nothing except watch as he fights the waves to reach the girl. As soon as he does, I turn around to begin walking back to the house and run straight into Hudson.

I look him in the eyes and gasp.

"It's you," I say on a whisper. My head feels like I've spent too much time on a merry-go-round and my vision is hazy.

His mouth is twisted up and his eyes unsure. "Of course it's me. "Rae..." he says slowly. "Where's Joey?"

"I...I don't know..." My head is still spinning. "But it was you, Hudson. You were the little boy."

"Rae," he says, taking me by the shoulders and shaking me. "Rae, where's Joey? Where's my daughter?" He shakes me again, harder this time.

"I don't...I don't know. She was in the water, but she was me..." He drops his hold on me instantly and sprints off toward the water, yelling a string of cuss words.

"You were him. You were the little boy," I say to myself.

"JOEY! Fuck! Joey!" I barely hear Hudson yell.

The thumping in my head feels like someone is taking tiny hammer and whack, whack, whacking away. I grab on to it with both hands and squeeze, hoping that maybe if I do it hard enough, the pounding will stop. It doesn't.

Next, I try my heart, because it feels like it's going to explode. That doesn't work either.

Everything *hurts*. Everything inside of me feels like it's being meticulously pulled apart—every little molecule of my being getting plucked from within, slowly and painfully, and it hurts so, *so* bad.

I feel like there's something I should be doing—anything other than just standing here—but I can't figure it out.

Then the anger sets in—all of it at once. I don't know what it means or why I'm so furious, but I'm shaking; I can feel my blood boiling. I clench and unclench my fists, ready to strike at whatever is near. I'm looking around, spinning in a circle, when I see what it was I was supposed to be doing all along.

Hudson grabs a small floating body and something inside me breaks—or snaps back together. I'm not sure which.

Holy shit. It's *not* a nightmare! It was real! My mother watched me drown. She *let* me drown.

Hudson saved me. I remember him clearly now—same dark hair, slightly longer and wet from the water. The look of panic on his face as he dragged me up the beach will be forever etched in my head now. Standing over me, he was drenched and breathing hard, and his eyes were still so beautiful. He watched as my dad cradled me in his arms. I remember him asking if I was okay, but it was so hard to hear him over my father's crying.

The hardest part, though? Watching him walk away and silently begging for him to come back to me.

He did. He *finally* did—but now I'm not sure he's going to stick around.

I take off running and reach him as he's dropping her onto the ground. I fall to my knees next to them, tears streaming down my face.

"She's not fucking breathing! Goddammit, Rae! What have you done!" he yells, pumping furiously at her tiny, unmoving chest.

I watch helplessly as he continues to pump. I watch powerlessly as he breathes air into the one person in this world that means the most to him.

Then suddenly, miraculously, Joey coughs and sucks in a huge breath of air, reaching for Hudson in an instant.

"Daddy!" she cries as he holds her securely, tears rolling down his cheeks.

As she falls apart in her father's arms, I sit there and watch, my heart snapping in two. She looks just like Hudson did—soaking wet, tears streaming down her face. She's breaking right in front of me and all I want to do is reach out to her, but I can't, and I'm not sure if I'll ever be able to again.

Hudson looks at me over her shoulder, tears streaking his face. "Shh. Shh. It's okay, bug. You're okay. Shh. Calm down, honey. Shh," he whispers endlessly to Joey.

This look—the one on Hudson's face right now—it replaces everything I saw as a kid. This is the look of a scared father, a broken man.

And *I* did that to him.

He slowly fades away from me because I know—*I know*—this is the end for us.

In that moment, my whole world falls apart.

I SPRING to my feet as Hudson comes walking back into the living room and over to stand in front of me.

"How is she?" I ask, wringing my hands.

"She's exhausted. Confused. Asleep." He sighs heavily and runs his hand down his face. "I'm not much in the mood to play nice right now, Rae, so I'm just going to cut straight to it. What the fuck happened out there? Why weren't you watching her?"

He's seething, and with good reason. I let him down. He trusted me with his most precious gift and I blew it.

"I... Shit. I honestly don't know," I tell him, biting my lip to keep from crying. I feel so ashamed right now. So embarrassed.

"Not good enough, Rae. I need more. Something. Anything."

I sit back down and wipe away the single tear that's managed to fall.

Breathe. In, out. In, out.

I start at the beginning.

"I've had this horrible recurring nightmare since I was seven. It's always the same: I'm drowning in the ocean as my mother watches. I see a little boy. Then I sink. I wake up sweating every time at that point. Until today, I assumed it was a dream, but it's not. It's a memory," I tell him. I see the moment it all clicks for him.

"I... You... I saved you. *You* were that little girl. Holy shit." His eyes grow dark and he frowns as he drops his head into his hands.

"Today I had a flashback of sorts, only this time, I wasn't me. I was my mother. I *tried* to move. I *wanted* to help Joey." His head pops up at the mention of her name, and just like that, he's back to being pissed. "But I couldn't. Deep down I knew something was wrong about taking her out there on my own, but I couldn't say no to her," I say, choking on the last word. "I promise you, Hudson. I would never, ever want to hurt Joey—never want anything bad to happen to her. I am so, *so* sorry."

He doesn't say anything; he only stares at me.

"Hudson?" I say, reaching out to him. He jerks back and it hurts so *fucking* bad. My tears fall harder. "I didn't mean for anything to happen—you have to believe me. I love Joey. I love *you*. You have to understand that."

His eyes get watery and for a second—just a split second—I think I'm getting somewhere with him.

"I think... I think you need to leave, Rae," he tells me quietly. He gets up and begins walking out of the room. Stopping halfway, he turns toward me slightly. "I'm not taking Joey anywhere tonight, and I think it would be best if you didn't stay here. You can either take my car or have someone come pick you up. I'd prefer the latter."

Then he leaves, taking my heart with him.

I call the only person I know who won't ask questions or even hesitate to make the drive.

"Hello?"

"Perry..."

"Rae? What's wrong?"

"Perry..." I try, my tears falling hard. "I... I need you."

CHAPTER 27

HUDSON

"JUST FUCKING CALL HER ALREADY, ASSHOLE!" Tucker yells at me from across my desk.

It's been over a week since I've talked to Rae, over a week since I've smiled at anything or anyone other than Joey. I've been nothing but a bundle of anger, which I feel I'm entitled to.

"It's not that simple, Tucker," Gaige tells him.

Gaige is right. It's a lot more complicated than that.

I feel so damn guilty for letting anything happen to Joey. I was too busy being wrapped up in my "perfect family" fantasy to see how freaked the water made Rae. It's all my fault. I should have never left her alone with Joey on the beach like that.

I know none of it was Rae's fault, but I'm still pissed at her for not telling it to me straight about the nightmare she was having or how afraid of the water she is.

I get that it was all a horrible reliving of a traumatic event in her life, one she had blocked out in a way. I can understand that anyone would break from something like that, but I let my kid— my world—be in the middle of it. That's not okay.

On top of all that, I'm embarrassed by the way I treated Rae after everything. I was so cold to her, so unaccepting of anything she said. I know she's never going to forgive me and I can't blame her.

So, I'll continue to wallow, because that's exactly what I deserve.

"Bullshit it's not! Hand me the goddamn phone and I'll do it. You just hit the green button next to her name. BOOM! Fucking done!"

"Tuck, man, chill. Take a deep breath," Gaige tries again, always the voice of reason.

"No. I won't 'chill'. He's spent the last week and some odd days doing nothing but moping about and chewing my ass for nothing. I'm damn sick of it." They're talking like I'm not even here now. "He needs to get his head out of his ass and fix his fucking personal life or leave that shit at the door. I'm done with it."

I barely listen as Gaige goes for another round, attempting to soothe Tucker in any way. None of it works.

"Oh, for fuck's sake, man. Shut up or get out of my office and go home. I'm tired of hearing this shit," I finally tell him.

He looks me dead in the eye. "No. I have work to do and—unlike you—I'm going to fucking do it instead of turning around to cry every five damn seconds. *You* get out. *You* go home. Go fix this shit or I'm done. I refuse to work with you like this. I love you like a brother, Hudson, but I'm tired of it. I'm tired of watching you beat yourself up over it." He sighs. "I. See. You. *None* of it was on you, man. *None* of it was really on Rae. Get your shit together!" he yells one last time before he stomps out of my office.

I stare after him, barely hearing Gaige say, "Tucker was right," before he leaves.

I sit and think. And think and think and think.

Then, something hits me. I grab my coat and keys and head

out the door, going to the one person I know won't feed me any bullshit, no matter what.

———

"MA! YOU HOME?"

"In the living room, dear!"

I walk around the corner to find her doing some weird, incredibly uncomfortable-looking yoga move.

"Damn, Ma. That looks rough."

"Quite the opposite. It's relaxing," she says, unfolding herself from the weird twisty thing she has going on and sitting down cross-legged on the floor. "Something you look like you need to do. What's going on, kid? Spill."

I sit down on the couch, facing her.

"I'm not sure I handled the Rae thing right," I confess.

"Ya think," she deadpans. I roll my eyes. "First, just because you're a giant doesn't mean I can't still spank your ass for rolling your eyes. Second, you're right. Simple as that."

I sigh. "How do you know that though?"

"What's my motto for everything?"

"Everything happens for a reason."

She nods, a small smile forming on her lips. "You saved her, Hudson."

I screw my face up, not sure what she's getting at. She pats my knee. "You'll get it. Don't worry. I'm going to go make some coffee. You want anything?"

"Have any whiskey instead?"

"I have coffee, coffee, or apple juice. Your pick."

I sigh. "Coffee is fine. Thank you."

She gets up and heads to the kitchen, leaving me alone with my thoughts. I wish she hadn't. Nothing is coming to me...at least nothing I *want* to think about. I groan and fall back onto the couch, closing my eyes and grasping my head as if that will make me see things better.

Fuck!

I *know* I need to forgive Rae. I *know* none of it was really her fault, but it's hard. It's hard to get over her not telling me about her nightmare or her fears. It's hard to look past the fact that she was supposed to be watching after Joey. I was gone for twenty-five minutes tops, and Joey almost drowns. What would have happened if I had been gone thirty minutes? Or, hell, even twenty-six minutes? Where would Joey be? Where would Rae be? What would I have gone back to?

I'll never know. I'll never find that out, and I'm so damn thankful for that...*but what if?* That's the part I can't get through my head, the part I can't get over.

I'm scared, terrified even, of something else happening to her under Rae's watch, but I know—my *heart* knows—I shouldn't be. This all happened because of what happened to Rae, and not any other reason. Rae's still a responsible adult, and she's damn good with Joey. I just need to get my head wrapped around that.

"You're thinking too hard about it," my mom says. I open my eyes to find her standing in the doorway. "Did I ever tell you about the time your dad left you in the car when you were about three?"

"What? No?" It comes out a question for some reason.

She nods and comes to sit next to me on the couch. "It's true. It was on a hot summer day, too. Windows up and everything. He had picked you up from daycare and I was still at work when it happened. I pulled into the driveway after work and walked inside. I knew almost instantly something was wrong because you always greeted me at the door. Your father was passed out on the couch, snoozing away. I called your name over and over again, getting nothing but echoes back. My yelling roused your father from his sleep eventually. He was panicked, completely freaking out, calling for you too. We never got an answer. The cops were called and everything. A police officer just happened to look inside the car window a half hour after they arrived."

My mouth falls open in shock. "What happened? How did dad forget about me?"

She shrugs. "He was exhausted, Hudson. We weren't in the best financial spot and were both working long hours. You fell asleep on the way home and he just kind of zonked out, forgetting you were in the back seat since I was the one to usually pick you up."

"Wow. I...I had no idea. I mean, I kind of remember the lights from the police cars, but nothing else. How did you two handle it?"

"Honestly? I was pissed for a long time. You were out there for over two hours, Hudson. That's a long time in a hot car. The police said we were lucky you were already asleep so you didn't panic or anything. That would have made it a lot worse," she tells me. "We didn't talk for almost two weeks. *Two weeks.* We lived together and were raising a kid together. That's a long time to go without talking. It was hard, but then I just realized one day you were safe; you were okay. That was enough for me. I never once stopped loving your father in those two weeks. In fact, I think it made me love him more. My heart did nothing but crave his the entire time. If anything, I think the whole thing brought us closer together."

Then it clicks for me. That's what I've been feeling this last week or so.

Emptiness.

Yearning.

I *need* Rae back in my life. She makes me smile, makes me happy. She makes me feel whole.

And I love her. Fuck, do I love her.

Joey's safe—happy even. In the end, that's what counts the most. The "what if" of it all doesn't matter anymore. It's time for me to find that happiness again—to get back what I had with Rae—because I don't know how much more of this separation my heart can take.

"You get that worked out?" my mom asks, smiling softly at me.

I blow out a breath and look her in the eyes. "Yeah, I think I did."

CHAPTER 28

RAE

PERRY AND MAURA have been knocking on my front door for the past half hour. I refuse to answer it. Actually, I refuse to move off this couch.

I know I'm fucked when I hear keys jiggling.

"Really, Rae? They're your best friends," Haley says, marching through the door.

Just like I have been doing for two weeks, I ignore her.

"Whatever," she mumbles, walking to her room and slamming the door. I don't even flinch or care because I'm still too pissed off at her.

Maura comes and takes a seat next to me on the couch. Perry paces.

"Rae," Maura starts gently. "You need to get out of the apartment. The only place you've gone is work. It's time."

I just look at her. "Are you for real? 'It's time'? Do you even realize how badly I fucked up? Do you even realize I almost *killed* a little girl?"

"Oh, come off it already, Rae! No one fucking blames you! I bet Hudson doesn't even blame you! You reacted—normally I might add—to an extremely fucked-up situation in your past. You've been unknowingly living with PTSD your entire life!

No. One. Blames. You," Perry shouts, his face growing redder and redder with every word.

Where does he get off being pissed at me? I bet he knew about it all along!

I glare at him. "Did you know, Perry? Did you know what happened to me? To my mother?"

"Don't you dare insult me like that. Fuck no, I didn't know! I'm just as pissed as you are at Haley and Uncle Ted," Perry exclaims, bellowing the last part loud enough so Haley hears him.

"FUCK OFF, PERRY!" she retorts.

I snicker. Perry notices.

"See," he says softly. "I know my girl is in there somewhere. Now, go shower. We're going to Lake Q. You need some thinking time away from the asshole in there."

Maura stands and holds her hand out to me. "I'll help you. Come on."

I sigh. "Fine, but I'm wearing my sweats."

———

WE PULL into my preferred spot at Lake Q and Perry and I climb out of the car. I grab my favorite blanket, spread it out, and get ready to settle down for some "me" time.

"We'll be back in an hour or so," Maura says from the passenger side of Perry's car.

They decided it'd be best if I had a little time to myself first. I wholeheartedly agreed.

Perry wraps his arms around me. "I love you, sweet girl. Remember that."

I watch him climb back into the car and drive away, leaving me with my jumbled thoughts.

I feel *so* bad for what happened with Joey. I know things

could have ended so much worse than they did, but that doesn't make all the guilt go away. Hudson had every right to kick me out, every right to end things. I deserve it.

Sitting down on my blanket, I pull my knees up and wrap my arms around them and just stare out at the lake. Like Maura said, this is the first time I've been anywhere but Clyde's since my birthday. Perry dropped everything to come pick me up that day, and I didn't even speak to him the entire way home. I didn't talk to anyone. It took me three days to tell Maura and Perry what happened.

Then I blew up at Haley and haven't talked to her since the moment she told me she knew my "nightmare" was a memory. She must have told my father I now know the truth, because he keeps blowing my phone up every night when he gets off work. He's stopped by the apartment twice, but never made it past the front door being slammed right in his face.

I am beyond pissed at them both. They lied to me—and everyone else—for years. Years! And for what? My mental health? Because they didn't want me to be upset? Makes me wonder how much of their concern was for me and how much of it was for themselves in case I ever found out. It's going to take me a long time to fully forgive them...if I ever do.

I may not have responded to Haley while she was talking to me, but I sure as shit listened.

She claims they let me believe it was all a dream because that's what I thought it was and they never corrected me, scared I'd have some sort of "reaction" to finding out the truth, especially since it happened on my birthday...the day before my mother killed herself.

I grew up thinking my mother never loved me. I was wrong. She did, she just didn't understand how to show it. After I was born, she was diagnosed with postpartum depression that lasted many months. Eventually it got to where things were good and there were a few happy years. I don't remember much since I was so young, but once Haley said it, I remembered my mother's smile. It was beautiful.

When I was five, she got pregnant again. That little piece of information surprised me because I didn't remember it at all, but Haley knew. Unfortunately, my mom lost the baby and her depression spiraled out of control, leading to her suicide.

I don't understand why they would hide everything from me. Was it because I was so young when it happened? Because of when she killed herself? Did they think I would have blamed myself? I think at first I might have—especially when I was younger—but there's no way I would have carried that guilt all that long. I understand depression. It's not something that can be helped, and I'd *never* hold it against someone.

But, because I was never told the truth, I've inadvertently been doing so my entire life. I've been blaming my mother. I've hated her for her lack of affection, for not loving me enough to stick around, for everything—but it wasn't her fault. None of it was, and I'll never get to tell her that.

"I don't blame you, Mom," I say quietly, out loud for the first time.

"Guess it's only fair that I don't blame you either, huh?"

His voice sends a shiver down my spine. I glance toward him and choke out a raspy gasp.

"Hudson."

CHAPTER 29

HUDSON

THE MOMENT I laid eyes on her sitting there in her sweat-pants and t-shirt, all curled up into herself, I knew I was making the right decision.

Perry called me the other day to tell me everything he knew about Rae's mom and how Haley and Ted hid it from her for years, letting her believe it was nothing but a recurring nightmare. He told me she hadn't spoken to either of them—or him—since the Wednesday after the beach.

I get it, and I completely understand her silence toward them. I'd be pissed too. Hell, I *am* pissed, but I also understand why they did it—at least Ted's involvement. He did what he thought was right to protect her. I'd do the same for Joey.

I just wish I had told her earlier that I didn't blame her for any of it, because seeing her like this hurts. And then I hear her talking to her mom? My heart broke. She seems so sad, so lonely. I don't like it.

I give her a small smile and motion to the spot next to her. She scoots over, so I fold myself down and stare out at the lake with her.

She's not doing well in the breathing department. Every breath sounds harsh.

"I don't blame you, Rae."

Her body shakes as she starts to cry. "You should, Hudson. You really, really should."

"How can I? You can't help what happened in your past. *Anyone* that has to face a traumatic event like that would break. It wasn't you out there, and I understand that. I promise, I'm not mad at you, Rae."

She sniffles, wiping at her face. "Then why haven't you called or anything?"

"Because I'm horribly pissed at *myself*," I admit on a sigh.

"But...but why? *You* didn't do anything wrong. Hell, you *saved* her!"

"I knew something was off before I left you with her. You were clammy the previous day and wouldn't look out at the water for more than a few seconds without breaking into a sweat," I tell her. "I should have known she would talk you into taking her down to the beach, and that's the last position I should have put you in. You weren't ready to face it on your own, and that's *okay*, Rae. It really is. It's my fault for making you face that on your own, and I'm sorry."

I peek over at her. She's staring at me with her mouth hanging open. I reach over with two fingers and close it for her.

"Flies, Rae."

She *smiles*.

She smiles.

In that instant, my world becomes whole again.

"I can't...I can't believe you blame yourself. That's kind of ridiculous."

I wink. "Ditto."

She huffs out a breath. "Well, aren't we quite the duo."

We sit in silence for several minutes, just staring out at the lake and trying to absorb all this...well, all this shit. It's been a wild ride from the beginning with Rae, and when you add in these last two weeks, it's been pure fucking chaos.

We needed the quiet, needed the break.

But we need each other more.

"I'm sorry, Hudson. So, *so* sorry."

I shake my head and swallow thickly. "I know you are, Rae, and I know now it truly wasn't anyone's fault. My mom kind of made me realize that."

She buries her face in her hands and groans. "She knows?"

"Of course. She's not mad you. Promise."

"What, uh, what did she say?"

"'Everything happens for a reason.' It's kind of her motto."

"That's it? That's all she said?" Rae asks, clearly shocked.

"She also reminded me that I saved you once." I bump my shoulder into hers. "You're welcome for that, by the way."

Rae smiles again. "Thank you, but I guess I still don't understand how that's all she said."

"At first I didn't either. I was confused, but then I realized that if I hadn't saved you, I wouldn't have met you. Point one for her," I joke. "If this whole thing hadn't happened with Joey, you would have never found out about your mom, or how we really met. You'd still be in the dark about that. You'd still think you weren't fit to be a parent because you never knew how it felt to be loved by your mother."

I pause for a moment to take a deep breath, knowing she may get upset over what I need to say next.

"I was pissed at you at first because you didn't tell me about your nightmare or your fear, but I understand why you didn't. You didn't think any of it was real. You went down to that beach to face it once and for all. You had no idea it would come crashing down around you. Boy did it, but now, Rae? Now you're free. You don't have that fear anymore. You're finally free from it all."

She's quiet again, and I watch her. Even with her face all puffy from crying, she's still beautiful. I can't believe I made myself miss two weeks of being with her, two weeks of her laughter and the weird things that randomly pop out of her mouth.

"What did you get out of it all?"

"That's easy—you, Joey, and an awesome hero complex."

She laughs freely then grows serious. "Is Joey mad at me?"

"Not at all. She knows things like that can happen in the water and that she was out too far. She thought I was mad at *her* for going out so far."

"Really?"

"Promise. She's asked about you every single day, begging me to call you because she misses you. Joey loves you, Rae."

"I love her too," she says with sadness in her voice.

I reach over, pull her hand from her legs, and scoot closer. "Rae, look at me." She does, and I can see the tears beginning to pool in her eyes. "I meant what I said that weekend. I love you. That hasn't changed."

Tears slide down her face. "How is that possible?"

"How can you even ask me that? It's so hard *not* to love you. You're smart, you're funny, you're *real*, and you're gorgeous. You're the perfect package. You have the strangest sense of humor and it meshes perfectly with mine. You... Fuck." I pause. "This is going to sound so damn stupid and I may as well just hand you my balls now, but you...you fuckin' complete me. I didn't even know I was missing anything until you. I had no idea my heart had any more room in it next to Joey, but you proved that it does. You share so much of that space with her. I don't know how else to explain it. It's just *you*. I love *you*."

Her tears are falling harder now. I wrap her in my arms and hold her until the very last tremor wracks her body.

She pulls away slowly and meets my eyes. Then she leans

in close and kisses me. It's soft and unsure at first, but I want more. *Oh, man, do I want more.* I flick out my tongue and she opens instantly for me. Grabbing the back of her head, I pull her with me as I fall onto my back, our kiss never breaking.

This is what I've been missing. I can feel my heart swell. I can feel myself become whole again. I needed this. I need Rae.

"Well?" I ask when we finally pull apart. She's laying half on top of me and I'll be damned if I'm not sporting a semi.

"I missed that," she says, brushing one more kiss across my lips.

"Me too," I chuckle.

"I love you too, you know. I really do. Thank you for accepting me as I am. Thank you for accepting my lack of filter, for letting me into Joey's life. You'll never understand how much all of it has meant to me. I'll never be able to repay you for it either."

"You could do it in kisses."

She laughs, and kisses me about a million more times over the next hour.

"What time is it?" she asks between kisses.

I pull out my phone, our lips still connected. "Eight." Kiss. "Thirty." Kiss. "Seven."

She giggles and pulls away. "I should head back home, and you should get home to tuck Joey in."

"Mood Killer strikes again," I deadpan.

We stand and I help her fold the blanket.

"Shit! Maura and Perry never came back! I need to call them." She pulls her phone out in a panic.

I reach over and put hand on hers. "It was a setup, Rae."

She rolls her eyes. "Of course it was. Fuckin' Perry."

"Actually..." I start. "It was Maura."

"That meddling little wench!"

I laugh. "She said it would be a cute throwback to our first date. Her exact words were 'blind reunion'. She was really proud of that one."

"You know...that wouldn't be a bad idea..." Rae taps her fingers against her chin.

"What's that?"

"Starting over." She shrugs. "Because that's basically what I've done. *We* can do it too."

"Hmm. Okay, deal. We'll start over then." I step into her and stick my hand out. "Hi, I'm Hudson."

She smirks, and it's wicked, nothing like I've ever seen. She steps forward, ignoring my outstretched hand, and looks me dead in the eyes.

"Shouldn't you at least buy me dinner before you screw me?"

I fall in love all over again.

EPILOGUE

RAE

"JOEY ELEANOR TAMELL, hurry your little butt up! We're on a schedule!" Hudson yells up the stairs.

It's New Year's Eve and Hudson's taking me "out". I think I've asked about a million times since he told me last week, even enlisting Joey's help, but the info is locked up tight. He won't tell me jack shit.

"I'm coming, I'm coming! Geez!" she shouts back, running down the hallway.

"No running, dude."

"You're so bossy," I tell him jokingly.

He shoots me a glare. "Don't even start, woman. I'll leave you here."

"Well, since I have no idea where we're going, I don't know if I should be upset by that or not."

He gives me his stupid smirk again. "Oh, you *so* should."

I stick my tongue out at him and reach for Joey's hand. "Come on, bug. I'm sitting in back with you. Your dad's mean tonight."

"He's getting so grouchy in his old age," she says seriously.

"Oh, sick burn," I say over my shoulder to Hudson.

"I'll leave you both here!"

Joey and I just shrug.

After we drop Joey off at Elle's, making sure to give her

extra kisses for the New Year, we head into Boston. I bounce in my seat the entire way, still having no clue where we're headed. There's only half an hour left until midnight and I'm starting to wonder if we're going to be late or not.

"Are we there yet?" I ask impatiently.

Hudson laughs. "You're worse than Joey."

"Well, if you would just tell me, I wouldn't have to ask a million times."

"Patience. We're like five minutes away."

He lied. It's ten after traffic.

We pull into a jam-packed parking garage and Hudson gets out and opens my door for me.

"Hudson, this is really lame. I've been to plenty of parking garages in my life."

"Shush. Come on. It's right up the street."

He lied again. It's up two streets.

A slow, warm feeling starts low in my gut as we cross an intersection. There's a small crowd of people milling around and I'm not sure what for. I just happen to glance up at the awning above them.

"HOLY FUCKING SHIT! NO WAY!" I scream loudly, causing nearly everyone on the street to look at us.

Hudson laughs hard.

"No, no, no, no! Are you shitting me?" I turn to him, still yelling.

He shakes his head, that stupid smirk on his face. "Nope. This is real. This is *very* real."

"My first Transit show! On New Year's Eve! Holy. Shit."

"You're welcome," he says smugly.

"Thank you, thank you, thank you! I love you!" I throw myself into his arms.

"I love you too, weirdo. Now let's go in before we're late.

We only have a few minutes and we don't want to miss the opening song."

Once inside, I glance around in wonder. It looks so small on the outside, but the inside looks huge. It's crowded; there are tons of people holding beers and laughing, and some are even dancing to the music playing over the speakers.

We push our way through the crowd, trying to get as close to the front as possible. We find the perfect spot just as the lights dim. The crowd erupts and the band takes the stage.

"10..." the singer shouts. "9...8...7...6...5...4...3...2...1! Happy New Year!" everyone shouts in unison.

Hudson wraps his arms around me from behind and kisses my neck softly.

"I love you, Rae. Here's to tomorrow," he says in my ear.

I smile.

Because this? This is bliss.

This is my tomorrow.

My forever.

My everything.

THE END
Psst...
Keep swiping to read a preview of Here's to Forever: A Novella, a continuation of Rae and Hudson's story.

Thank you for reading HERE'S TO TOMORROW!
I hope you loved Hudson and Rae and little Joey.

But their story isn't over...

HERE'S TO FOREVER picks up shortly after Here's to
Tomorrow and continues their story.

Maura's happy with Tanner...or is she?
Find out who steals her heart in HERE'S TO YESTERDAY!

ACKNOWLEDGMENTS

I'm not sure how to start this, so here goes nothing!

The Marine, you're the best damn husband (or guy) I could have asked for. You make me smile daily. I can never repay you enough for all the laughter and joy you've brought into my life. Thank you for not knowing how to spell lesbian, because without that, we'd have never met.

sMother, you're my favorite sMother and my best best friend. I really did mean everything I wrote to you in that drunken rambling note. I love you. Thank you.

Bonnie Rae—my B—I adore you. Your friendship means the world to me. Thank you for always being there for me, even when all I want to do is talk about hot guys (*cough* Nick and Brandyn *cough*). Just...thank you, hooker. Thank you for being you and for being weird just like me. You already know you've inspired Maura and I hope that when you read the next book, you see how much you've grown, just as she does.

Twinsie, do I even have to say anything? You know I love you, girl. Kiss my babies for me!

Caitlin. Oh, Caitlin. You're an amazing editor and I'm SO glad I found you. Thank you for everything.

Fake Mrs. Will Cooper (AKA Mrs. Walker Wannabe), Chelle, Kristin, and Laurie...thank you for taking a chance and beta reading for me! You're all awesome and helped a ton! This book would've been missing quite a few pieces without you all.

Assholes, you know exactly who I'm talking about. You

crazy ladies light up my day a good 5 out of 7. I hold you all high on my list of Okay People. Thanks for all the laughs and for threatening to kick my ass when I need it!

Dawn Billings, you are amazing. You were the first person to ever read my book the whole way through. You have no idea how much your begging for more kept me going. Thank you for loving my words and pushing me to finish.

Dawn Ramkissoon, your constant support is appreciated beyond belief. Thank you for being there for me to vent and for sprinting with me when I need it. NOW GO WRITE!

Even though I know this will never get read by them, I have to thank the band Transit that inspired the setting for this book. You dudes kept my head (and heart) in the game all throughout writing. Thanks for the sweet tunes! Oh, and everyone else, GO LISTEN TO THEM! They are amazing!

To my sister, who makes fun of me and laughs with me just like Rae and Haley.

And to everyone that I'm forgetting because I so know I'm forgetting someone...thanks, dudes! All your support means the world to me.

Finally, you, the reader. Thank you for taking a chance on me. I hope you fell in love with Rae and Hudson and their weird mouths just as much as I did. Don't worry...you'll see them again soon. Maura's up next!

With love and unwavering gratitude,

Teagan

OTHER TITLES BY TEAGAN HUNTER

ROOMMATE ROMPS

Loathe Thy Neighbor

Love Thy Neighbor (Coming December 2020)

SLICE SERIES

A Pizza My Heart

I Knead You Tonight

Doughn't Let Me Go

A Slice of Love

Cheesy on the Eyes

TEXTING SERIES

Let's Get Textual

I Wanna Text You Up

Can't Text This

Text Me Baby One More Time

HERE'S TO SERIES

Here's to Tomorrow

Here's to Yesterday

Here's to Forever: A Novella

Here's to Now

STANDALONES

We Are the Stars

If You Say So

Want to be part of a fun reader group, gain access to exclusive content and giveaways, and get to know me a little more?

Join Teagan's Tidbits on Facebook!

Want to stay on top of my new releases?

Sign up for New Release Alerts!

ABOUT THE AUTHOR

TEAGAN HUNTER is a Missouri-raised gal, but currently lives in South Carolina with her Marine veteran husband, where she spends her days begging him for a cat. She survives off coffee, pizza, and sarcasm. When she's not writing, you can find her watching various TV shows, especially *Supernatural* and *One Tree Hill*. She enjoys cold weather, buys more paperbacks than she'll ever read, and never says no to brownies.

www.teaganhunterwrites.com